BEAUTIFUL MUSIC

Olivia and Will sat close together on the piano bench, turned into each other, so that the distance separating them was brief. Her gaze moved over his face. She continued to be amazed that one man could possess such masculine beauty, and she saw such profundity in the tropic warmth of his blue eyes, she nearly drowned. "I don't..." her eyes automatically lowered to his mouth, "know what to make of you."

"I'm just a man, Liv," he said, his voice husky. The keen handsomeness of his face grew sharper with unmistakable desire, as his own gaze traveled along her face, down her neck, over the bare expanse of her shoulders and chest, and wherever his eyes moved, she felt her skin heat in response.

"I know..." she breathed, but then her breath deserted her as he leaned closer, bringing his rough, hot palm up to cup the back of her neck.

The heat of his hand traveled all the way down into the liquid core of her, and she nearly gasped aloud at the contact. She let him draw her closer and tilt her head, then she felt his lips move against hers....

LADY X'S COWBOY

Zoe Archer

LEISURE BOOKS NEW YORK CITY

To Zack, for everything.

A LEISURE BOOK®

February 2006

Published by

Dorchester Publishing Co., Inc.
200 Madison Avenue
New York, NY 10016

ISBN 0-8439-5666-6

Visit us on the web at www.dorchesterpub.com.

I am a pore cowboy, I've got no home,
I'm here today and tomorrow I'm gone;
I've got no folks, I'm forced to roam,
Where I hang my hat is home, sweet home.
—*Diamond Joe*, Traditional Cowboy Song

But "what am I to do with
my life?" as once asked me one girl out of
the numbers who begin to feel aware that, whether
marrying or not, each possesses an individual life,
to spend, to use, or to lose. And herein lies
the momentous question.

—Dinah Maria Mulock,
A Woman's Thoughts About Women, 1858

Chapter One

London, England
1883

"Don't come any closer," snarled Black Jack Cutler, leveling his Colt .44 pistol. He cocked the hammer of his well-used and deadly weapon. The sound echoed in the tiny cabin like a hundred lethal snakes waiting to strike.

Lorna Jane swallowed past the hard lump of fear that had lodged in her throat as she stared down the barrel of the gun. "You won't shoot me, Cutler," she cried, "because I know the secret of the map! And the secret is—"

"Lady Xavier! Lady Xavier!"

Sighing, Lady Olivia Xavier tucked *Lorna Jane of Glittering Gulch; or The Map of Don Diego* by Captain Frederick Livings into her reticule and attempted to smile at the woman approaching her. Olivia had been hoping to wait for her carriage undisturbed so she could catch up on the latest escapades of the often hapless Lorna Jane. But that was not to be. Her brewery, Greywell's, had the immense misfortune of being located almost directly across the street from Prudence Culpepper's Eternal Flame Mission. Though Olivia usually managed to avoid Prudence through judicious scheduling, sometimes their paths did cross.

Now Prudence, determined, gray and hulking like an iron-clad battleship, bore down on Olivia as she stood on the curb outside her brewery.

It was nearly six o'clock, and everyone at Greywell's had gone home. The night watchman was not due for another hour, which meant that after she completed her paperwork and locked the gates behind her, Olivia was alone.

Prudence locked the doors to the mission behind her and gave them a sharp tug for added security. There was nothing of value inside the mission—unless the thieves of Wandsworth were after stacks of Bibles and armloads of bunting donated and sewed by the fine ladies of the Eternal Flame Good Works Society—but Prudence rarely left anything to chance, including trapping Olivia in conversation when an opportunity presented itself.

"Lady Xavier," Prudence said, "I had one day hoped you would finally come to one of our little meetings." She gave Olivia a look that was at once smug and censorious, one of Prudence's specialties.

"I have often meant to," Olivia answered politely. "But business has kept me away."

"Business?" Prudence's expression left no room for doubt that she considered the thought distasteful, at the least.

"My brewery does keep me exceedingly busy," Olivia

said. She looked up and down the narrow street for her carriage. Where the devil was Arthur? She needed rescuing from the good intentions and harsh judgments of Prudence Culpepper.

"Most women would have ceded the actual running of a business to someone more suitable for the position," Prudence reminded her. "When Lord Xavier left you this brewery, I am certain his intention was not to have you sully yourself with such vulgar matters."

Olivia felt her patience begin to fray. Everyone had something to say about the terms of her late husband's will. It wasn't uncommon for a man to leave his wife some interest in a business venture or two, but it certainly was unusual for that wife to involve herself in the daily running of the business, especially if that property was a brewery.

"Why, Mrs. Culpepper, I had no idea that you could communicate with the dead!" Olivia said. At Prudence's bewildered look, she explained, "How else could you possibly know what my husband's intentions were?"

"Such impudence," Prudence huffed, inflating.

"I find your judgment of my actions impudent," Olivia returned. She was very, very tired of this conversation, since she had been having it for the past three years. Once Olivia left off her two years of deep mourning, everyone had had an opinion as to how she should spend her time. Her parents urged her to move in with them and pursue a life of quiet emptiness and widowhood. Her friends wanted her to attend parties, operas and outings. And society bulwarks such as Prudence wanted her to fill her days with time-consuming charity work that produced little gain for those who actually needed it most.

"How can you defend your actions, Lady Xavier?" Prudence demanded. "Your business provides the lower classes with the means to ruin. Have you not read the temperance tracts?" She fumbled with her enormous reticule for just such an item, but Olivia held up a hand to stop her.

"I run a brewery, Mrs. Culpepper, not a gin palace. I ensure that the beer I produce goes to upstanding pubs that provide honest, hard-working men and women a place to relax and enjoy themselves after a long day. Besides," she added pointedly, "I fail to see how providing corsets and religious tracts assists the deserving poor."

"Those pitiable wretches haven't the sense to tend to themselves," Prudence said tightly. "We must give them moral guidance to see them through the dark wilderness of their lapsed state. I do not think that offering demon drink will improve their lives."

"I offer employment at my brewery to those who seek it," Olivia replied. "Men and women."

"You would take a woman out of the sacred domain of her home?"

"I would give a woman a means of sustaining herself and her children, particularly if she has no husband. Can you say the same, Mrs. Culpepper?"

Just then, Prudence Culpepper's carriage clattered to a stop at the curb and she snapped to her coachman, "You're late! Everyone has gone."

"Sorry, madam," the coachman said without any remorse. A footman jumped down to open the carriage door for Prudence. After helping his mistress inside, the footman turned to Olivia, but a look from his mistress held him back.

"I shan't offer you a ride," Prudence said. "You may let your modern views provide you with a means home."

Olivia would rather stare down the barrel of Black Jack Cutler's .44 than be trapped in a carriage with Prudence Culpepper for more than four miles.

"Thank you for your trenchant assessment," Olivia replied dryly.

Prudence pressed her thin lips together as the footman jumped back to his post on the carriage. With a frown, she rapped sharply on the roof. The carriage lurched forward and Olivia happily waved it off.

As soon as she was alone, Olivia gave a very unladylike roll of her eyes and started to reach for her dime novel. Finally, peace. She'd already sat through a long meeting with the brewery's managers and chemist before she'd endured Prudence Culpepper's shrill jeremiad. She wanted some quiet time, just her and the savage outlaws of the American West.

Night was falling, however, and she was finding it difficult to read the book's print. Where could Arthur be with the carriage? He was running rather late, and she started to grow worried. Wandsworth, located on the southern bank of the Thames, wasn't a notorious slum like Whitechapel, but it was still very far from genteel Bayswater.

Peering into the settling fog, Olivia suddenly became aware that she wasn't alone. She'd nearly dismissed the feeling as exhausted nerves, but then three figures emerged from the growing shadows. Cold apprehension crept up the back of her neck. The men walked deliberately toward her, and she fought the urge to step back against the locked gates of the brewery. *Don't show fear,* she reminded herself as she tipped up her chin. These men might just be factory workers heading home.

But no. They wanted her.

"Evening, madam," one said, tugging on the brim of his hat. Though his tone was polite, his face was hard. He and his two companions gathered in a tight semicircle around her.

"Good evening," she managed to reply.

"You alone?" another asked. He had slumped shoulders and watery eyes.

"No," Olivia answered.

"I don't see nobody else," said the third man, a collection of knobby joints. He looked around slowly and insolently before letting his eyes rove over her with the same disrespect.

"My carriage will be here any minute," she said with more conviction than she felt.

"It ain't here yet," said Hard Face, "so we got a few minutes to talk."

"I don't see how we have anything to talk about." Olivia tried to keep her voice steady, as though she were merely telling Cook to order a roast today but no chops, thank you. As she did so, she began to edge away from the men. She didn't know what they wanted, but it couldn't be good. And she didn't intend to stand around and let them threaten her.

"I think we got a lot to talk about," Slump Shoulders answered. He moved faster than he looked capable of and grabbed hold of her arm. Shocked, Olivia dropped her novel. It made a quiet plop onto the pavement.

The pressure of his fingers made Olivia's insides roil with disgust. "Let go of me!"

"Not until we deliver our message," Hard Face said. "The man what gave us our marching orders, he ain't too pleased about you staying on here."

"He means the brewery," Knobby explained.

"And he wants you to reconsider his offer," Hard Face continued. "Otherwise, things could get kinda ugly."

An even uglier realization dawned. "George Pryce sent you," Olivia said, horrified.

"We didn't mention no names," Slump Shoulders said.

"But I know exactly who you are talking about," Olivia snapped. Anger, fast and unchecked, began to flood through her. She could feel herself begin to shake with it. "And you can go right back and tell him to stuff his offer and his hired toughs right up his overbred bum! Now *let go of me*." Olivia tried to snatch her arm away, but Slump Shoulders held her fast. She swung her reticule. It connected with Knobby's face, then burst open and scattered coins in the street.

Hard Face decided it was time to make a play and lunged for her. A strangled scream tore from her throat as she braced for impact, extending her free hand like a claw. She was prepared to fight as hard as she was able, use any means available to her to gain some kind of advantage. But before Hard Face reached her, a dark shape intercepted him, throwing him to the ground with a thud. Stunned by this new development, Slump Shoulders released her.

Both Olivia and the other men watched in astonished surprise as Hard Face struggled on the rough pavement with another person—someone whom no one had seen or heard approaching. They wrestled

7

back and forth until the newcomer sat up a bit and began punching Olivia's would-be assailant with vicious accuracy.

"The lady don't want your company," he said between punches, and Olivia felt her heart stop. He spoke in the distinctive flat drawl of an American. She'd met a few businessmen from Boston and New York and their wives when her husband was alive, but unless she was wrong, this man, her protector, wasn't from Boston, but from the *West*.

Her assailant's companions managed to rouse themselves from their shock and launched themselves at the American. Olivia thought for certain that the odds would be too great for him, but she heard him say with a laugh, "Come to join the party, huh, boys?" Good lord, he seemed to be enjoying himself.

The way he fought, it did seem like a game. She couldn't tell much about the American—he was wearing a long duster and, yes, she realized with a bubble of hysterical glee, a Stetson—but he seemed much bigger and more solid than Pryce's toughs. He punched Knobby in the nose and the fellow tumbled over backward, howling and clutching his face.

"Damn English nose," the American chuckled. "Made out of pure deadwood."

Slump Shoulders charged, but the American landed an elbow in his stomach. When the man bent over in pain, the American landed a solid uppercut to his jaw and laid him out flat.

"And you got a belly like an Arkansas sow," the American added, grinning.

Hard Face unsteadily regained his feet and tried to feint at his opponent, but the American had size and speed to his advantage. Neatly sidestepping the man, he stuck out a boot and tripped him. Hard Face's head made a thump on the ground.

The American swung about, fists ready, but no one stood to meet his challenge. "Don't quit now, boys," he said, still laughing. "I'm just gettin' my juices flowin'."

"We don't want no more of your juices," groaned the knobby man.

Olivia wasn't certain, but she thought the American looked disappointed.

"Then y'all better apologize to the lady," he said.

A chorus of moaned *Sorry*'s rose up from the pavement.

"I don't want your apologies," Olivia said. She was still jittery with rage, and it strained her voice. "I want you to deliver a message of my own. Tell Pryce that I won't stand for his bullying. Tell him my answer is no, and that's final."

"Now get the hell out of here," the American commanded, "before I hog-tie and brand your sorry asses."

Muttering and swearing, the men gathered themselves and slumped away, arms around one another's shoulders for support.

The American quickly turned to her. He had such a zeal and talent for fighting, she nearly expected those powerful fists of his to swing at her as well. "You okay, ma'am?" he asked instead, his voice now low and concerned. It was such an abrupt transformation, it was almost as if he had become another man. What a puzzle. She still couldn't see much of his face, which was shadowed by the wide brim of his hat and hidden behind an enormous mustache, but he loomed over her by at least a half a head. She wished she could see his eyes, yet somehow she could feel them on her, palpable and alert.

"I think so," she managed, still reeling from the odd turn of events. Olivia struggled with a peculiar desire to wrap her arms around him, this cheerfully bloodthirsty American who was as gentle as a wolfhound by the fire.

"You know those boys?"

Olivia's mouth thinned wryly. "I've never met them before, but I know who sent them."

"I bet they'll think twice before tangling with you again."

"You deserve all the credit. Thank you."

He tugged on the brim of his hat. "Anything for a lady." She sensed those eyes of his on her, warm and assessing, taking in the details of her clothing, her face, even the ridiculous hat the modiste had insisted was the latest rage in Paris, and an answering flush began to spread through her body. His gaze felt completely different from the violating leers of the toughs. It was both gentlemanly and uncivilized. "You *are* a lady, ain't you? I was startin' to think that maybe all the talk of fine English manners was nothin' but a dry wind blowing from the south."

A little laugh jumped up from her belly. This man had a very colorful way of speaking, but she liked it, much more than the empty bubbles of conversation provided by the gentlemen of her acquaintance.

"Some may call me a lady," Olivia answered; then, because he was so candid, she could not help but add, "Although sometimes I am not sure what that really means."

"Believe me, ma'am," the American said gravely, "I ain't never met a *real* lady 'til I met you." His words slid together, his Western drawl a combination of dark whiskey and honey.

"Thank you," Olivia said again, blushing. She had heard greater compliments, of course—ornate phrases covered in gilding and polished until they took on the sharp brightness of a blade—but it was this American's simple statement that suddenly gave her an intense rush of pleasure unlike anything she had experienced before. Perhaps because it had been so honestly rendered, and by a man who probably didn't give compliments very often. He looked too rough, too rangy and lean for such nonsense. But it didn't feel much like nonsense to Olivia right then.

The American suddenly narrowed the space between them by reaching down and picking up her discarded novel. She took an involuntary step backward. "This yours?"

Olivia looked down at the book in his large, callused hand. Its yellow paper cover looked faintly ridiculous contrasted with the foggy industrial streets of Wandsworth, and infinitely fragile and transitory compared with the weathered strength of his hand. Across the front of the novel was the title, as well as an illustration of a maiden tied to a post with a cowboy riding to her rescue, guns drawn and ready for action. The cowboy on the cover wore a long duster and a Stetson and sported a giant, untamed mustache. Olivia looked back and forth between the cover and the man now holding the book and felt herself grow hot and shivery at the same time.

He's a cowboy.

"I . . . I . . ." she heard herself stutter.

He peered closer, and for the first time Olivia saw his eyes. They were a bright azure blue, the blue of

Montana skies, the Rio Grande reflecting the Texas sun, and any number of places she had read about but never seen. Until now. Slowly, she took in the details of him. His hat was a battered tan Stetson, stained from exposure to the elements, with a braided leather hatband, its brim wide enough to shield him from the sun and rain. His long brown canvas coat looked equally worn, its bright blanket lining patched in places. At his neck, he had knotted a red kerchief. He also wore a shirt of soft blue cotton flannel with horn buttons and a plain black vest with pockets. She sensed, rather than saw, that he filled his clothes with lean, hard muscle, the kind gained from honest work under hard conditions rather than an expensive gymnasium or useless sport.

Olivia couldn't help it . . . her gaze trailed lower.

"Where's your gun?" she managed to ask.

"My what?" He looked down. "It's in my room. Didn't think I'd be needin' it. I thought England was supposed to be civilized."

He had a gun. A gunbelt. Oh, my.

"You sure you're all right?" he asked, a crease appearing between his brows. She saw his other hand come up, as if he meant to touch her face, but he stopped himself and let his hand drop to his side. She wanted to tell him it was all right, even though it wasn't, but she was pierced with a powerful longing to feel the rough hitch of his skin against hers, sliding down the smooth curve of her cheek.

"Yes," she managed. "A little shaken up, is all."

The American straightened to his full height, and Olivia took stock of the width of his shoulders and the natural grace with which he carried himself. "It ain't smart for a woman like you to be alone in a place like this," he said gruffly. "Where's your husband?"

"Gone. I mean, dead. I mean . . ." Olivia stammered. She couldn't understand where her poise had gone. Though she was a bit rattled from her encounter with the toughs, it still couldn't explain her muddled thoughts and complete inability to speak coherently. She was thirty-two years old, for goodness's sake. Far too old to stutter like a girl fresh from the schoolroom.

The American removed his hat and looked solemn. "My condolences, ma'am."

"It's all right," she said. She sounded terribly breathless. In the twilight she saw that the American had sandy hair, a bit unkempt but clean. There was no way to tell how old he was. His jaw was square, and she followed its line into the strong column of his neck. Olivia clenched her hands into fists to keep from pressing her palms against the skin of his throat. She wanted to feel the energy of him. He had the strength and power of someone quite young, not to mention the enthusiasm for violence, but in his gaze she could see more than a lifetime's experience. She wondered what he had experienced. "It was years ago."

"Glad to hear it," he said with a wry, almost boyish smile.

"You are the first person to say so," she answered back smartly, without offense.

He broke into a wide grin. "You're full of pepper."

"Is that a good thing?"

"Ma'am, it's a great thing."

She felt spellbound, liquid, but intensely aware. He still held her novel, but she wasn't prepared to claim it just yet. She wasn't completely sure whether everything that was happening—everything that had happened—wasn't some dream from which she would be roused in a moment by Sarah, her maid, who would pour her chocolate and give her a stack of the day's correspondence as morning sunlight filled her bedroom.

And then the strangest image sprang into her mind. In her vision, she wasn't alone in her bed. The American was there, too, without a scrap of clothing. Come to think of it, she was naked, too.

She prayed that he could not read her mind, but she thought she detected the faintest trace of a flush in his tanned cheeks.

The clatter of carriage wheels broke her reverie.

"My lady!" Arthur cried. "I am so terribly sorry to have kept you waiting—"

"Where the hell have you been?" the American demanded before Olivia could speak.

Her coachman blinked in astonishment and the footman jumped down.

"I should haul your ass down from there and beat you five ways 'til Sunday," the cowboy continued to rant. Arthur shrank back on his post and looked at Olivia with questioning, terrified eyes.

"Some men tried to accost me," Olivia explained.

"They would've done a lot worse if I hadn't shown up," the American snarled. "And on account of you," he pointed an accusatory finger at Arthur, "bein' too busy polishing your forehead."

Arthur gingerly touched a finger to the offending brow. "The carriage threw a wheel, my lady," he said. "And we couldn't fix it for love or money." He looked extremely upset. "I will understand if you want my resignation—"

"Damn right!" the American interrupted.

"You will *not* swear in the presence of Lady Xavier," Arthur insisted haughtily.

"I'll cook up your guts and serve 'em for church supper," the American shot back. "With cornbread and greens."

"Enough!" Olivia said, stepping forward with outstretched palms. She first turned to Arthur. "You ought to have checked the wheel before you left." The coachman bowed his head in acknowledgment of his failure. "Don't let it happen again. I was fortunate that Mister . . ." She looked at the American, realizing that she didn't even know his name.

"Coffin, ma'am," he supplied. "Will Coffin."

A flutter moved through Olivia's throat. What an unbelievably appropriate name. "Yes . . . Mr. Coffin. It was quite fortunate that you happened to come by. Most providential." Everything seemed to be turned upside down. Cowboys in London. Impossible. "And what *are* you doing here, Mr. Coffin?" It felt nice to say his name, a bit dangerous, sharp and exotic in her mouth.

"I'm stayin' across the river," he said, not fully understanding. He tilted his head east. "I think they call it Wapping."

"You came here all the way from Wapping?" she asked, amazed. "That's quite a distance."

"I like to know what I'm dealin' with when I go to a new place." He was so large, so unlike anything or anyone she had ever known, he continued to amaze her. "I'm in some flophouse they got down by the docks. I was gettin' the lay of the land when I heard the doin's over here and thought I'd see what was what."

15

"I'm very glad you did hear the *doings,*" Olivia answered. She smiled at him and realized that it was one of the first genuine smiles she'd given anyone in a long time. And she didn't even know this man. "I feel I must offer you some kind of reward for your kindness to me."

"Reward?" he asked with a frown.

She considered where he said he was staying, a "flophouse," which did not sound particularly pleasant or accommodating. And Wapping certainly wasn't known as one of the finer neighborhoods. So she did what she had been trained to do: throw money at people. "Of course, a reward. Some money, perhaps. Arthur?" she asked, since her few shillings were lying in the street.

"Yes, my lady," the coachman said, and reached into his pocket. She would reimburse him later, since she never traveled with more than a sovereign. Everything was on account, and everyone accepted her credit. She was the widow of a businessman, a successful business owner, and more likely to pay her bills than a peer's spouse.

"Keep it," Will Coffin said.

Olivia looked at him with surprise. He was angry. And angry in a different way than when he was fighting the thugs. This was a deep, personal anger that vibrated off him like an inaudible sound.

"But—"

"I don't want your money."

"I've insulted you."

Will Coffin put his hat back on, and what she had seen of his face became obscured. She suddenly felt very foolish and gauche, younger and more awkward than she had in years.

"Ma'am," he said, stepping back. "I've got to get back before this damned fog turns me blinder than a mule in a mineshaft."

"Really, Mr. Coffin, can I not—?"

"You get on home, and don't go walkin' by yourself in mean territory."

Before she knew it, her footman was helping her into her carriage. "Can I at least give you a ride?" she asked, though again she was violating the rules of propriety by inviting a man into the carriage with her.

She need not have worried. Even as the words were leaving her mouth, Will Coffin tipped his hat, a definitive dismissal. But courtly, in its way. Like him, a strange amalgam of coarseness and chivalry. Again she felt his eyes on her, one final, measuring gaze that swept over her in a warm tide. She kept one hand braced on the open carriage door as Will Coffin turned and disappeared into the foggy London evening. Strange how such a big man could vanish so completely. She strained and could just make out the fading sound of his boots against the pavement. In his wake, the commonplace and often irritating fog became a spectral coda, an annoyance turned enigmatic through his presence and absence.

"We really ought to go, my lady," Arthur said.

Olivia barely noticed when the footman closed the door after her and the carriage began to move north, across the river and back to Bayswater, back to everything familiar. She kept staring out the window, hoping to catch another glimpse of Will Coffin but finding in his place only fog.

Chapter Two

George Pryce entered the Three Graces Pub on the Strand looking for his failed henchmen. He was furious, more furious than he had been since they'd tried to throw him out of Cambridge for cheating. His father's authority kept him ensconced at university for two more years, but the outrage remained.

He slid into an empty booth at the back and ordered a beer.

"Greywell's or Bass, sir?" the publican asked.

"Bass," Pryce snarled. His mood blackened even further. It always came back to that damned brewery. He still lived with his parents, the last remaining son at home. His three older brothers had all married and set up their own prospering households. They had taken up mundane responsibilities such as sessions of Parliament, arguing bills and calculating interest. But as the fourth son of an earl, Pryce did not desire that which his brothers had been so eager to claim. He loved his life of leisure, the only true life of a gentleman as far as he was concerned.

But still Father would fix him with his piercing, critical glare and demand to know what his youngest son was doing with his life. Apparently, being a gentleman wasn't enough of a profession for Henry Pryce, fourth Earl of Hessay, nor his sons.

His beer arrived, and George took a deep drink. Bass was one of the most profitable breweries in all of England, with warehouses in Edinburgh, Paris, London and Dublin. He could only dream of such wealth now. George Pryce often bemoaned the fact that he wasn't born a hundred years earlier, when the thought of a man of his station actually *working* was considered vulgar and beneath him. But now everyone in society was possessed with a mania for practicality and usefulness—Pryce blamed sober Victoria and the ink-stained captains of industry who now held the reins of the kingdom.

So he cast about, seeking the easiest way to make some money of his own. It *was* a bit galling that at thirty-five he still drew an allowance. One morning, after reading the cricket scores in the *Times*, Pryce saw an article trumpeting the fortune that could be made effortlessly in breweries. And he had his answer. All he had to do was find some little brewery and buy its owner out.

Trouble was, the brewery he wanted was owned and operated by a presumptuous widow who wouldn't see reason. Pryce wasn't accustomed to people saying no to him. In fact, his father's money and influence made sure no one said no. If there was one thing he had learned about the rise of the disgusting merchant ranks, it was that they respected money.

He remembered his days at Eton and how the sons of those merchants would receive lavish presents from home on their birthdays, or when they performed well on their examinations, or at just about any bloody time their revolting parents thought to pet and praise their noxious offspring. Pyrce received nothing from home except angry letters from his father when, yet again, his son had failed to live up to expectations. On his birthday he was always sent the same gift: a Bible covered in Spanish leather, the passages about filial duty underlined in his father's bold hand.

Pryce came to hate all those boys, and their families, too, the upstart class that struggled so hard to show themselves worthy. Of course their marks were better than his—they had something to prove. As the son of a nobleman, Pryce didn't need to struggle and strain to distinguish himself. He was already distinguished by birth. It was his responsibility, his *duty*, to show Britain and the rest of the world that those born into the aristocracy embodied and cherished the ideals of gentility. This meant that he must elevate himself above the muddy roads of commerce. His income—such a sordid word—ought to arise from the land, the lifeblood of England, not banks and machinery. But this didn't seem enough for his critical father. Knowing that he could never please Henry Pryce with his academic or business triumphs, his son George made sure that he excelled at living the proper and genteel life of a gentleman, a life of cultured idleness.

Yet everywhere he went—at the races, the opera, balls, even the club, for mercy's sake—Pryce was forced to rub shoulders with new, purchased titles or, even worse, those who relied solely on their pocketbooks to gain entry and never bothered with titles at all. Pryce was, at best, coolly polite to these men and their overdecorated wives, brash sons and grasping daughters. All the while, he nursed a growing and poisonous hatred of those whose fortunes had brought them into the closed world of the British aristocracy.

So Lady Olivia Xavier's refusal was particularly infuriating. But Pryce was confident that the men he hired yesterday would help make up her mind at last.

And then he'd received word from his men. When the scribbled note arrived that morning, his confidence fell and his outrage grew.

"What the hell happened to you?" Pryce demanded as a trio with bruised and swollen faces sat down opposite him. "Don't tell me Lady Xavier did that."

"She didn't," Bill Dunsby mumbled. "Some daft American did."

"American?"

The publican hovered nearby to take their orders.

"Greywell's," the three men chorused.

"I'm not buying you drinks, you idiots," roared Pryce. "Piss off," he said to the publican. Dunsby and his companions looked disappointed.

"He came out of nowhere," he said, "an' beat the stuffing out of us."

"Pathetic," sneered Pryce. "One man defeating three? What do I pay you for?"

"You didn't see 'im," whined Davey Stoke. "As big as an ox, and four times as strong. And all the time laughing, just laughing at us, like he was stepping on ants."

The beginnings of a sharp and unrelenting headache stabbed behind Pryce's eyes. "Get out," Pryce snarled, pinching the bridge of his nose.

"What about the rest of our money?" Dunsby complained. "You said you'd give us half before and half after."

"I didn't anticipate you failing so spectacularly. You'll get only what I've paid you." When the men started to object, Pryce added softly, "I have many friends of influence at the Metropolitan Police, and just one word from me could see you three scum on the treadmill for the rest of your lives."

Muttering and cursing, the three men pulled themselves out of the booth and left the busy pub. Once alone, Pryce ordered a stiff glass of whiskey. Beer was not enough.

Lady Olivia Xavier would have to see things his way, American or no American. Eventually, she would learn that it was impossible to say no to George Pryce.

Will knew something about fog. And snow, and rain, and sandstorms, and just about every other weather that nature sought fit to bedevil a cattle drive. After a life spent almost entirely out of doors, a little thing like the heavy yellow fog rolling off the Thames didn't bother him much.

But here he was, wandering around London, more adrift than he'd been during that hellish two weeks crossing the Atlantic. Partly because of the fog, partly on account of the twisting, bewildering streets that defied logic and had strange names like Middlesex, Houndsditch and Threadneedle. At least Denver had the good manners to be laid out on a grid. And the streets were numbered. Even his brief visit to New York City hadn't been so confusing. London could try any man's patience when it came to figuring out the lay of the land. But he knew that given time, he could learn London as well as he learned the Goodnight Loving Trail. That wasn't his goal, though.

Will had only a scrap of old paper in his pocket to serve as his compass in London, and it wasn't doing him a lick of good. He'd made about as much progress today as he had the day before—meaning, nothing. He wasn't giving up, all the same.

As he walked up and down the streets of this odd city, he couldn't shake thoughts of that pretty English widow he'd met yesterday. No, she wasn't pretty. She was damned beautiful. Will had seen over a hundred actresses in his day, rouged and powdered and wearing next to nothing as they performed their fancy dances to the roars of the crowd. Yet not a one of them matched the pure loveliness of the English widow. Lady Xavier, her servant called her.

Will walked toward his hotel, rolling himself a cigarette as evening started to fall. He'd bought himself some kind of meat pie from a shop down the street and carried it in a paper sack, his dinner for the night.

A couple of soiled doves passed him—they looked the same as the girls in Leadville, and every other town he'd ever been in—so he wasn't mistaken in their question.

"Lookin' for a bit o' fun, lovey?" one asked, swaying closer to him.

"Yeah," her friend added, "you could 'ave the both of us for a quid."

"I don't know what a quid is, ma'am," Will said, "but even if I did, I'd have to say no, thanks."

Both women started to laugh. "An American!" they cried together. "We ain't never met an American before."

Will tipped his hat. Even whores were ladies underneath it all, and he never stopped treating them as such.

"You from Texas?" the older one asked.

"Colorado, ma'am."

"Is that in America?"

"Last I checked."

"That case, we'll give you a turn on the house," the younger one said. "A welcome-to-England prezzy." She wrapped her thin arms around Will's elbow and pressed her bosom against him. Her friend followed suit and began playing with his mustache. He wasn't the least bit tempted.

"Thanks all the same, girls," Will said, carefully disentangling himself from both and setting them back on the street. "I do appreciate your hospitality, but I just ain't up for company right now."

The women pulled faces of disappointment, but they both shrugged as they pulled their wraps tighter around their shoulders. "If you change your mind, come to the King's Head an' ask for Jennie and Kate," the older one said. "Mind you don't forget."

"I won't. Have a good evenin', ladies." Will gave his hat another tip. With cheerful waves, the women left in the direction of the docks.

Will continued toward his hotel and got back to the business of his cigarette. He hadn't had a tumble since New York, but he wasn't like other men coming off the trail, following their johnsons to the nearest bordello and squandering their money on paid company. He liked women. No, he *loved* them, their talk, their laughter, the way they looked at the world that sometimes defied all logic, but sometimes a man had different priorities besides bouncing mattresses.

That girl in New York, she'd worked in some factory and thought it'd be great fun to polish the sheets with a real live cowboy, and Will had been happy to oblige. His body had liked it fine enough. There was something to be said for a city girl's sophistication. But he'd found afterward, slipping out of her boardinghouse with his boots in hand, that he was getting a bit weary of these one-night fandangos. They were missing something, but he didn't know quite what.

His mind turned suddenly toward Lady Xavier. He hadn't been wrong—she was a lady from the top of her silly feathered hat to the tips of her expensive little leather shoes. Her blue dress had to have been made of silk, and it covered a slim and curved body. It wasn't the cost or cut of her clothes that made her a lady in Will's estimation. She carried herself like a falcon—noble, elegant, so keenly beautiful it made a man's eyes ache to look at her.

Will struck a match against the brick front of a building and lit his cigarette. He took a soothing drag of smoke into his mouth and blew it out. Thank the lord he'd remembered to pack good old Bull Durham tobacco. Who knew what kind of peculiar stuff they smoked here in England? Probably something boiled.

"Ches-nuts! Hot, roasted chestnuts!" a passing vendor cried. A few children rushed forward to buy them, then ran off with their snacks.

Lady Xavier's hair was darker than chestnuts, thick and glossy like a raven's wing, coiled neatly at the back of her head. He'd been dying to take it down from its pins and run his fingers through it. He knew it would be softer than the silk of her dress. Her skin was smooth and fair, unmarked and perfect.

The shape of her face showed she came from good

stock. A clean, neat jawline that led a man right to her mouth, which was full and wide, the color of crushed raspberries and near to heartbreaking when she smiled. Unlike women who put clothespins on their noses to get the look of the upturned beauties from *Harper's* or *Frank Leslie's Illustrated Newspaper*, Lady Xavier had a straight, fine nose, just shy of assertive. She had the kind of nose, Will mused, drawing on his cigarette, that didn't turn away from unpleasantness.

Will neared his hotel. He'd traversed London enough to know that he'd managed to find one of the lowest, roughest and most shoddy hotels in the whole city, but it was cheap and it had been blissfully near where his ship docked. All he'd wanted when he staggered off that tub was someplace that didn't pitch like a bronc.

Now it wasn't the motion of the ship that unsettled him. It was the lady's eyes that kept haunting Will as he walked through London, as he lay down last night and all the times in between. They were the precise color of the sky just as night eased into morning. He'd seen that color a lot when he'd had last watch on the drive, and it always took him by surprise that something like a color could fill a body with pleasure. But he hadn't counted on seeing that gorgeous shade of violet-gray in a woman's eyes. He could lose whole days of his life looking into Lady Xavier's eyes.

Despite all this, it wasn't her beauty that kept her returning again and again to his thoughts. Some cattle baron had once bought a glass vase from a company called Tiffany in New York and made sure all them men who worked for him had a chance to see it, to show them what success had gotten him. It was a pretty thing, to be sure, a mass of colors that fair glowed under the gaslight, but it was empty, and an empty thing just wasn't worth much to Will.

Lady Xavier wasn't empty, though. Like he had told her yesterday, she was full of pepper—spirit, grit, gumption. He saw it in the way she tried to hold off the mudsills hassling her. She didn't scream, didn't faint, just held her ground. She had more nerve than a sodbuster's wife facing down a raiding party, and even now it made Will smile. What made him smile even more was the sass she showed afterward, firing back at him with those fine words of hers, that high-class accent that made him feel like he'd drunk a fifth of fine whiskey.

Will waited outside his hotel to finish his cigarette. All the ranch wives had frowned on him taking tobacco indoors.

Lady Xavier was, Will realized, watching the smoke uncurl from his cigarette, the kind of woman a man—hell, *this* man—wouldn't mind setting up housekeeping with. When the time came.

But then she'd offered him money for doing what any man with a speck of integrity should do, and Will understood that Lady Xavier really was as beautiful and remote as a high-flying falcon. He'd been angry at first that she'd thought so little of him as to try to pay him off like some kind of hired hand. But he saw that she was just being what she was, a lady, and he was just a cowpuncher who didn't even know his parents' names. Yet.

A lamplighter made his way down the street, only a bit more than a boy behind his dirty face and bulky clothes, and in his wake the street turned into an ugly, sulfurous alley, narrow and grimy.

Will might be able to afford a better lodging house, but sometimes a body didn't know when his money was going to run out. It was better to practice economy. Sooner or later, he'd have to buy a ticket home. He was comfortable with hard living, so a few rats and dripping storm drains didn't ruffle his feathers.

Crushing the remains of his cigarette under his boot heel, Will smiled grimly to himself. Lady Xavier wasn't used to rough company, even though she was ace-high for standing up to those bulldozers yesterday, and he felt pretty certain she would find his bunking-down arrangements less than satisfactory. He turned to head inside.

And ran right into trouble of his own.

The hotel was one shade better than a mining camp bunkhouse, with faded, torn wallpaper, warped floorboards and ceilings stained black from gaslamps. The walls were so thin Will could hear his neighbor's every sneeze, scratch and snore. And every now and then Will was awakened by the sound of a scarlet lady practicing her trade in the room above.

None of this seemed to bother the management. They had no problems with the drunken sailors and assorted blowhards who came and went through the hallowed halls. Americans, on the other hand, were unwelcome. They'd been sour on him since the moment he took a room three days earlier, and it was only because the rent was so cheap that Will stayed.

As he entered the hotel's lobby, he saw the desk clerk talking with a duded-up fellow, both casting baleful looks in his direction. Yesterday there'd been a bit of a dustup when the desk clerk whined about Will's boots making too much noise coming up and down the stairs. Will did what any sane man would do; he'd ignored the clerk and gone to bed.

But it seemed that the greasy little clerk had called in the big guns. Which explained Mr. Fancy Pants, wearing an embroidered vest stretched across his belly, giving him the once-over.

Will wasn't up for whatever those two had planned, but the portly Brit blocked the staircase up to Will's room.

"You must remove yourself immediately," he droned. Unlike the desk clerk, this dude had the swanky accent of Lady Xavier, though without the class. "I own this establishment, and such behavior will not be tolerated."

"What the hell are you talkin' about?" Will demanded, bracing one hand on the banister.

The Brit looked as put-out as a frog in the dry season. "Swearing, for one thing. I have received numerous complaints about the manner in which you speak."

"There ain't nothin' wrong with the damned way I talk," Will growled.

A disdainful snort shot out of the owner's pointy nose. "And furthermore," he continued, "I refuse to provide lodging for some ill-bred ruffian." He pointed to the bloodstain on the cuff of Will's coat with a pale bloated finger. "Brawling! That is evidence of your brutish behavior."

Will looked down at the blood and almost smiled. "It ain't mine."

"You *attacked* someone," the owner squealed, his eyes widening.

" 'Cause they were on the shoot with a filly up yonder," Will explained, his patience growing thinner by the minute while his slang thickened. "Damn it, I just want to eat my supper, then lay down and sleep for a hundred years thereabout, so just hobble your lip and step aside."

"What in heaven's name are you talking about?" The owner turned paler, his large face jiggling like aspic as he worked himself into a lather. "On the shoot? Filly?"

"There was a lady out in the street and some mudsills—bad men"—he said with forced patience—"were givin' her some trouble. I just wanted to even the score."

"A lady," the owner sniffed doubtfully. "You mean a trollop."

Will's hand shot out and tightened around the silk of the dude's neckcloth so fast that the man could only gasp in fright as his feet nearly dangled over the stairs. "She was a *lady*," Will insisted, his voice low and dangerous. "And if you insult her, too, then I'll have to feed you your teeth. Hear me?" He gave the owner a slight shake to enforce his point. Releasing him, Will added, "I don't see what the fuss is about. It ain't like you're runnin' the Ritz." He looked around at the dilapidated front parlor, which contained one dying palm tree, a yellowed painting of a cow and a man passed out on an uncomfortable sofa with a bottle cradled in his lap.

"You will remove yourself at once," the owner gasped, "or I will fetch the constabulary immediately."

Will fought the urge to sigh. It was time to cut his losses. Frugality was one thing, but it was another to put up with jackasses. He'd heard once that discretion was the better part of valor. Now was as good a time as any to put that into practice. "Fine." He started to walk past the owner but the man squawked.

"Where are you going?" he demanded.

"To get my things out of my room," Will said. "I'm gonna clear out—"

"Absolutely not! Leave at once."

"I gotta get my saddle, at least."

The owner turned red. "Saddle? In your room? This is not a stable."

"Stables smell better. Now get outta my way." He took a step, but the owner blocked him. The desk clerk appeared to try to add some muscle. Will considered himself someone with a pretty long fuse, but he felt it burning up by the second. "Am I gonna have to clean your plow, too, junior?" Will asked through his teeth. The clerk whitened.

Just as he was getting ready for his second fight in as many days, the front door behind Will opened and closed. He wouldn't have paid it any mind, except both the owner and the clerk goggled over his shoulder like fish on a riverbank.

"I'm not interrupting anything, am I, gentlemen?" asked a soft female voice.

Will had only met a few women during his short time in England, but he knew that voice as sure as he knew his own dreams. Turning around, he saw a sight that made him goggle as much as the dude and his crony standing on the stairs.

Will had never seen a more incongruous or surprising vision than Lady Xavier, pretty and rare as a peach in December, standing in the mildewed, faded lobby of his fleabag hotel. He wanted to snatch her up and run out into the street to keep lowlife dirt like the greenhorns behind him from even looking at her. She was dressed as smart as they come in a burgundy dress and black velvet coat, with a delicate pair of leather gloves and a hat with a turned-back brim, trimmed in burgundy ribbon. Will had never seen a woman in such elegant clothing before, and certainly no one else who could wear them as naturally as their own skin.

With wry amusement and a hint of confusion in her lovely face, she surveyed the scene in front of her.

"Madam," the owner said, hustling his bulk down the stairs as fast as he could. "Can I be of some assistance?" He looked plumb flabbergasted but tried to cover it up with sweet talk.

Which was better than Will—who could only stand and stare like a green kid on his first visit to a saloon.

Lady Xavier looked past the owner at Will. Her direct gaze sent a hundred fireflies of awareness skittering through his body. What the hell was going on?

The owner caught the direction of her gaze and said, "Please take no notice of that hooligan, madam. The Bentley Arms is a respectable establishment and we are having him removed from the premises immediately." The owner glared at Will, daring him to argue in front of a lady.

"Removed?" she asked, frowning a little. "Has he done something wrong?"

The owner slid his eyes around the room, trying to drum up complaints against Will and finding nothing. "Regardless, he is leaving *right now*."

"Goddamn it, I'm gonna get my gear and then I'm leavin'," Will growled. Lady Xavier had already seen him kick up a row with the toughs the day before, but he didn't care for the idea of her seeing him brought low.

"Fetch the bobby," the owner squealed to the desk clerk, and the little man began to scuttle toward the door. Will took several threatening steps, causing both the owner and his crony to shrink into themselves, but Lady Xavier's voice stopped them all.

"All this is quite unnecessary," she said dryly. "Mr. Coffin is a friend of mine."

"He is?" the owner and the clerk asked together.

Will knew better than to question her, though he could hardly call protecting her from a couple of rowdies the basis of a friendship.

"Who are you?" the owner managed to ask through his shock.

She gave him a look so cold it could freeze chile peppers. If Will had ever doubted that she was high-born, the arctic aloofness of her voice convinced him otherwise. Only folks certain of their place in the world could talk or look the way she did at that moment—completely untouchable. "Lady Olivia Xavier, and who are you?"

"H . . . Horace Whitbridge, my lady."

Still as cool as a Dakota breeze, she continued, "Mr. Whitbridge, if you do not want to earn my lasting enmity, you will allow my friend Mr. Coffin to retrieve his belongings from his room at once." Though nobody in his right mind would argue with her, she added, "And if you insist on fetching a constable, I will happily report this shambles you call a hotel to the authorities. Believe me when I tell you that I know many members of Parliament who would happily close down this establishment and any other properties you may own."

Whitbridge gulped. "Of course, my lady. Whatever you wish, my lady. In fact," he added frantically, "there is no need for Mr. Coffin to leave. We'll happily accommodate him for as long as he needs."

Will was about to turn his offer down flat. He'd rather sleep at the docks than spend another night in this dive, but Lady Xavier—Olivia, what a name—beat him to the punch.

"I wouldn't board my dog in such foul conditions," she said frostily. Turning back to Will, her whole attitude changed. With a smile that made Will's chest hurt, she said, "Shall we be going?"

Will had to bury his own grin as he bounded up the stairs—as loudly as he damn well pleased—and grabbed his rucksack and saddle from his room. His heart was racing, and it had nothing to do with the three flights of stairs. Damn, she was *here*. At his sorry shack of a hotel. She'd come looking for him. He didn't know why or what he planned to do with himself once he cleared out, but none of that seemed to matter. He didn't even spare his dingy room a second look as he hustled back downstairs.

It hadn't been a mirage. She was still there, trim and fashionable, and still cool as a duchess. Her eyes widened slightly at the sight of his saddle draped over his shoulder, but other than that, she behaved as if she went to rundown flophouses in dangerous neighborhoods to bail out Colorado cowboys every day.

"Shall we, Mr. Coffin?" she asked with a pert smile. The owner and the clerk continued to stare. She looked expectantly at his arm, and he realized that she was waiting for him to offer it to her.

"Abso-damn-lutely," he answered, sticking out his elbow.

As the owner gasped, Lady Xavier laughed softly and placed her fingers lightly on Will's arm. He almost jumped. She wore gloves and he was bundled underneath his coat, shirt and underwear, but he felt her touch all the way to his boot heels. He was ready to jump out of his skin when Lady Xavier came within breathing distance.

And then they were out on the curb. Night had fallen, but the street was full of curious faces peering at the fancy carriage parked outside the hotel.

Reluctantly, Will separated himself from Lady Xavier. "Thanks, ma'am," he said, touching his fingers to the brim of his hat. "I thought I was gonna have to teach those boys their ABCs."

"I should thank you," she said, her voice a touch gravelly. "And apologize."

Will frowned in surprise. "Ma'am?"

She gazed down at the space between them. "I was unforgivably rude to you yesterday." She tipped up her chin, her face beautiful and grave. "I was wrong to offer you money instead of treating you properly. Like a gentleman."

A startled chuckle rumbled up from his chest. "I ain't never been called a gentleman before. Lots of other names."

"But you are one, Mr. Coffin. You were brave and gallant, helping a woman you don't even know. Most would have ignored the problem, but you didn't. That makes you a gentleman." A crease appeared between the dark arches of her brows. "And I apologize for not considering that."

Where he was from, people didn't use soft words very often, and hardly ever about him, so hearing himself described in such a fashion, and by a woman like Lady Xavier, didn't sit easily on Will's shoulders. He shifted uncomfortably.

"How'd you find me?" he asked suddenly.

She must have sensed his awkwardness because her answer was light and cheerful. "You told me that you were staying 'by the docks,' so I had my footman make some discreet inquiries about any Americans staying in Wapping. There were several Americans in the area, although I had to investigate them all before locating you." She looked around, taking in the dirty, crowded streets and unsavory establishments lining them. "It has been a very educational day."

Will suddenly understood what all this meant. It was clear she was out of her element—she belonged far away from Wapping, in grand houses with servants and beautiful things. She had traveled far from home, with considerable risk to herself, if yesterday was any indication, in order to find him and right a perceived wrong. He was stunned.

"And now you've lost your lodging," she continued, "though I can't say it was a great loss. You ought to delouse yourself as soon as possible."

"Maybe later," he said, still amazed. "But I've got to find someplace else to sleep before it gets too late."

Now it was Lady Xavier's turn to look surprised. "Find someplace else? But I thought it was understood."

A prickle of worry danced down Will's spine. In his experience, when women had that look on their face, trouble was soon to follow. "What's understood?"

As though it were the most obvious fact in the world, she answered, "You're staying with me."

Chapter Three

The decision had been made in an instant. As soon as Olivia and Will Coffin left the squalor of his lodgings, she knew immediately what she was going to do, what she had to do. She only hoped the sureness in her voice didn't betray the uncertainty in her heart.

And so, without knowing much about him beyond his name, she invited the American to lodge at her house for the night.

"After all," she explained as they rode toward Bayswater, "there are no fewer than four unused bedrooms, and it would be a terrific waste to leave them unoccupied." Another plan was ripening in her mind, but she wouldn't give voice to that—not yet.

"Four, huh?" Coffin said, tugging thoughtfully on his mustache. "Seems like a lot of land lying fallow." Still, she could see that he wasn't entirely convinced.

She leaned forward and added, "Please, Mr. Coffin. You would be doing me a great honor."

Her heartfelt request seemed to win him over.

"You sure I won't be causin' you any trouble?" he asked.

"None whatsoever," Olivia answered firmly. Which wasn't entirely true. The physical logistics could be easily managed, yet she could not help wondering what the society wags would make of Lord David Xavier's widow giving temporary accommodation to an American man she had met, literally, on the streets of Wandsworth only the day before. It could cause a minor scandal.

"I won't refuse your hospitality, ma'am," Coffin said with a grin, which she felt rather than saw across from her in the semidarkness of the carriage. "It'd be downright churlish of me to say otherwise."

"That's very obliging of you, Mr. Coffin," she answered, and somehow a smile worked its way onto her own mouth. He did that to her—made her want to smile without really knowing why.

"I've got somethin' that belongs to you," he said.

Olivia raised her brow in astonishment. "What?"

He reached into the pocket of his long coat, forcing him to lean forward a bit. Olivia pressed herself lightly back into the squabs without thinking. He was such a big man, his size and physical presence nearly overwhelmed her. Will Coffin had an air of living on a much larger scale in landscapes that could barely be contained by her imagination. She would be frightened of him if she didn't know that he was, by her own words, a gentleman. Yet as he moved back to pull something from his pocket, she felt herself relax a fraction. There was something unpredictable and raw about him that thrilled her even as she recoiled from its strangeness.

"This is yours, ain't it?" he asked, holding something out to her.

She looked down and saw the yellow paper cover of *Lorna Jane of Glittering Gulch* in his large hand. Olivia flushed. She didn't admit her love of the cheap little books to anyone. They were the reading material of the great unwashed, those without literary discernment or taste, who valued sensationalism over intellectual refinement. Whenever anyone asked what she was currently reading, Olivia mumbled something about Trollope or Ruskin's edifying essays, while *The Laughing Ghost of Killcross Manor; or, Love's Revenge* sat silent and accusing in her bedside table.

Will Coffin had already put the book into her hand, and she stared at it with hot cheeks.

"It's all right," he assured her easily, leaning back. "I know it's yours. I just thought I'd return it to you."

Olivia's fingers tightened around the now-battered novel as she looked up at Coffin's rangy body stretched out in her carriage. "What makes you so sure it's mine?" she heard herself challenge.

"I didn't think any of those mudsills we met yesterday were much for readin'," he answered with a laugh. Then she sensed a sharpening in him, a honed perception, as he added, so low she thought she misheard, "And it smelled like you."

"I beg your pardon?" Olivia asked, more stunned than offended.

Will Coffin straightened, then shifted around on the seat, which had been, only moments earlier, perfectly comfortable but now could not fully contain the length and breadth of him.

"I forgot to give it back to you yesterday. So I took it with me, and that's when I noticed."

"That I smell like a book," Olivia finished.

"No, the book smells like you. The jasmine perfume or toilet water or whatever it is you call it, and orange, and somethin' else. You," he concluded.

"Ah, well," was about all Olivia could manage as she slipped the book into her reticule. It was such a personal observation—no one she knew would ever admit to having their own scent let alone acknowledging someone else's. Surely in their six years of marriage, David had learned the different notes of her own smell. But such knowledge was intimate, reserved only for a spouse and valet or maid.

Somehow, Will Coffin knew her enough to trace her scent—and the visceral animality of this turned Olivia's blood hot and sluggish.

"You like readin' about cowboys," he said.

When she didn't answer, he pointed to her reticule. The corner of his mouth turned up and disappeared under the wide brush of his mustache.

She didn't prevaricate. "Cowboys, pirates, buried treasure, abducted princesses, haunted woods," she enumerated proudly. "All of it."

He whistled in appreciation. "I didn't know ladies read stuff like that."

"They don't. At least," she said with a shrug, "they don't admit it to anyone. Most claim that such reading is beneath them."

"You don't think so," he pointed out.

She shook her head. "I like being entertained. And I love reading about places I'll never go and people who lead lives more exciting than mine."

"Like cowboys," he said with a grin.

"Like cowboys," she answered, smiling right back.

They could have gone right on smiling at each other if the carriage hadn't stopped in front of her house.

"Here we are," she said as the footman opened the carriage door. "Princes Square. Home."

Will stepped out of the carriage and stared up at the biggest pile of stones he'd ever seen outside of the Denver Opera House. But nobody called the Opera House "home." When Lady Xavier said that she had four spare bedrooms, he'd imagined narrow little halls with cots, the kind of accommodation he normally got when staying at a two-story ranch. But this place had to have four stories at least, not counting the basement, where he could see a mess of people bustling around in a kitchen, and the tiny lights at the very top. It wasn't a particularly wide house, but it sure was tall.

"You live here alone?" he asked Lady Xavier as she stood beside him.

"It's only me," she said. "And the servants, of course. Which makes for around twelve altogether."

"Jee-sus," Will breathed. He would have stared indefinitely, but out of the corner of his eye he saw two of the servants trying to take his saddle down from the roof.

"Easy, boys," he said, stepping forward. He carefully grabbed the saddle from their hands and cradled it against him. "I'll take that."

Lady Xavier gazed at him, puzzlement in her lovely violet eyes. "Wouldn't that be better off in the stables?"

"This here saddle cost me two months' wages,"

Will explained, lovingly running a hand down the tooled leather skirts and silver conchos. "I took it with me from Denver to New York and over the Atlantic. So if it's all the same, I'll keep it close by."

Will saw Lady Xavier nod, and the servants backed off. He didn't mind. From the look of things, folks in London didn't fully appreciate the value of a good saddle, and if they thought him peculiar, it didn't make much difference to him. He knew that a man's saddle was one of his most prized possessions, and damn if he'd let a little something like English folly mess up his priorities.

Besides, Lady Xavier looked as though *she* understood. Whether it was just politeness on her part or real understanding Will didn't know, but he did appreciate it. He was quickly beginning to see that Lady Xavier was a lot different from anyone else he had ever met, English, American or otherwise. And she was definitely the most interesting woman he'd ever known.

"Show Mr. Coffin to the Vetiver Chamber, Herbert," she said to one of the servants pulling Will's bag and Winchester down from the roof. She wasn't imperious, but she wasn't embarrassed to give someone directions, either. A middle-aged man and woman in uniform stood on the front steps and bowed and curtsied in greeting as Lady Xavier ascended the stairs.

"Mr. Coffin will be staying with us this evening," she said, gesturing to Will as he came up behind her. "Have Lily and Sarah draw a bath for him. Is there anything you'd like particularly for dinner, Mr. Coffin?" she asked.

"No, ma'am. I'll eat just about anything so long as it's dead enough."

"We'll be sure to give the capons an extra throttling before serving them," she said with dry humor as the servants bowed away. She turned and followed them, expecting him to do the same, but he stared after her for a few seconds.

Goddamn it if he didn't feel a tug at the front of his britches. It was the same tug he'd felt in the carriage when he'd admitted that her damned book smelled like her. He didn't know what in the name of Abraham Lincoln he was thinking, sniffing after her like a wolf on the hunt. She wasn't a pretty piece of corsetry he could woo and lay without much ado. She was a damned lady, someone so far above him that he couldn't see her with a high-powered telescope, and he was a no-name cowboy deadbeat who was going to spend one night under her roof and then find himself someplace more his style to stay.

"Coming, Mr. Coffin?" she called to him. "Dinner is in half an hour and we don't want to keep Cook waiting." Even though he knew he should just grab his saddle and go, he followed.

When Will Coffin joined her half an hour later in the drawing room, he was bathed and combed and wearing what she suspected were his best clothes. She saw his eyes flick to her dinner gown, green velvet and lace, which she had selected precisely because it was one of her oldest and most simple dresses. However, compared to his well-worn white cotton shirt, red-and-gold-striped vest and black wool jacket and pants, she might as well have been clad entirely in peacock feathers.

"Are you settling in all right?" she asked with a bright smile.

"Ma'am, I've never seen a home as pretty," he said, returning the smile. "Though nothin's half as pretty as the lady who lives here."

She laughed off his easy compliment as a bit of western hyperbole. Instead, Olivia focused her attention on the man standing in her drawing room. His coat and hat were gone, and the gaslight, tempered by frosted glass shades, revealed a face that, Olivia suspected, was exceptionally handsome beneath the large mustache. She could see the fine, angular planes of his cheeks, high and defined, and the square line of his jaw before it disappeared under the mustache's unruly bristle. He did need a haircut rather badly, and his clothes were store-bought and well used. But for all that, he captured her attention in a way she was not fully able to comprehend.

The threat of George Pryce seemed very far away at that moment. She felt herself exhale for the first time in several months.

"Shall we go to dinner?" she asked.

"Surely, ma'am." He stuck out his elbow and she rested her fingers as lightly as she could on the hard muscle of his arm. Olivia did not think her etiquette books would endorse running her hand up and down Will Coffin's tough, lean arm, even though that was what she wanted to do very badly.

"This is the dining room," she said, as Mordon, the butler, ushered them inside. She watched Will Coffin look at the long mahogany table surrounded by twelve chairs. Despite the place settings, it seemed empty and unused, and even though it was well-maintained, there was something derelict about the table, down to the enormous silver epergne squatting in the middle. "We used to eat in this room quite a lot when we entertained, but since David died, I mostly take my meals in the morning room, which is much less formal."

"I don't blame you," Coffin said. "It could get awful lonely in a big room like this."

Which was true. Olivia had tried valiantly to eat alone with nothing but the company of the servants and eleven other chairs, but she'd grown so uncomfortable that she'd lost weight. The doctors had feared for her health, but once she switched to the morning room, her appetite returned.

She now took the seat the footman pulled out for her. Will eyed the footman with distrust as he offered him the same service.

"It's all right, Mr. Coffin," she assured him. "That's Lawrence's job."

Once Coffin had settled himself, he looked down the length of the table. He sat at one end, Olivia the other. "Are we expectin' any other company?"

"No, it's just us," Olivia answered, and felt a peculiar shiver at the word *us*. She hadn't used it in a long time.

"Then how come I'm sittin' all the way in East Jesus and you're all the way out there?"

"I . . ." Olivia gazed up and down the expanse of the table, where five large mahogany chairs separated her from Will Coffin. It did seem ridiculous, the space between them. "This is how we normally took our meals."

"Hang on a minute." With a clatter, Coffin collected his plate, silverware and napkin and relocated himself at Olivia's elbow. She resisted looking at the servants, even though they were too well-trained to show shock or disapproval. But Olivia was certain the kitchen would be full of talk later tonight.

"Ain't that better?" Coffin asked, settling in and grinning. She smiled right back at him.

"Much," she answered.

Let them talk, she thought to herself. She hadn't enjoyed a meal so much in years and it hadn't even begun.

"I read some of that book of yours," Will said.

"Which book?" Lady Xavier asked, laying her soup spoon to the side of her bowl. She'd only taken a few sips, while Will'd had to fight the urge to tip the rim right up to his lips and drain the damned thing. If he ate this good every night, he'd wind up as fat as a heifer ready to calf.

"The book with the cowboys and the dumb girl, Liza June."

She laughed. "Lorna Jane. Yes, she often reminds me of a less intelligent vole, poor thing. She never quite thinks things through."

Some servants quietly removed their soup bowls. Will had never been waited on before—at least not with this much ceremony, as though everything he'd touched had turned into a milagro—but the servants came and went with such silent reverence it made Will wonder if he *had* performed some miracle without knowing it. Did they save his bathwater, too?

"Whoever writes those books don't know a thing about cowboyin'," he said.

"I don't read them for their verisimilitude," she said with a smile.

"All the same," Will said, "they give people the

wrong idea about pushin' cows. Stampedes in the mornin', Indians on the warpath at noon and wild-fires at night. Plus lunk-headed Lorna Jane runnin' around without a lick of sense, gettin' kidnapped, tied up and lost regular as Old Faithful." He shook his head. "If I'd had to contend with half the stuff those books write about, I'd be too plumb tuckered out to herd cattle. I'd just sit under a cottonwood tree and wait for someone to tell me the Comanche are diggin' up the tomahawk and, by the way, Lorna Jane's lashed to the train tracks again."

"I'm a little disappointed," Lady Xavier admitted, though her face was cheerful. "I had hoped that some of those stories were true. Especially the Buffalo Bill novels."

Will snorted. "Bill Cody is a big blowhard."

"You've met him?" she asked, eyebrows rising.

"He wanted me to ride in some rodeo, what'd he call it? A Wild West show in Omaha."

"Sounds exciting."

"Playin' cowboy ain't for me. I got my fair share of the real thing."

"And no 'lunk-headed' girls to rescue, either." She added with a pointed smile, "Unless you count me."

"You ain't lunk-headed," Will said. "You're the boss."

He thought he saw a little flush creep up her cheeks, but the gaslight flickered.

"What brings you to England, Mr. Coffin?" she asked suddenly. Will watched carefully as she helped herself to some chicken from a dish a servant held out to her. He knew that there was no way he could manage all the rules needed for a fancy dinner, but he was determined not to show himself too much of a green-horn where high society was concerned.

"I'm lookin' for some people," he said. The servant came around with the dish and Will did his best to follow Lady Xavier's lead.

Her face lit up. "Are you tracking down the men who did you wrong?" she asked. "Are you out for justice?"

"You've read too many of those dime novels, ma'am," he said, laughing. "I ain't no vigilante."

She struggled to keep the disappointment from her voice. "That's good." After taking a sip of wine, she asked, "If I may ask, who are you looking for?"

Will was so hungry he wanted to cram the whole chicken right into his mouth, but he reminded himself that he wasn't in the bunkhouse anymore, and he didn't have to worry about rotten bastards like Omaha Dave or Frank Bell getting to all the food before he had the chance. Forcing himself to cut a genteel bite, he said, "My family."

"You don't know your family?" she asked, and her lovely purple eyes widened in horrified surprise. Starved as he was, Will thought Lady Xavier was a damned sight more appetizing than the roast bird he was chewing, and that was saying a lot because he'd never tasted anything finer.

"No, ma'am. Never have. When I was a little 'un, my folks were killed by a dynamite blast."

She placed her soft fingers on his sleeve. "I am very sorry."

Damn it, was he blushing? "Thanks, ma'am, but it was a long time ago. I don't even remember it." He regretted when she took her hand away, but at least it allowed his heart to stop racing like a runaway train. "They didn't know too much about sodbusting— farming—but were tryin' to make a go of it in the

Rockies. They had some dynamite and nobody told them that they shouldn't bring it inside. Near the fire."

"Oh, no."

Will nodded ruefully. "Yeah. The whole cabin went up. Only reason I wasn't killed, too, was on account of me playin' out by the woodpile."

"How did you survive?"

"A miner heard the noise and could tell the difference between a planned blast and an accidental one. When he got to the homestead, he found me buck naked, covered in ash and messin' around with a coffin-handled Bowie knife. Since my folks were dead and there wasn't anything to show who I was or what my name might be, he named me."

Her food was now completely untouched as she stared at him. Will couldn't decide whether he liked having her look at him or whether it was like staring right at the sun. "I was wondering how a man could be named Coffin."

"I've gotten a few jokes over the years, but once folks get to know me, the undertaker gags stop."

"And what did the miner do with you after he found you?"

"He raised me." Will smiled sadly, thinking about his old friend. "He called himself Jake Gold, but his real name was Ya'akov Goldberg."

"That sounds Jewish," she observed.

Will immediately tensed. "You got a problem with that?"

Her eyes rounded again. "My grandmother was Jewish; my father's mother. Sarah Speigelman." Her expression darkened, a surprisingly fierce thing. "Some people stopped speaking to my grandfather after he married her, but he said they were fools." She looked down at her plate, toying with her food. "I was sorry when she died. She was a beautiful woman."

Will said, *"Punkt vi ir,"* Like you, surprising himself, both at the compliment and his language choice.

But she was more surprised. *"Ir redt yidish?"*

"A kleyn bisl." A little.

The expression on her face was comically astounded but very pleased. He'd completely ambushed her, a thought that gave him no small pleasure. They were both a little different from expectations, and Will liked it. It gave him, for the first time in a long while, the feeling of belonging, but belonging to a small, select group—their separate club apart from everyone else.

"A cowboy raised by a Jewish miner," she marveled, her eyes warm as her fingertips touched the rim of her glass. "What a marvelous story."

Will shrugged. "It makes a good tale, but the life was hard. Jake mined his whole life, waitin' for the big score, but it never came." He took a deep drink and marveled at the feel of the wine on his tongue. "This is great stuff," he said, admiring the dark red liquid. "I ain't used to such a fine vintage. Usually what passes for wine in Colorado could take rust off a wagon wheel."

She laughed, saying, "We're much more refined here. We use our wine for cleaning tarnished silver," and Will laughed, too. After playing with her food a bit more, she asked, "When did Mr. Gold die?"

"Six months ago." He looked down at his plate. "I've seen a lot of death in my years, and I'd grown almost used to it, but sometimes it catches a body hard. That's what happened when Jake died." He looked up and saw not pity in her eyes but empathy. He'd never told anyone how he felt about Jake dying, but he knew that Lady Xavier was exactly the person who would understand and not poke fun.

"I felt as though a horse had kicked me in the chest, and even now I can't quite catch my breath, thinkin' about old Jake."

"You loved him," she said simply.

Those were words Will didn't speak, but he felt it just the same. "The *alter bocher* loved America but missed his home in Krakow. He told me he'd been squirrelin' his catch away and gave me the key to a safety deposit box at a bank in Denver. I found ten thousand dollars in it."

She looked impressed, but Will knew that money like that couldn't mean much to her. He figured the furniture and gewgaws in this dining room alone cost over ten thousand dollars, what with the silver monster sitting in the middle of the table and the heaps of silver knives, forks and spoons that glinted everywhere like the Comstock lode.

"What did you do with the money?"

"Nothin' . . . yet."

This news caused her more astonishment than anything. "I know what you're thinkin'," he said ruefully. "Some beat-up, dusty cowboy would piss away his windfall on whores and rotgut inside of a few months."

"No!" she said immediately, then added, a mite shamefaced, "Well, possibly."

"Jake told me, just before he died, that I was different from a lot of the cattle-punchers," Will admitted. With a shrug, he said, "Maybe I am. Haven't quite figured it out yet."

"I'm glad you haven't spent the money," Lady Xavier said, her voice quiet but warm. She looked at him, open admiration in her eyes. "I'm very glad, indeed. Now, let's finish our dinner before Cook gets insulted and threatens to quit again. You must be very hungry."

More than you know, Will thought.

She had never seen her home through someone else's eyes. As she and Will Coffin moved through the rooms and halls where she had lived for the past eleven years, the configuration, size, shape and even the smell became foreign to her, so that as she entered a different chamber in the house, she could anticipate what he would feel, sense his reaction even before he spoke.

It was curiously intimate, and also unsettling. Not unlike finding a stray animal in the woods and having it follow you home warily, nosing under the furniture and disrupting order and stability with its undomesticated energy.

That was Will Coffin, padding cautiously into the apartments of her house and taking everything in with a feral, perceptive gaze. When they had settled back in the drawing room, Olivia felt strangely awkward. From an early age, she had been trained in the proper forms of what a hostess should do with her guests, but all that seemed like empty, ridiculous ceremony now. Why on earth would Will Coffin, a rough man of the Colorado Rockies, want to drink sherry and play euchre? It seemed frivolous, a means to waste time, and from the sound of things, time was short for men like him.

Lately, her own life had been so exhausting, so enervating. Running Greywell's had always taken her time and energy, and now George Pryce was making things incredibly difficult. It was a lot for one woman to shoulder by herself, almost overwhelming. But having Will Coffin in her home helped all that fade to the back of her mind, if only for a little while.

"Whiskey?" she asked, standing by the decanter.

"Yes, ma'am." He hunkered down by the fire and stirred the smoldering logs with the poker, his gestures practiced and experienced. He was so focused on his task that she actually caught him off guard when she came to stand beside him, bearing two glasses of single-malt scotch.

"You joinin' me?" he asked, straightening to his impressive height.

"My late husband used to drink this after dinner, but it was only until after his death that I thought to give it a try. It's not a drink for ladies, but I like it."

He took a glass from her and winked. "I promise not to tell."

No one had flirted with her in so long. And certainly not in such a bold fashion. What an incredible feeling this was, as though she were ten, fifteen years younger.

"To new friends," she said, holding up her glass for a toast.

He seemed to like the sound of that. "Here's how," he said, and their glasses made a chiming sound in the still room. She felt it like a ringing bell in her own heart.

"You never answered my question, Mr. Coffin," she said after taking a sip of whiskey. It slid down her throat and pooled warmly in her belly, but she wondered if it was the scotch that made her feel that way or the lanky, raw man beside her. When he looked at her questioningly, she explained, "How is it that you are in England?"

Coffin took a drink of whiskey and gazed into the fire, contemplative. "Jake left me a note in that safety deposit box. He told me to get out of pushin' cows while I still had all my fingers and toes. He said I had too much goin' on upstairs to sit on the back of a horse the rest of my life, and he wanted the money to be a way out."

"Do you agree with him?"

He shrugged. "A body can't cowboy forever, I know that. Eventually, a man's gonna wind up dead. And the railroads are makin' men like me unnecessary. Soon enough, there won't be any cattle drives anymore, and I'll be just another blowhard sittin' in the saloon, spinnin' yarns."

"So what are you going to do?"

"That's what brought me out to your lovely country, Lady Xavier," he said, a smile disappearing under one side of his mustache.

Coffin reached into the inside pocket of his jacket and produced a brittle, blackened piece of paper. It looked to be damaged by fire and years of use. Setting down his glass on the mantel, he carefully unfolded the paper. It astonished Olivia to see him handle something so tenderly and with such care—his hands seemed capable of immense strength and yet he opened the paper as gently as if he were holding a baby chick.

"Careful, now," he warned as he handed the paper to her.

Also setting down her glass, Olivia took the sheet

and scanned it. It was written with a man's sure hand, but the ink had browned and faded.

> *"Dear Mr. Hardene,*
> *We have at last settled and the baby is fine. Tomorrow we will start blasting out some of the larger rocks so we may begin clearing our fields. It is so different here than in London, but we are determined to make a new start. Please be sure to let my father know that—"*

"That's all there is," Will explained. "The only thing my parents left me is that little scrap."

"You want to find them," Olivia said, understanding. She returned the letter to Coffin and he put it away. She leaned back against the side of the fireplace and felt a touch of the cool marble against her shoulders. "You want to know about where you come from before you determine where you're going."

He frowned in contemplation, absently stroking his mustache. "I hadn't thought about it like that," he said slowly, then nodded, "but it makes sense." He gave a little snort of recognition. "Me comin' out here to figure myself out. Yeah, I guess that's what I'm doin'. You sure are quick, Lady Xavier," he added with admiration.

"You probably understood that already," she demurred, "though not knowingly."

He stared at her for a long time, and the only sound in the room came from the pop of the fire and the ticking chinoiserie clock. His stare was direct, penetrating, more keenly perceptive than she would have liked. But approving, too, that look. He came to stand in front of her, then braced his hands on each side of her. His arms were long, so he did not hover too close, and yet he *was* close, closer than any man had been to her in years.

"You're the only person I've met who's been able to figure that out," he said. "All the fellas I know back in Colorado think I'm off my rocker. They think I should just open my own ranch and quit lollygaggin'."

She felt it, too, this thing between them, a small, secret understanding that drew them together. She ought to slip out from under his arms. She ought to tell him to stand back—no gentleman would lean so close to a lady—but she could feel the warmth of his body over hers and she saw the growing interest in his eyes, the bright spark of primitive awareness that found an answer deep in her own belly.

"I think you are doing the right thing," she told him. Her breath wouldn't come fast enough. Had someone slipped laudanum into her drink? She felt profoundly drugged, fluid.

"I think so, too," he said. His voice was even rougher, a harsh rasp full of grit. Then he leaned down farther, his arms bending out to the side, and he kissed her.

And she kissed him back. Their mouths met, a light brush at first, and then became more definitive, slightly wet. She tasted whiskey and tobacco on him; the careful exploration his lips and tongue were conducting were a counterpoint to these aggressively male flavors. The brush of his mustache against her top lip felt faintly, pleasantly abrasive. Again he surprised her. So much more refinement, if such alert sensuality could be called refinement, than she had anticipated. And it felt so *good*. She heard a rumble come from his throat. Ah, mutual pleasure. Her hands at the small of her back tingled with it.

Pleasure was too mild a word. Olivia hadn't felt such marvelous unfolding sensations since . . . long before David died.

That was when she stopped, turned her head and broke her mouth away from Will Coffin.

"Lady Xavier—" he began, dropping his arms.

She wasn't about to let him speak. "I have to get to bed," she said. She started to rush toward the door but made herself slow down. "It's late, and we've had a long day. I must get some sleep." At the door, she added, "If you have need of anything, just ring for the butler. But I—good night."

And then she was literally running for her room.

Will watched silently as she left—darting out as though she were leading the stampede. He cursed himself when she had gone. Stupid, clumsy dope, slobbering over her, like he'd never been near a woman before.

He was a fool who was completely stumped. Lady Xavier had him as lost as a pirate ship in the Rockies. He couldn't figure out what it was about her that had him tied up in knots. She was handsome, the handsomest woman he'd ever seen, and she could laugh and smile in such a way that it made his eyes sting with gratitude. But under all that, there was something else, a fine sharpness he'd never known anywhere else.

Will's gaze fell on a small framed photograph on the mantel. It held a place of honor between two vases of yellow flowers. He had a good idea who the man in the picture might be, so he went back to examine it, drawn by morbid curiosity and—what? Jealousy? But that couldn't be.

All the same, Will stared down at the face of David Xavier, the face of a man who'd been dead for years.

The picture Lord David Xavier took was clearly meant for family, for a wife. He was sitting in a chair, wearing some kind of long silk robe over his clothes to show that he was taking his leisure. The man wasn't large, but he wasn't overly small. Just average. He had a slight paunch filling out his expensive waistcoat and a fine watch chain looped around the buttons.

His face interested Will the most. Not unkind, and tending toward shrewdness, handsome in a soft, well-kept way. The lines around the eyes showed a man who'd squinted a lot. His medium brown hair was thinning at the sides and would have eventually given way to baldness had he lived. All in all, David Xavier looked like a man in possession of a large amount of money, a goodly bit of power and a lot of self-satisfaction. Will couldn't blame him—the man had what most wanted. Including a beautiful, clever wife.

Will found himself absently stroking his mustache. Xavier had a mustache, too. Not that that was unusual; most men sported some kind of hair on their faces. It was a sign of maturity, of manly pride. Will had started getting his first beard when he was fourteen. Eager to prove himself a man and able to work, he'd let it grow in and hadn't been bare-faced since. Only once before had he shaved his face completely, and he'd gotten so much ribbing from the boys in the bunkhouse and catcalls from the girls in town, he'd grown his mustache back as soon as he could.

That'd been six years ago. He didn't know what he'd look like without it. Someone else. Someone different.

Different from David Xavier.

Chapter Four

A stranger walked into her breakfast room.

Alarmed, Olivia rose nearly out of her chair, her morning toast and tea half consumed, to summon Mordon. Her butler never let strangers in without at least announcing them, and she wondered what he could have been thinking to admit this unknown young man.

And then the stranger opened his mouth and Will Coffin's voice came out. "Whadya think?"

Olivia slowly lowered herself back down, stunned beyond words. He had shaved off his mustache either last night or this morning. The transformation was astonishing. And disquieting.

If she had suspected him handsome before, now she had full proof that Will Coffin was one of the most magnificent-looking men she had ever seen in her life. It was no wonder his kiss last night had felt so marvelous—his mouth was perfectly sculpted, just shy of being too full, too sensuous—and all tempered by the clean, sharp severity of his good looks. And somehow his eyes were lighter, more intense, drawing her own eyes immediately to them by the purity of their cool blue blaze.

Oh, God, this stunning man had stayed the night in her home? And she had kissed him? A disaster.

Seeing the dismay on her face, Will Coffin grimaced. "That ugly, huh?" he asked. He paced to a mirror over the sideboard and looked disapprovingly at his own reflection, touching the tips of his fingers to his clean upper lip.

"No, no," Olivia said. "Not ugly at all, Mr. Coffin. You're quite . . . agreeable." Which was the equivalent of calling the Pyramids headstones.

Still staring critically at himself, turning his face from side to side, he muttered, "I don't know what I was thinkin'."

Her modest breakfast room was filled with him. She ought to have taken her morning meal in the dining room—at least in that large, formal space, she would be less aware of his outsized masculinity, which took all space and left little air to breathe. Shaving his mustache had not domesticated Will Coffin at all. Now, he was like a well-groomed lion standing in front of the rosewood sideboard, ready to pounce.

Something else occurred to Olivia as she watched him critique himself. "If I may ask, how old are you, Mr. Coffin?"

He turned and faced her with a wry smile. "Call me Will. This 'mister' business makes me feel like a trail boss, which I sure ain't."

"Very well." She struggled to compose herself. Everything was growing more complicated by the second, and if she asked him the question she'd been thinking about all night, she would have to keep her wits. "How old are you, William?"

He grinned, and her heart contracted. It did not seem right that one man could be so attractive, especially *this* man. "Just Will, ma'am. Jake never got around to the rest of the name. But to answer your question," he continued, thoughtfully and hypnotically running a finger back and forth over the expanse of fresh skin above his top lip, "I don't know. When my folks died, I was about knee high, but there weren't no records of my birthday, so I just kinda estimated."

"And what is your estimation?"

"'Bout twenty-seven, twenty-eight, or so." He shrugged. "It never made a difference. Long as I could push cows, none of the foremen ever cared how old I was. Are you all right? You don't look so good." He took a few steps forward, and she pressed herself back into the cushions of her chair.

"I'm fine," Olivia said, though she knew she looked ashen. She tried to recover by drinking her tea, a futile gesture. "I just . . . did not expect you to be so young."

He chuckled, moving back, and she swallowed. "Where I come from, I'm an old man. Folks like me are lucky to live so long."

Olivia smiled wanly, then stared down at her plate, where her toast had grown hard and cold. She doubted she could swallow another bite, anyway. Despite what Will said, he really *was* young, four or five years younger than herself, and between his age and his good looks, Olivia's carefully wrought plans were beginning to appear unfeasible.

But what choice did she have? Things were starting to grow desperate.

Managing to recollect herself, she said brightly, "Why don't you help yourself to some breakfast, Mr. . . . Will? I'm sure you didn't mean to start your day with my discourtesy."

"Nothin' discourteous at all," he said, and his manner was so affable, she knew she would have to be on her guard. She watched as he took a plate from the sideboard and heaped it with eggs, bacon, fried bread, tomatoes and sausages. The Sevres china looked fragile and childlike in his large, square-fingered hand, something to decorate a well-appointed doll house. "You eat all this yourself?" he asked, sitting down beside her. "If so, I'm plumb amazed. You're no bigger around than an aspen sapling."

She shook her head. "Of course not. But since you're here, I thought you might appreciate something more substantial than my usual marmalade and toast."

And it did appear as though he appreciated it. Will began to shovel food into his mouth with the speed of a fireman stoking coal into a train's firehole. He must have felt her eyes on him because he abruptly stopped. "Sorry, ma'am," he said with a sheepish grin. "No chuckwagon can compete with the grub you got here."

"Don't apologize," she said. "I'm glad you enjoy the food. And perhaps," she hesitated, then continued with more conviction, "you might call me Olivia. 'Ma'am' makes me feel a trifle old."

"Old? You?" He shook his head in disbelief. "You're as fresh and lovely as a field of columbine. But if it's Olivia you want, I'm happy to oblige." He sipped his coffee and smiled. "This ain't Arbuckle's, that's for damned sure."

She decided to let him finish his meal in peace before springing her proposition on him. As critical as the situation was becoming, she did not spend years at finishing school in Geneva to rudely accost her guest with projected schemes. So they ate quietly together—or rather, he ate and she sipped her tea. She thought briefly about correcting his hunched-over posture, which indicated that he was protecting his food from any scavengers, or the way he held his cutlery like weapons, or even the napkin he had tucked into the collar of his shirt. Olivia had no intention of playing Pygmalion with Will Coffin. He was not her project, her raw clay to be formed and shaped to her liking. Besides, table manners notwithstanding, she rather enjoyed him the way he was. Even though his youth and appearance had unsettled her, Olivia found the experience of breakfasting with Will much more agreeable than she had anticipated. Almost homey: domestic, yet with a frisson of wildness—somewhat like taking tea with a slightly trained grizzly bear.

"Y'know," he murmured after popping a whole slice of bacon in his mouth, "I never really ate like this before, but maybe my folks did, or their folks. Seems kinda strange that all this"—he gestured around the elegant little room with his knife—"is buried in me somewhere."

"Breakfast rooms?" Olivia asked.

Will grinned. "Naw. England. I was raised a Colorado cowpuncher, but there's this vein of Englishness in me that could be waitin' to be discovered. Like the silver in the Rockies. Somethin' fine stuck in the middle of hard rock. Funny, ain't it?"

Olivia looked at him, assessing. Maybe, if he wasn't

wearing his outrageously foreign Western clothing, and if he didn't open his mouth to let his honeyed twang wrap around every word, and if he didn't saturate a space with his expansive democratic personality, he might, just might, pass for an Englishman—in the fairness of his coloring and the precision of his bone structure. But there were a lot of *if*s that needed to be negotiated before that hint of Englishness could come through.

Olivia had never been overly fond of the English archetype. National pride dictated that the women of England were to love the Anglo-Saxon sons of their home country, but for her tastes, those men often seemed delicate and retiring, a bit like Bunthorne in Gilbert and Sullivan's *Patience*. Picturing Will carrying an oversized sunflower and wearing velvet knee breeches made Olivia smile. Absurd, incongruous.

Will saw her smile and must have thought she found the idea of him as an undiscovered treasure amusing. "Yeah," he said, slightly dispirited as he poked at his eggs, "funny."

"Oh, no, Will," she said quickly, "I was thinking of . . ." She didn't know how to explain the ridiculous notion of Will, the cowboy, in aesthetic dress. "That is, I think that you could have a great deal of Englishness in you."

He brightened, and she realized that in many ways, Will Coffin was rather young. "You think so?"

"I do, but I wouldn't be so quick to cast off your Americanness just yet. I think it's rather nice."

Will said with a grin, "Thanks. But I'm pure cattle pusher, through and through, an' I'm glad 'bout that. I just wonder, sometimes." He shrugged and took a big bite of toast.

"I can't imagine what it must be like to know nothing about yourself," Olivia said thoughtfully. "No father, mother, brothers or sisters. Just an empty, clean expanse of history on which to shape yourself as you please." She thought about her own family and David's, and a whole world that knew who she was and what she was going to be even before she had been born. "It must be wonderful."

"Sometimes." He drank down the last of his coffee. "And sometimes . . ." Will looked out the mullioned window that faced the back garden, an unguarded longing in his eyes that made her heart feel brittle. "Sometimes I wanted to send a photo home to my folks like the other boys did at the end of the trail, but Jake moved around and there wasn't anybody else."

She wanted to apologize for his solitude, even though she hadn't been responsible. She wanted to take that longing away from his eyes. She wanted a lot of things, things she hadn't known she wanted until very recently.

Instead, she suggested, "Shall we take a turn in the garden? Most of the flowers have gone, but it's still lovely this time of year."

He visibly shook off his melancholy, transforming from a man in search of something into an easygoing cowboy. "That's another thing I ain't done," he said with a grin, standing up and then pulling out her chair, "take a turn in the garden. Sounds fine, indeed."

She hoped he would still think so after she waylaid him.

"October in London can be rather gray, I'm afraid," she remarked. She ran her fingers over the glossy green leaves of a neatly trimmed hedge, and Will could see where the blossoms had withered with the coming of autumn.

"It ain't so bad," he said, but he was looking at her, not the hedges. His boots crunched loudly while her dainty little shoes—though he couldn't see them—hardly made a sound at all. They strolled down the narrow gravel paths of her little back garden, and though she did not take his arm, they kept gently bumping up against each other until Will was half loco. She hadn't said anything about their kiss last night, and Will had learned enough to know that if a lady didn't want to talk about fooling around, she wouldn't appreciate a body bringing it up.

But the funny thing was that it *hadn't* felt like fooling around. It had felt different than stealing kisses from the church-going daughters of the ranch owners, and it was a hell of a lot different from the rough tumbles he would get in town with more worldly women. He'd felt a little something stir inside him when he and Olivia kissed, and it wasn't just his John Thomas.

Don't think bosh, Will reminded himself. He kicked his toe into the path and sent a few stones clattering. There couldn't be anything going on with him and an actual lady. Especially since the night was past and it was getting on for him to grab his gear and go. He still had a lot of work ahead of him.

"If we had met a few months earlier," she continued, "you would have found my garden a much more beautiful place."

"I like it," he said, "as it is. Kinda reminds me of the public gardens in Denver. Tidy, but smart. A little smaller, a'course." He felt a bit like a giant, like that fellow Gulliver, towering over the trim hedges cut into refined blocks, and just as clumsy, though he suspected Olivia was more the source of his ungainliness than the garden. Any minute, he felt he would go tumbling into a flowerbed.

"Naturally. Perhaps when you get the opportunity, you should visit Hyde Park. You ought to find its wide-open spaces to your liking. People even go riding there. I do, when I have the time."

It pleased him to think she was a horsewoman. He didn't think he could really like a body who couldn't sit a horse—it seemed unnatural, somehow. He hadn't ridden in nearly three weeks, a fact that made him almost sick with longing. No self-respecting man could call himself a cowboy and be on foot for so long.

"Maybe if I get the chance," he answered.

"And you brought your own saddle," she added. "Which looks a trifle different from English ones."

"That's 'cause mine is meant for workin'."

She'd led him toward a little stone fountain, which was dry and had a few dead leaves resting in its bowl. She picked out the leaves and scattered them on the ground, but she did this so diligently that Will suspected something was on her mind. "This is one of my favorite spots back here."

"It's powerful pretty," he said slowly. She wanted to tell him something, something she was having a hard time saying. Will had a suspicion what that might be, and it made him a bit low, though it wasn't a surprise.

"It dates from the eighteenth century," she continued. She kept looking at the fountain, which was a fine little thing, nicely carved with leaves and flowers, but surely not deserving so much concentration. She avoided meeting his eye. "It once belonged to Sophie, Viscountess of Briarleigh. She was a famous botanist.

Some of her theories are still being used today." A small, melancholy smile curved Olivia's lips. "She was lucky. She had a husband who believed in her and enough fortune to ignore society. Things were different then."

"Sounds like a remarkable woman."

Olivia nodded. She chewed on her bottom lip, and Will was torn between trampling all the pretty shrubs in order to flee and taking two steps around the fountain and laying his mouth right down on hers. She probably wouldn't cotton to him kissing her again, since it seemed she was readying herself to give Will the mitten and tell him he could never take any liberties with her again.

"Lady Briarleigh could speak her mind," she said darkly. "I wish I had the same fortitude."

He knew what she wanted to say, though politeness or breeding kept her from saying it. "Look, Lady Xavier," Will burst out, tired of waiting, "I'm planning on packin' my plunder this mornin'. You don't gotta tell me to scoot."

She looked up at him, shock and dismay in her eyes. "No," she said quickly. "That's not what I want at all. I hope I didn't . . . Lord, no!" She gestured to a small stone bench. "Please sit, Will. I just want to talk to you for a few minutes."

He took a seat gingerly, feeling mighty relieved and also beef-brained. It seemed that every opportunity he managed to prove what a yokel he really was. She continued to stand by the fountain, but at least she looked at him now. Glancing down, Will noticed that he took up the whole bench, which was probably meant for two people. Everything here in England seemed so much smaller than back home. He felt like a big, lumbering draft horse in a country of ponies.

"What do women do where you live, Will?" she asked.

He frowned. "Do?" he repeated. "You mean, for a livin'?"

"Exactly," she said, nodding. "Do they stay at home? Do they work?"

Will reached up to tug thoughtfully on his mustache, realizing when he touched the bare top lip that it was gone. His heart sank. That had been one of the stupidest things he'd ever done, if Olivia's horror-struck look had been any indication. But he'd just wanted to start fresh, be someone different for a while. He should have known that you couldn't make a sirloin from chuck.

"Some have jobs, I guess," Will said meditatively. He snapped off a dead twig and began to flip it along his fingers. "There ain't too many women out West, so they can pick and choose what they want to do. One lady I met ran the town newspaper, and another owned the dry goods store. 'Course," he added, "a lot either work at or own cathouses."

"They don't mention that in Mr. Ingraham's novels," she said with a nervous laugh.

"I don't expect they would. Don't want impressionable ladies readin' about soiled doves."

"No, indeed." She picked at a spot of moss on the fountain. "But would you say that women in Colorado have freedom? Freedom to pursue lives outside of their homes?"

"Some do," Will answered cautiously. He wasn't sure exactly where she was leading, but it was starting to make him a mite suspicious. He longed for a good piece of timber and a whittling knife. When he got antsy, he carved, and he thought he could probably carve a whole armada of wooden ships about now.

"I . . ." She struggled to find the right words. "Let me put this another way . . ." She braced her hands against the fountain and leaned against it. "In those books I read about the West, there were often farmers who were being forced off their land by evil cattle barons, or bad railway men, or someone else who wanted what they had. And those bad men used whatever means they had at their disposal to get what they wanted, even if it wasn't right, even if someone got hurt."

"I think I know what you're talkin' about." He added, "Those are just books, though. It ain't real life." Will did know of a few instances where sodbusters had been run off their land, but it happened a lot less than the melodramas and dime novels made it seem.

"But for me, it *is* real life," she said. She came quickly around the fountain and sat beside him on the tiny bench. She moved so fast, he didn't have time to scoot over, and even through her layers of petticoats and skirts, he could feel her leg pressed against his. But she didn't seem to notice. He almost toppled into the bushes.

"My brewery is in danger," she continued. She looked at him intently, and Will found he could not turn away. "Those men you beat the other night were only a small part of a bigger problem. And I fear that the man who sent them will only become more and more desperate as time goes on. He wants Greywell's very badly."

"Why don't you just sell him the brewery?"

She shot to her feet, energy and outrage crackling

through her like an electrical storm. "Because it's mine," she said hotly. Pacing in the small enclosure around the fountain, Olivia reminded Will of a caged mountain lion, spitting mad and ready to fight. "Because no one thinks I should have it. Because people think a woman shouldn't be in business, especially not a woman of my 'station.' Because," she concluded, turning to face him, "I will not be bullied. Not by George Pryce, not by anybody."

He could feel her force like a tornado tearing down the prairie. It was hard not to go to her, give her a little squeeze of encouragement, but there was no way on this green earth that such a gesture by him would be welcomed by a lady like her. Still, Will found himself admiring her gumption, which she had in spades.

The twig in his hand snapped, and the sound made them both look down in surprise. He tossed it aside.

She forced herself to take several deep breaths, letting the hot color in her cheeks recede. "Suffice it to say, Greywell's belongs to me and I have no intention of letting anyone take it away from me, regardless of their tactics."

"Sounds like you been guardin' the henhouse for a while," Will said.

"George Pryce is worse than a fox," Olivia said darkly. "At first he simply tried to buy me out, and when I refused, he started threatening me, my family. But the other day was the first time he made good on those threats. He thinks his breeding can get him anything, that it justifies any behavior." She clasped her arms and held them against her chest. "I am certain it will only grow worse."

Will stretched out his legs. He wasn't used to keeping them inactive for so long. "So just report him to the sheriff, or the judge, or whatever you got here. They'll throw Pryce into the hoosegow and your problem's solved."

She pressed her lips together, clearly frustrated. "Come with me," she said suddenly, and began to walk hurriedly back toward her house. Will followed at a goodly distance, both out of self-preservation and also, he admitted to himself, to keep himself away from her. He kept wanting to reach out and touch her, just a little bit. She seemed to him both powerful determined but also very alone, a combination he was finding difficult to resist.

Back inside, she picked up a fresh newspaper sitting in the breakfast room. After flipping through the pages for a few moments, she folded the paper back to one section and held it out to him.

"Read this," she said in a voice that would not be argued with.

He did.

The Kennford Gallery was highly honored yesterday by a visit from George Pryce, youngest son of the Earl of Hessay. Mr. Pryce opened the newest exhibit of several esteemed painters from the Royal Academy, guaranteeing success for these artists. Mr. Pryce and his venerated family have been patrons of the arts for nearly two hundred years, and it is well known that the earl's late father passed several legislative bills in Parliament in support of arts funding.

"So everyone thinks Pryce is of the first water," Will said, tossing the paper down.

"Not only him but his whole family. Men like him

can trample people like me in a moment. Exactly like he is doing now."

"But you're a lady."

Her laugh was prickled like a cactus. "My husband bought his title. He became a baronet through money, not blood."

"Unlike Pryce." Will paced toward the window and stared at the severely trimmed garden he and Olivia had just left. Most everything in England seemed broken to the saddle, contained. Except Olivia. When he turned to look at her, there was enough fire in her eyes to melt a Dakota winter.

"Precisely. And one thing about England, Will, is that she loves her noblemen. David got his wealth through textiles, and my father was a banker. We're new money. Even though people like David and my father have fortunes greater than many of them, the aristocrats will always come first. Believe me, I know." She sank down into a chair and appeared, for the first time, weary. "When Pryce first began making his threats, I tried to go to the authorities, but he'd gotten to them first. They laughed me out the door."

Will went over and looked again at the paper. There was a small engraving next to the article that showed a gent with full mutton chops and a top hat, someone a touch overbred for Will's liking, and a bit smug around the mouth.

"That him?" he asked.

She nodded.

"Looks like he could stand for a dose of strap oil."

She smiled a bit at this. "How I wish I could give it to him."

"Somebody oughta."

"I agree. But I cannot. Certainly not alone. I need to find someone who can. And I think I know who." She stared at him directly. No, she had no idea how lovely she was, solemn and serious and full of vinegar. "I need you, Will."

He blinked, straightened, banging against the heavy wooden table and making the china and silver jangle. He wished her request was based on a different need, but he knew what she was talking about. "To fight Pryce? What the hell can I do? If you're new money, I'm new nothin'. A cowpuncher with holes in his socks."

"I can mend those holes. Or buy you new socks."

"You know what the hell I mean. I live in the saddle and ain't got no home." He dragged a hand through his hair, rattled. "I can't hold a candle to some society upper-cruster, not when it comes to fine manners and peacockery."

"That's exactly why I need you." She rose and stood in front of him. "I don't want fine manners or posturing. You defeated Pryce's thugs. You know how to handle yourself. You can help me protect my brewery."

"Two fists can't fight a well-heeled dude," he objected.

"It's not merely brute strength but a quality of mind, a will to survive. And if you have anything, it's that will."

He almost smiled at the pun of his name, but he felt himself being drawn underwater. He began to pace, jarring the crystal in the chandeliers and vibrating the mirrors. The whole room might fall apart.

"I can make it worth your while," she said softly.

Will jerked his head up sharply as he wheeled around. "I don't need your money."

"We already settled that two days ago," she said. The tiniest smile touched her mouth. "I had another payment in mind."

Chapter Five

Will Coffin stared at her as if she had just suggested she dance naked down Oxford Street, and from the looks of things, he wasn't entirely averse to the idea.

"Well, ma'am," he said, his drawl thickening as he rocked back on his heels, "that's a mighty interestin' notion, and don't think I haven't considered the prospect myself, but seein' as how you're a lady and I'm some tumbleweed rollin' through town, it might not be so wise. For your sake," he added hastily.

And then she understood, and it was her turn to redden and stammer. "Oh, Lord, no . . ." she said. How horrible. He thought she was offering him her bed, with her in it, in exchange for his help with Pryce. "That's not what I meant at all. I'm sorry if I—"

He held out his hands, as if to push a wall up between them. A flush crept into his tanned cheeks. "No, I should apologize for leapin' to conclusions—"

"I must have made a dreadful impression on you if you thought—"

Their voices overlapped, until Olivia's staunch, enforced politeness won out. "What I meant was that I would assist you in finding your family," she explained. "I do not come from such noble background as George Pryce, but I am well connected. It would be much easier for you if you allowed me to help in your search."

He still appeared deeply embarrassed by his assumption but tried to push it aside. He worked a toe of his boot into the thick oriental rug. "I doubt you'd know my folks," he said. "They could be livin' in the streets."

"I might not know them personally, but let me assure you that I have excellent tools at my disposal for locating people. An English lady with many contacts can succeed where an unknown American cannot," she added. "As for that other thing," she said, forcing herself to continue, "as for last night . . ."

His attention was fully focused on her now, keen and interested. He wanted to know what she made of the situation. She wasn't a prude and, yes, she had liked the kiss very much. But neither one of them could afford to let the spark that existed between them grow bigger. It had to be extinguished—for many reasons.

But she would only tell him one reason, for now.

"If you help me, if you and I collaborate to fight Pryce and find your family," she said, and she felt grateful that her voice was steadier than her nerves, "we cannot let what happened last night happen again. It would complicate a working relationship that many would already see as . . . unusual." There: She'd said it. And it didn't sound so bad to her ears.

A wry, slightly mocking look came into his eyes as

he folded his arms across his broad chest. "No sparkin' with the help?"

"Well . . . no." Her bed had remained empty since David's death, and those five solitary years had been long ones. She did sometimes miss having a man beside her at night, yet that yearning had been unfocused, transitory. Will Coffin had reawakened something inside her last night, something bright and living, demanding satisfaction. It could not be appeased, however; not with him. It was impossible.

"Yeah, I figured as much," Will said, his mouth twisted slightly. "Ranch hands sleep in the bunkhouse, not the big house. No mixin' with the boss's women."

"In this case," she reminded him, "*I* am the boss. And that is precisely why I need you to help with Pryce." She wanted to bring the conversation back to a topic she felt more comfortable with, something she could fully understand and sort out. "I run Greywell's capably," she said without conceit, "which came as a surprise to many, including myself. But I cannot contend with a man like Pryce."

"So get one of your highfalutin friends to do it," he said, slightly cross.

"They cannot or will not. They're afraid of him. They have too much to lose and no skills with which to defend themselves. But you have talents none of them have: cleverness, adaptability, nonconformity." Which was all true. He still looked dubious, and for several panicked seconds she thought he would refuse her outright. If he did, what would she do? Surely Pryce's next move would be even more hostile than the last, and she didn't know if she could hold out against him.

"You don't have to answer right away," she said, trying at least to stall for time. She gripped the back of a chair and leaned against it. "Take a little while, think over what I've said. Maybe in a day or two—"

She did not get the chance to finish her sentence. Mordon cleared his throat politely in the doorway.

"There is a gentleman from Greywell's here to see you, madam," he announced, "and he says his business is quite urgent."

"Show him in."

But the visitor did not wait for her butler, instead dashing into the breakfast room with his cap clutched tightly in his hand. He stood just inside the door. Olivia recognized him as John Stevenson, one of the brewery's deliverymen. He was gasping for breath.

"Mr. Stevenson, what is the matter? Can I get you some water?"

Panting, the man shook his head. "No . . . thank you, madam. But . . . I . . ." He bent over and rested his hands on his thighs, wheezing.

"Easy there, compañero," Will said, walking around the table and giving Stevenson a few hearty thumps on the back. "Get your wind and then let fly."

Poor Stevenson, who'd never read a dime novel, had no idea what Will Coffin was talking about, but after a few gulps of air, he managed to straighten up. "There is trouble at Greywell's, madam," he finally said.

"What kind of trouble?" Already on the alert, she felt herself grow taut with apprehension, gripping the top of the chair tightly.

"The delivery vans and drays can't get through to the pubs. Whenever they go, they get turned back."

"By whom?"

Stevenson shook his head. "Don't know, madam.

Men. Men with clubs. They threaten the drivers and say they'll bash their heads in if they try to make the deliveries. So the vans have been sitting in the yard all morning."

If she had not been so well-trained in the art of proper comportment, Olivia would have cursed. And cursed loudly. "George Pryce, again," she muttered instead. She had not been mistaken in her assessment. The man was now hell-bent on ruining her.

"What'll we do, madam?" Stevenson asked, imploring. His cap was almost crushed into a ball in his hands.

She clutched the back of a chair again, thinking hard. There had to be another way to make their deliveries, but how?

"Them drivers oughta fight back," Will said, breaking the silence, "show some gumption." Both Olivia and Stevenson looked at him in surprise.

"The men had clubs, sir," Stevenson answered.

Will rolled his eyes. "Then give the drivers guns."

"Guns, sir?" repeated Stevenson blankly.

"Yeah, you know, firearms, equalizers, barkers—guns."

"This is England, Will," Olivia explained. "People only carry guns to hunt."

His look was level and serious. "Then maybe it's time we started huntin' bullies."

"You aren't going to actually *shoot* anyone, are you?" Olivia asked as they rode quickly toward Greywell's. She eyed the rifle resting across Will's legs with a combination of apprehension and curiosity. The only firearms she was at all familiar with were the polished and engraved hunting rifles her father kept on display in a locked cabinet in his study, but those guns were purely decorative. Seeing something so deadly and, from the looks of the worn and smooth butt, well-used, was a startling experience.

Will Coffin laughed and shook his head. " 'Course I'm not gonna shoot anyone, I just want to show your delivery fellas how to make a big show, scare off the mudsills."

She breathed low in relief. "I have to admit, I wasn't particularly eager to replicate that aspect of those dime novels."

"The way them books talk," Will said, smiling, "you'd think there weren't any people left alive out West—all we do is run around and plug each other." The idea made him chuckle.

She wished she could emulate his insouciance about the upcoming conflict but found it more difficult than she had imagined. "Don't you?"

"I use this Winchester for huntin' and protectin' cattle against wild animals," he explained. "Maybe once or twice I shot it into the air to scare off some rustlers."

"And what about your pistol?"

"My Colt? The same. Most towns don't even let you wear 'em in the streets. Sheriffs make you drop 'em off when you come in and pick 'em up when you leave." He held open his coat. He wore no gun or gun belt. "See? I ain't even heeled now."

"So no showdowns on Main Street?"

He couldn't help but laugh at the note of disappointment in her voice. "That's pure fiction, ma'am."

"And you've never shot or killed anyone?"

The merriment in his eyes fled immediately as his laughter died. "I didn't say that."

"Oh." She looked down at her hands, clutched in her lap. God, what to make of this man! Everything about him made her feel a bit small, even though she knew that wasn't his intention. He didn't frighten her somehow, but she knew, if he had to, he could become as feral as a wolf.

And she was a lapdog, fed on scraps from the master's table. But weren't all women of her class trained and obedient pets? Moral, loving and biddable? As she worked in her brewery, Olivia began to agree with the radical female writers whose works were condemned at tea parties. She desired more than a favored spot at her master's feet, whether that master was David or the upper echelons of society. And she was willing to defend that desire. But it was getting harder and harder to do so, especially alone.

The carriage went through the iron gates of Greywell's into the yard, where more than a dozen delivery drays and vans stood waiting. They were all full of carefully stacked barrels, ready for distribution to the forty pubs licensed to sell Olivia's beer. Ordinarily, the sight of so much industry made her chest expand with pride. But it was well after nine in the morning, long past the time the deliveries should have been made. If she couldn't get the beer to the publicans before noon, when many working men took their lunches, it could be disastrous for the long-term success of Greywell's. She had to be a reliable supplier; that was a primary rule of business.

And the drivers knew it, too. They stood next to their wagons, holding the horses' reins, shifting and uneasy. She could see the relief on their faces as her carriage pulled into the yard and came to a stop. She only hoped she could be worthy of their trust.

After Arthur helped her down, she turned to address the drivers. She saw their curious, cautious eyes turn to Will Coffin standing beside her, and she could not blame them for their wariness. Wearing his Stetson and his long duster, his Winchester rifle balanced on his shoulder, he was the epitome of an American cowboy. And the drivers were the embodiment of the English working man.

The anxious hum died as Olivia spoke to the drivers. "Gentlemen," she said loudly, holding up her hands to get their attention. Everyone grew quiet and watchful, even, it seemed, the draft horses. "I understand that there has been some difficulty making the deliveries this morning."

"They tried to beat me face in!" one driver called out, and a rumbling chorus of agreement followed.

"I ain't gonna make no deliveries if me face's beat in," another added angrily. "An' who'll feed me wife an' kiddies?"

More rumblings, growing in hostility, ensued. Olivia knew the men had to be kept calm. Otherwise they would turn more ugly and unpredictable than anything Pryce could devise.

"Compose yourselves," she said forcefully. Surprisingly, the drivers obeyed her. It rather astonished her that people—men especially—would ever follow her orders, but Olivia was beginning to realize that she had more power than either she or her late husband had given her credit for.

Gesturing to Will beside her, she said, "This is Mr. Coffin. He is here to help us make sure we make our deliveries on time."

" 'Ow's 'e gonna do that?" someone demanded.

Will stepped forward, and Olivia could actually see

the drivers, some of them outweighing Will by two stone, move back in deference. He had a natural authority that was difficult to reconcile with his lowly upbringing, and for the first time Olivia wondered if perhaps his origins were less humble than either of them suspected.

"Boys," Will said with a wide, Western smile, "let me introduce you to my good friend Winchester."

For a country that prided itself on its far-reaching empire, Will marveled that no one had thought to ride shotgun when making dangerous deliveries. Hell, Wells Fargo had been doing it for more than thirty years.

"Just have a body sit with you with a rifle across his knee," Will explained to the men gathered around him, "and if anyone tries to bulldoze you, give 'em a taste of what for."

"I'm not gonna shoot anyone," a man hollered.

" 'Course you ain't." Didn't anyone in England have a lick of sense? So far the only person he'd met who had any brains at all was Lady Olivia Xavier, and he couldn't fault a gentle-born woman for not knowing the way of guns. "Just give 'em a warning shot across the prow and they won't give you any difficulty."

The men continued to look dubious. "Don't be a bunch of old croakers," Will chided them. "These mudsills think they got you beat with their heavy sticks, but nothin' can top a genuine Winchester rifle for convincin' someone to leave you alone. Hell, you don't even have to load 'em. Just point and act like you mean it."

"We can't arm all these men," Olivia said quietly beside him. "It would be much too expensive."

"All it takes is one man with one gun to send the right message. Now," Will said, addressing the crowd, "who's it gonna be?"

Still, they didn't move. "Goddamn it," Will growled, "I'll show you how it's done." He pointed a finger at one driver, a big bruiser wearing a bowler hat. "You an' me are gonna make a delivery."

The man nodded, even though Will could see him swallow in fear. Clearly nobody in England knew how to fight a dirty war like this. They weren't familiar with the underhanded tricks and schemes ambitious men used to get what they wanted. Everything with them was up front, marching in formation like some army from the Revolutionary War. But England had lost that war, while America, hiding behind trees and being sly, won. And nobody was craftier than a cowboy. Charles Goodnight hadn't become a cattle baron by asking please and saying thank you.

As Will went to sit next to the driver, Olivia came over and took hold of his arm. He was priming himself for a tussle, but even getting ready for a fight, her touch managed to unsettle him more than anything else he might face. His stomach immediately took up residence in his lungs when her fingers rested on his sleeve.

"Be careful, Will," she said softly, and even though the yard was full of hustle, each word from her mouth branded him. Genuine worry creased her brows and deepened the violet of her eyes. "If it gets too dangerous, come back. Don't worry about the delivery. We'll figure something out."

Will couldn't help wondering whether her concern was real, or if she was playing him. She already knew that he couldn't be bought, but he did have a soft spot for helping women—he'd bailed her out once before; why not again?

Will had seen plenty of pretty-faced cheats work a man without batting an eye and had learned to spot a fleecer at an early age. He wasn't anyone's dupe, not even a fancy filly's. But somehow he knew, just looking at Olivia, that she didn't sucker folks, and she wasn't suckering him. Her worry was for real.

Outside of old Jake, nobody had really given two licks about Will. It floored him that this lady, who didn't really know him from Adam, could care about him at all. No matter what happened, today, tomorrow or whenever, Will didn't think he could ever forget that.

But Will didn't like to show his serious side to the world. So instead of thanking her as solemnly as he felt, he just grinned and said, "I'll be fine as cream gravy. By noon, every bank clerk and pot-bellied tycoon'll be guzzlin' Greywell's beer with their luncheon."

She tried to return his smile, but she was clearly very troubled. Olivia looked around the yard and, seeing that no one was watching, pressed a quick kiss to Will's clean-shaven cheek, before hurrying away.

Lordy, he was a goner.

"Let's get this wagon rollin'," he said, vaulting up beside the driver. He kept his hands tight around the Winchester to keep from touching the spot where her lips had pressed against him. Couldn't get moony just when things were about to become interesting.

Neither he and nor the driver spoke as they drove across the river and into the city. Some of the places they rode past looked vaguely familiar to Will, but he'd covered a lot of ground on foot over the past few days, and being on top of a wagon jingled his orientation. It wasn't long, though, until they turned down a narrow street behind a saloon. Will felt his whole body tense. The street was still and silent.

Four rowdies stepped out from a doorway and blocked the way. Sure enough, they were holding big clubs. Will smiled to himself with relief. He knew how to fight once his enemies had shown their faces. It was the waiting that got to him. As the wagon slowed to a stop, the toughs slapped their clubs in their hands threateningly.

"Didn't we tell you to turn 'round?" one snarled.

"Else we're gonna bash yer 'ead in," another added.

Will laughed. After everything he'd seen and been through back home, these customers were plain amateurs. "With them little sticks?" He chuckled. "Go on and play. Me and my friend got work to do."

The toughs exchanged looks, clearly not expecting someone to argue with them, let alone try to get through.

"Now what?" one asked another.

"I guess we 'it 'im."

With a shrug, the first man raised his club and started to swing it toward the driver. As he brought it down, there was a loud bang, and then the man held only a few splinters of wood. Eyes round with shock, he looked up and down the barrel of Will's Winchester, pointed right at his face.

"This Yellow Boy here's a repeater," Will said, bringing down the rifle's lever and cocking the hammer. The empty cartridge clattered onto the street. With a satisfying click, he brought the lever back up and chambered the next round. "So I can sit here all day and pick you boys off like buzzards. Or you can get lost. You choose."

Another man took a tentative step forward, but Will brought the Winchester around fast. "Don't try it, compadre. Although," he added almost thoughtfully, "you'd be less ugly without a head."

"I didn't get paid to get me 'ead blown off," the man holding the remains of the club said, panicked.

"Me neither," his companions agreed. Like a flock of startled geese, they took off down the road, honking in fright.

"Be sure to tell Pryce and his other desperados that Lady Xavier don't cotton to being threatened," Will shouted after them, standing up in the seat. As he sat back down, he caught the driver's stunned expression. "Just havin' a little fun," he said.

"You're a crazy son of a bitch," the driver answered.

"Crazier than you know." Will grinned, thumping him on the back. He thought about Olivia waiting back at the brewery and his heart began racing faster than it had been when facing off against the hired guns. "A lot crazier."

They finished their delivery and sped quickly back to the brewery to report their progress. Just as Will and the driver steered into the yard, Olivia's carriage came rolling by, then stopped alongside them. Her slim hand opened the window and Will's breath caught as she poked out her lovely, elegant face. He didn't understand how she could have remained unmarried for so long. Any man of her class with brains should have been pacing outside her door like a hound on the scent as soon as she'd become available again after her husband's death.

"It's all over London," she said, her eyes bright with excitement, "how you fought off those thugs.

And you were right: We don't need to arm anyone else. All the deliveries are being made right now. We just had two men go instead of one. You have Pryce's men running scared."

"Glad to hear it," he said. He was starting to find he liked pleasing her, and he'd never sought anybody's favor before. It was definitely time to grab his kit and hit the trail. "Headed home?" He thought to catch a ride back with her and pack up.

She shook her head. "I received word that more of Pryce's ruffians are threatening a publican who sells my beer. I'm on my way to the pub to get rid of them."

Will stared. "Alone? Ain't you takin' somebody with you?"

"Everyone's making deliveries," she explained.

Cursing under his breath, Will jumped down from the delivery wagon and pulled open the door to her carriage. "I'll go," he said curtly. He jerked his head to indicate that she should get out of the carriage. "You stay here."

"This publican is a very good customer of mine," she said, eyeing his rifle. "He would be scared out of his wits if you came in with guns blazing and had a showdown right in his pub. I doubt he would purchase from us in the future," she added dryly.

"Olivia, I don't think—"

"It's not your decision to make," she said, and there was that grit of hers again, giving no quarter. "Greywell's is my responsibility, and there are some things that I must do myself."

Will tried to argue, but he saw that there would be no quarreling with her. Short of pulling her bodily out of her carriage, she would insist on coming along.

Lady Olivia Xavier didn't do things with a lick and a promise, he'd give her that. He sat down opposite her, shutting the door after him. "Well, if you don't care a continental, let's go see the elephant."

She rapped sharply on the roof of the coach and they were off. "How you talk," she said with a little smile.

"Ain't nothin' wrong with the way I talk," he answered. Then, less sure, "Is there?"

"Not a bit."

Oh, he could sit across from her all day and watch her smile. Prettier than the stars over the mountains, and warmer than a summer's campfire. She could make a man wish for things he had no right wishing for, and the longer he spent in her company the more he began to wish.

There was no time for fancy, though. Before too long, they'd pulled up in front of another saloon—pub, they were called here—and Will was priming himself for another tussle.

"Leave the gun," she advised as they got out of the carriage.

He didn't like the idea but did as she asked. If he had to, he knew how to fight with his fists and anything else handy. But she wanted to do this her way, so he'd let her—for now.

They walked into the pub looking like two folks on a Sunday outing, Olivia on his arm and smiling affably. The pub was full of dark wood and brass, with mirrors behind the bar and leather chairs set around polished wooden tables. It was a sight finer than any saloon Will had ever seen, a place a gentleman might bend an elbow with his chums rather than a spot where some patched-up cowpoke would snort rotgut and find a scarlet lady for some mattress bouncing.

The pub was empty except for the man behind the counter and two beefy blowhards leaning across it with blood in their eyes. At Olivia's cheerful, "Good morning," all three turned to look in her direction.

"M . . . madam," the publican stammered, "we are not yet open for business." Even as fear strained his voice, there was a note of befuddlement in his words, and Will understood that even dandy pubs like this one didn't cotton to serving highbrow ladies. They just didn't belong.

"I'm not here for a drink," she announced and began walking forward. Will dogged her steps. If she was frightened, she sure didn't show it. Coming up to the bar, she reached across to shake the pubkeeper's hand. "I am Lady Xavier, owner of Greywell's Brewery."

"Fred Cowling," the publican answered. He shot nervous eyes toward Will and then the hardcases looming nearby.

"This is my associate, Will Coffin," she continued, and Will shook hands, too. Olivia then turned her keen, cool gaze toward Pryce's hirelings. If Will had thought her approachable in the carriage, now she suddenly looked as icy and unreachable as a queen on a throne. Had he been the unlucky son of a bitch on the business end of that look, he'd have withered away on the spot. It was a stare more chilling than any Winchester, Colt or Gatling Gun.

"Gentlemen," she said to the toughs, and it was clear by her voice that she considered them anything but, "I have business to attend to with Mr. Cowling; *private* business."

The men looked at each other, puzzled. Whatever they had been expecting, it wasn't a slip of a lady telling them to get lost.

"We ain't finished 'ere," one said.

"I believe you are," Olivia insisted, her tone cutting and cold.

"But—"

"If you have any further business of your own to conduct, I suggest you take it up with Mr. Coffin." Seeing his cue, Will gave his best killer grin, the kind that said he'd be happy to chew off their ears and use them for target practice. Pryce's men actually turned pale. "He would be delighted to discuss whatever concerns you—outside."

" 'E's the bloke what nearly shot Jimmy's 'ead off," one hissed to the other. They both swallowed audibly.

The publican looked back and forth between Will and Olivia and the thugs, plainly ill at ease. Olivia, meanwhile, was composed and frosty, a touch impatient for the annoying interlopers to be on their way. Will heard a clock ticking in the silent pub; even the noises from the street had petered out.

"Well?" Olivia demanded icily.

One tough looked at the other and then bolted for the door. "I'm off!"

"Me too," his companion cried, running after him.

As their footsteps clattered into the distance, Olivia turned to Mr. Cowling. Her voice warm but businesslike, she said, "Perhaps you should fetch your record books from your office and we may determine if your supply of Greywell's is enough. I want to keep my customers satisfied."

The publican nodded readily and scuttled into the back office. As soon as he disappeared, Olivia let out a long, unsteady breath, and Will could see that her hands were shaking as they clutched her little bag.

"I believe in poker, that is what they call bluffing,"

she said with a tremulous smile. She sat down heavily on a nearby stool as though her legs had suddenly given out from under her.

Will shook his head, thunderstruck. "Remind me never to bet against you."

Chapter Six

Crawcook, Pryce's valet, finished tying his master's cravat, adjusting the folds carefully. His master was a demanding one and would often make Crawcook undo his handiwork and retie the whole thing if even the smallest pleat wasn't perfect.

Fortunately, sir was too distracted today to make even a cursory inspection of his cravat, else Crawcook was certain he would have made him reknot the silk necktie simply to prove that he had the power to make him do so. Sir had been distracted quite a bit lately, and Crawcook was grateful for it.

"Watch fob," his master demanded, and a case of fine Swiss and Austrian chains was presented for his inspection. After making a selection, Crawcook took the fob and affixed it to the jeweled watchcase sir had received from his father, the earl, after finally completing his studies at university.

Just as the valet was holding out his master's worsted wool jacket, there came a tap at the door. It was Len Banks, the footman.

"Begging your pardon, sir," Len said with an apologetic shrug, "but there are two . . . em . . . gentlemen in your study wishing to speak with you."

"Tell them I'm busy," sir snapped.

"They say it is urgent and will not leave."

Sir purpled with anger, and Crawcook didn't envy them being on the receiving end of his master's wrath, which could be terrible indeed. Instead of having two of the burly underbutlers remove the visitors, sir said hotly, "I'll be down in a moment." He shoved his arms into his jacket, tugged irritably on the sleeves and then strode from the room without another word.

Len and Crawcook exchanged glances and immediately followed their employer. They kept a discreet distance and then waited for him to go into his study before sidling up and pressing their ears to the closed door. The heavy wood made it difficult to hear everything, but Crawcook was an adept hand at eavesdropping and was able to make out a goodly amount.

". . . what the *hell* are you talking about?" roared sir.

". . . 'ad a *gun,* sir . . ." a voice answered, and from the sound of it, a voice from Whitechapel.

". . . nearly blew me 'ead off, sir," another voice chimed in. Len and Crawcook glanced at each other and shuddered with glee. Two men from the East End visiting sir—there would be good talk at the servants' table tonight.

Sir gave another snarl, and Crawcook thought he heard something heavy being thrown and hit the wall. ". . . incompetent! . . . disgusting American . . . trollop of a widow . . . something else must be done."

"What . . . ?"

". . . Maddox . . ."

Crawcook and Len traded looks of gleeful shock.

Not Maddox! The man was well known even to servants of the gentry. He was a horror, a monster, high-priced and ruthless.

And then the servants had to scatter into the recesses of the house, because the old countess was coming down the hall. They dove into a nearby hallway and listened carefully. The countess rapped on the door to sir's study.

"I say, George, we must leave immediately if we are to make the Duchess of Walford's tea party," she called.

"I'll be along shortly, Mother," sir answered after a pause.

"*Now,* George," she said, in a voice that Crawcook and Len both knew too well. She sailed off back toward the front of the house, and both the valet and the footman pressed up against the wall to keep from being seen when sir jerked open the door of his study.

"I'll deal with you two later," he barked to the men in his office, "so leave by the servants' entrance and never come into my house again." He stalked away and shortly after the East Enders, grumbling and swearing, vanished.

Both Len and Crawcook had to suppress the giggles that rose up in their throats. They must wait until sir and his dragon of a mother were out of the house before scampering belowstairs with their story. And it was a marvelous story. Who would ever believe an earl's son mixing with blokes from Whitechapel? Who, exactly, was the disgusting American and the trollop of a widow? And why was sir summoning Maddox? These were mysteries the servants would ponder for hours.

* * *

"You have heard so much about this place; perhaps it is time I showed it to you," Olivia said as she and Will entered the brewery. "Here is Mr. Huntworth, the esteemed manager. How are you today, Mr. Huntworth?" she asked as a round, alert owl of a man approached them, blinking behind thick spectacles.

"Much better, thank you, Lady Xavier, since you and your associate solved our distribution problem," he answered brightly. He ran his sleeve over his smooth forehead. Olivia made quick introductions, and outside of a fleeting look of consideration the manager gave Will, no one seemed to question his presence. Which was very well, since Olivia wasn't quite sure of herself around him anymore.

She had been so glad to see him return unharmed from his delivery, it had taken considerable self-control to keep from launching herself at him and covering his face with kisses. Perhaps having him assist with the protection of the brewery wasn't such a good idea, after all. She was beginning to like him too much. Yet the weariness that had been dogging her for so long was beginning to lift, largely due to Will Coffin. He helped her face down George Pryce, and he didn't question her right to run a business—unlike most people she knew. Such relief.

But Will couldn't be more distant from her—socially, financially, geographically and just about every other way she could imagine. He was temporary, nothing more. And eventually, she would go back to running Greywell's alone. The prospect wasn't as cheering as it had been only a few days ago.

"I shall take a look around, Mr. Huntworth," Olivia decided. "Just to make sure everything is running smoothly."

The manager seemed used to the idea. "As you wish, Lady Xavier. Let me accompany you."

"Why not come along, Will?" Olivia found herself asking. "At the very least, you can see how beer is made."

He was hesitating. He hadn't decided whether to help her or not, and Olivia herself was torn. His assistance would be invaluable—he had scared off Pryce's henchmen several times and seemed to know how such wars were waged—but she was becoming aware that the more time she and Will spent together, the more he intrigued her. And Lord, she didn't need more of society's disapproval. Running the brewery had made life difficult enough as it was.

But she would lose Greywell's without him. He needed to stay.

"Sure," he said at last.

She made her inspection with Mr. Huntworth and his omnipresent clipboard. Will stayed beside her and gazed around at the enormous rooms and machinery.

"This spread you got sure is considerable," he said on a whistle.

"I thought so, too," Olivia admitted. She checked the pressure on a boiler and nodded in satisfaction to Mr. Huntworth. "When I found out that David had left me the brewery, I didn't know the first thing about making beer. So I took a tour of Greywell's and was absolutely astonished. The first thing I noticed was the smell."

Will took a deep sniff. "Like a big loaf of bread." He sniffed again and made a face. "A big, angry loaf."

Olivia laughed. "I don't notice it anymore, or so I tell myself. I can only wonder what *I* must smell like." And then she remembered that Will did know what she smelled like, he'd told her so the second time they had met, and it brought back the same rush of intimate awareness she'd felt that day.

Will must have felt it, too, because he abruptly turned and pointed to the giant tuns in the middle of the room. "What're these?" he asked.

"Mashing tuns," Olivia explained, grateful that neither of them had spoken any further about her personal scent. "We mix the ground malt with liquor—that's what we call water—and then mash it for two hours."

"Lady Xavier had the tuns fitted with steam-heated jackets to keep the temperature exact," Mr. Huntworth said proudly. "The latest in modernization. Come and see."

Greywell's was a smaller, local brewery with only one brew house, but Olivia could see that to many unfamiliar with the process, and with industrialization in general, the six-story structure could look like a castle built of copper kettles and huge fermenting vessels. In his clean, worn Western clothing and Stetson hat, strolling past enormous refrigerators and fermenting vessels, Will looked incongruous, a wilderness spirit rattling among the man-made. He had an outsized wildness about him, even at rest, that the machines hissing and humming around him emphasized rather than diminished.

How absurd all this must look to him, she thought, as Mr. Huntworth demonstrated a specialized thermometer. How prideful and transitory, compared to the mountains where he came from.

But Greywell's was impressive, too. She'd worked hard to make it one of London's most modern breweries. There were rooms and rooms, some with giant copper drums and others with long, open coolers where fans created breezes to bring down the temperature. And there were her many employees, male and female, all as invested in the success of the brewery as she.

"Let me show you the pride of Greywell's," Olivia said, leading him toward their covered well. "Water is the most vital component of brewing," she explained, as Huntworth lifted the wooden cover. "We are lucky enough to have our own well."

"It goes eight hundred and fifty feet deep," Huntworth chimed in.

"Eight hundred and fifty feet deep?" Will repeated. He peered down into the dark expanse of the well and yodeled, then laughed at the echo. "That's halfway to China."

"Australia," she said, also laughing. "Every day we do a chemical analysis to make sure that the mineral content is exactly what we need for our different beers."

"I thought beer was beer."

"So did I, but I came to learn otherwise. We make five here: a porter, a stout, a strong, and mild and pale ales."

"All Londoners drank stouts and porters," Huntworth said, "or so we thought. We weren't making much of a profit when Lord Xavier bought us, but when Lady Xavier took over, she had us add gypsum to the water so we could produce the Burton ales everyone's become so fond of lately."

"They're lighter and brighter than heavy porters, and easier to drink," Olivia explained.

"Can't be a brewer anymore without making a pale ale," Huntworth concluded. "And Lady Xavier knew it, even if we didn't."

She shrugged to dismiss his praise, even though Mr. Huntworth's compliment meant quite a bit to her. Winning Lawrence Huntworth's good opinion had been an uphill battle at the beginning. Getting anyone to listen to her had taken every ounce of strength and determination she had possessed, and even some she didn't but had to pretend she did. And after she had won over the people at Greywell's, she'd had to weather the storm of public opinion. And now the threat of George Pryce.

Glancing over at Will, she saw frank admiration in his crystalline blue eyes, heating her as much as a steam-powered engine. He had not questioned her role at Greywell's, but she still enjoyed earning his respect.

Huntworth waved them ahead as he stopped to talk with one of the workers.

"You sure know a lot 'bout brewin'," Will said as they moved away from the well. His boots rattled the floorboards, sending tiny vibrations through Olivia's own feet and up her spine. "Didn't know that ladies did that sorta thing."

"I had to spend two years in mourning for my husband," she explained. "One year in deep mourning and another in half mourning. I had to refuse all invitations and saw no one except close relatives. That's what society dictates."

"Society!" Will said with a snort. "What the heck is that? Just a buncha stuffed shirts sittin' on their inbred hindquarters. Can't even wipe their own noses."

She shook her head. "That's not true. If I go against society, the consequences could be horrible. Absolute social exile. No one would see or speak to me, and I couldn't travel anywhere without scandal following me. It would be like becoming a ghost—completely invisible to everyone but doomed to wander the earth." She shuddered. "I chose two years of inactivity rather than face that fate."

"That sounds duller than a week-long Bible meetin'."

Olivia shot him a quick, secretive grin, and said on a whisper, "It was! I missed my husband, but I found myself just sitting, day after day, with nothing to do but contemplate my solitude. It was as though"—she glanced around, careful to be sure that no one was listening—"I had been buried, too. Buried alive." She pressed a gloved hand to her pale cheek. "I'm not supposed to say things like that."

"It's the truth, ain't it?"

"Perhaps that is what makes my feelings so unforgivable."

Will faced her, right in the middle of the floor of the brewery. "It ain't right to take a healthy, spirited woman and stuff her away like an old horse blanket," he said, surprising them both with the heat of his voice. "The Navajo Indians mourn for four days, then they wash their hair with water and yucca root. Then mournin' is over. They can join the rest of the world. Doesn't sound so bad to me. And I don't give a flyin' fig for what anybody else thinks 'bout that. 'Specially *society*."

Several of the brewery employees stopped what they were doing and stared at Will and Olivia. She, herself, was stunned by the vehemence of his words, the angry, crackling energy that filled his rangy body standing so close to hers.

She took hold of his arm and began to lead him forward, away from the ogling employees, and felt his muscles bunch underneath her gloved hand. A strong one, Will Coffin. Stronger in his convictions than most people she knew, and unafraid to speak them. But what was his anger right now directed toward? Society? Or the thought of her in mourning for David? She wasn't entirely certain.

"All the same," she continued, "I knew that, in addition to my settlement, David had left me a brewery. So I began to read about them when no one was around. I had a good deal of time, so I read everything I could in trade publications about the history, the latest technology, all of it. When the time came to leave off my mourning, I had resolved to take a struggling little brewery and turn it into something profitable."

"And she has," Huntworth put in, coming up behind them. "We were skeptical at first, but Lady Xavier has tripled our earnings."

"All luck," she said with a self-deprecating shrug.

"No, Lady Xavier," Huntworth said, politely shaking his head. "Though I would never have admitted it before, a woman may possess more talent than she is given credit for. But," he added hastily, "I would never say such things to those radicalists."

They had reached the end of the large room and stood in front of a frosted glass door with the word LABORATORY painted in gold on the front.

"This is another of Lady Xavier's innovations," Huntworth explained, opening the door. Long shelves lined the small room, each covered with scientific equipment—tubes and microscopes, glass cases and scales. Two men in long white coats tinkered away with the equipment. Will looked even more incongruous here, amid the fragile laboratory equipment and harbingers of the modern world.

"Mr. Maidford," Olivia said to one of the men, who looked up quickly from the experiment he was conducting, "how fares your research?"

"Very well, Lady Xavier," he answered readily. "I almost have this strain of yeast isolated. In a few more days I believe I will have a new species ready."

"We'll beat those chaps at Carlsberg," Mr. Huntworth said. He added, for Will's benefit, "In Denmark, just this year, they have already introduced the first absolutely pure brewers' yeast culture, but we aren't far behind, are we, Lady Xavier?"

"Thanks to Mr. Maidford's assistance," she answered.

Will whistled softly. "I didn't know that chemistry had anythin' to do with beer."

"Brewing is all chemistry," Olivia said. She bent down and put her eye to the lens of a microscope, then motioned Will to do the same. He pushed his hat back and looked, then jumped back in astonishment.

"It looks like an empty blob of water," he said, flabbergasted, "but it ain't. Tiny critters live in there."

"Several years ago Louis Pasteur wrote a fascinating book on the subject, *Études sur la bière*. He's doing amazing work with yeast and the reproduction of microscopic organisms."

"We've all read it," Maidford said before diving back into his work.

Will picked up a test tube, which looked like a toy in his hand, and studied its contents. "Funny," he murmured, swirling the yeast sample around. "A cowpuncher doesn't know about half this stuff when he bellies up to a bar and orders a beer. He's just hot and thirsty. And then there's all this"—he gestured around at the spotless laboratory—"makin' that drink possible."

"Science and progress is amazing," Olivia said.

More carefully than she would have thought possible, Will replaced the phial in its holder. Ruefully, he said, "Yeah, but science and progress is also puttin' guys like me out of work."

"I never realized," she said, surprised.

"They don't write 'bout that in dime novels."

"If you'll excuse me, Lady Xavier," Mr. Huntworth said with a respectful bow, "I must return to the brewery floor."

"Of course. Mr. Coffin and I will see ourselves out."

Once the manager had gone, Olivia and Will left the laboratory and began walking through the lower rooms toward the front gate.

"You're a gambler, awright," Will said after a pause. When she appeared mystified, he explained, "It looks like this whole place has been one big roll of the dice for you."

"I hadn't thought of it that way," she murmured thoughtfully.

"This is a fine spread you got here," Will said. "And it looks like you really made the place."

"Mr. Huntworth exaggerates my contributions."

"Doesn't sound like it to me."

"Well," she conceded, "I did invest a good deal of time and energy into Greywell's. At first I did it to fill my time, give myself something to do with the long hours and endless days. But in time I came to love my work. I felt, at last, as though I had found a purpose. If I were to lose all this . . . ." Her voice trailed away as her brow furrowed.

"Olivia—"

"Pryce wants Greywell's because he believes brewing is easy money," she said, interrupting him. She burned with outrage, incensed, forceful. "That's what he told me at our first meeting. He just wants cash. And I also think he wants whatever isn't his, like a child. If you have something that he doesn't, and you won't give it to him, he throws a tantrum." She shook her head. "A dangerous tantrum that could ruin me."

Will sighed and stopped walking. He leaned against the wall and looked out the large window into one of the yards that surrounded the brewery, arms folded across his chest. Men were unloading empty barrels from wagons and rolling them down the pavement to be filled up again inside. She watched the activity, too, standing beside him. He'd withdrawn, and she could almost see the furious activity of his mind as he absently watched the yard. He might not have the education of the men she knew, but Olivia understood Will Coffin was just as intelligent, if not more so, than those men.

"Will?"

"Aw, Liv," he muttered, and the shortening of her name glimmered through her, "you got me in a bind." He turned to look at her, and the pale gray light sculpted his face like an artist's brush. The square line of his jaw worked reflexively in thought. "I ain't keen on takin' up someone else's fight. It makes a body's life too messy."

She tried to mask her disappointment and said levelly, "I see," but it was a failing struggle. Her throat tightened. He would leave. She would face Pryce alone. The tiredness that afflicted her began to seep back into her bones.

He turned to look back at the yard, still full of activity. His eyes moved restlessly, not lingering on any one thing too long. "But," he continued, "life's messy, no matter what."

A stab of hope, almost painful, pierced her. "What do you mean?"

Will shifted his gaze again to Olivia. "I wouldn't be much of a man if I saw a lady in need and turned my back on her. I don't want to turn my back on *you*, Liv. It'd be plumb wrong. And," he added with a wry smile, "I wouldn't be worth my salt in them cowboy books you read if I didn't hold to the 'code of the West.' I'm a better man than blowhard Bill Cody, that's for damned sure."

For a moment, she only stared at him, and then she threw her arms around him. "Thank you, Will," she breathed against the back of his neck. First, she only experienced pure, unadulterated gratitude. Her exhaustion slipped away. And then, she became aware of something else. She smelled him, through her mouth and nose. Soap and tobacco and the warm undercurrent of male skin. Olivia was seized with the desire to run her tongue along the strong curve of his neck, discover what he tasted like, too. But then she remembered.

Don't spark with the help. That was the rule. *Don't make this any more complicated than it already is.*

Before his own arms could come up, she stepped back.

"We shall get to work right away locating your family," she said quickly, taking hold of his arm. She hoped he didn't see the pinking of her cheeks, but she could see a flush in his own and knew her face was even more transparent. They began to walk again to the front of the brewery. "I promise I will help you find them. It doesn't matter if they are marquises or mudlarks," she vowed, "we will track them down."

They had reached the door marked OFFICE and she continued, "There is a friend of mine who will be very helpful in our search. He is extraordinarily informed about all levels of English society."

"What does he do?"

"Graham Lawford?" Olivia looked slightly mystified. "I don't know, actually. Something that has to do with the government. If you ask me," she added softly as Will bent closer, "he's a bit shady."

Will narrowed his eyes. "Can we trust him?"

"Of course," she answered, confident. "I have known him for many, many years. He was a friend of my older brother's at university and he spent holidays with my family because we liked him so well."

"If you say so," was all he answered, and opened the door to the office—

To find Graham standing there, glaring at Will and looking quite dangerous. He was wearing his usual attire of a charcoal gray suit, immaculately tailored to his large frame, without much ornamentation save the silver watch fob on his black silk vest. With his dark hair, light eyes, severe aquiline nose and cheekbones and penchant for somber clothing, Graham always made an impression. If she didn't know him very well, Olivia would have been intimidated by his air of intensity. But this was Graham, and too much time had passed for her to feel any more trepidation around him.

She could feel Will tense up immediately beside her. She thought for half a moment that the two men might spring on each other like wolves.

"Graham!" She came forward and took his hand, trying as best she could to dispel the tension. "I was just about to write you. What brings you to Greywell's?"

Still squinting at Will, Graham answered, "Some of my men told me there had been some trouble here this morning." He broke his eyes away from Will and looked down at Olivia, and his gaze turned from cold and hard to warm and affectionate in an instant. "I came as soon as I could. Are you all right?"

"Yes, marvelous," she answered. "Will . . . Mr. Coffin was here, and he handled the situation wonderfully." Turning to Will, she smiled and motioned for him to join them. Will took a few guarded steps forward. "Graham, may I introduce Mr. Will Coffin from Colorado? Will, this is an old friend, Mr. Graham Lawford."

"Pleasure," Will said tightly, shaking hands.

"Likewise," Lawford replied through his teeth. They each released the other's hand as though dropping something dead onto the floor.

"You said you were going to write me," Graham said, turning to Olivia. She could see him immediately shift into the role of protective older brother. "Is there anything you need?"

"As a matter of fact, yes. Mr. Coffin and I require your services, if you can spare the time."

"For you, anything," Graham answered directly, which seemed to imply that he wasn't interested in helping Will, only Olivia.

She explained as concisely as possible the nature of Will's search, with Will filling in a few details where necessary. Graham listened attentively, nodding and asking a few questions. Will showed Graham the scrap of letter his father had written, clearly unhappy to part with the document. But Olivia saw that he was grudgingly pleased to see Graham handle the letter very carefully, acknowledging that it was, as far as Will was concerned, a priceless family heirloom.

"Unfortunately, it isn't much to go on," Graham finally concluded. "But," he added when Olivia looked downcast, "I have worked with far less. I'll have to borrow this letter for a few days to analyze it."

"What's there to analyze?" Will demanded, suspicious. "It's just a letter."

"Among other things, Graham is an alienist," Olivia explained. "He uses a rather unconventional analytical approach to discover things about people."

"I can study the kind of paper the letter was written on, the ink, even the handwriting, to see who wrote it and where they came from," Graham said. "It's a new science, but it has been used in certain investigations for Scotland Yard."

"All right," Will said, grudging respect in his voice. "But I want it back."

Tucking the letter into his pocket, Graham gave a slight bow, almost mocking. His words, however, were serious. "As you are a friend of Olivia's, I will do everything in my power to assist you. And your letter will be returned, unharmed. Now, if you will excuse us, I need to speak with her in private."

She could see Will hesitate, unwilling to leave her in the company of a man he so obviously distrusted, but Olivia gave him a reassuring smile. "It will be fine. You can wait for me outside, if you like. Or the carriage can take you home and Graham can give me a ride back."

"I'll wait for you," Will said, and she thought he directed his last words to Graham, "and we can ride home together."

The look Lawford gave him would have torn a lesser man into vulture feed, but Will didn't back down. With a big grin that he didn't quite feel, staring right into Lawford's chilly eyes, Will left the office, closing the door behind him. He almost lingered outside the door to catch whatever they were saying to each other, but he wasn't such a low-down bastard that he'd snoop. Reluctantly, he went outside to the front yard, where Olivia's carriage waited.

Throwing himself on the plush seat and stretching out his long legs, Will realized the angry churning in his gut wasn't his breakfast repeating on him. It was jealousy, plain and simple. He'd never really experienced it himself, since there wasn't much out on the trail to get jealous about. And the women he knew weren't worth that kind of botheration. Heck, there'd never been anything or anyone he'd wanted badly enough to get green-eyed about.

Seeing Olivia with Lawford was starting to change everything, though. They looked mighty handsome together, two dark-haired folks dressed in rich duds, as though they stepped off the cover of *Harper's*. And the way Lawford talked was like Olivia, elegant and refined, not like the lower accents of the people who worked at Greywell's, or even her servants. Clearly, Olivia and Lawford came from the same world. And they knew each other. She called him an "old friend." The way Lawford tried to stare Will down meant NO TRESPASSING, KEEP OFF.

He'd been a cowpuncher almost his whole life. The wind blew him around like a tumbleweed. It didn't bother him. He was the man he was. But then, near the time Jake had died, Will had started to be badgered by an odd feeling. The feeling that there was something else he wanted, something that just brushed the tips of his fingers, and if he reached out to grab it, he would only push it farther away. He thought maybe going to find his family would help get rid of his discontent, let him know who he was. It still might. Then he could go back to Colorado, finally settle down. Marry even, if he found the right girl. It seemed like a sensible plan.

But meeting Olivia made him wonder what he was chasing. She had a passion for her work and a dedication that he envied, even though it seemed to cost her quite a heap to pursue it. And she fascinated him like no other woman ever had before. So smart, so beautiful, with such backbone. She was able to understand, even when he hadn't, what he was really looking for—not his kinfolk, but himself.

"I'll be jiggered," he murmured in the empty carriage. She was amazing.

He'd come to England to find his family, to get a sense of himself, and instead found a woman he could never have.

Chapter Seven

"Good God, a *cowboy?*"

Charlotte Gough, usually one of the most gracious and refined people Olivia knew, openly gawked at Will as he came into the salon.

"I am so sorry," Charlotte said, blushing at her own rudeness. "Please forgive my lapse in manners."

"No offense taken, ma'am," Will said affably.

"Charlotte, may I introduce Will Coffin?" Olivia said dryly. She entered her salon and drew off her gloves, giving them and her bonnet to Mordon, who then took Will's hat and coat and discreetly faded away to get tea for Olivia's visitor. "Will, this is Mrs. Charlotte Gough. Charlotte and I went to school together, and," Olivia added dryly, "we are such good friends that she occasionally stops by unannounced."

Charlotte tipped her fair head in acknowledgment of the breach of protocol. "Yes, I know it's terribly discourteous of me, but, Olivia, I have heard such rumors about you, I had to see you right away."

"What sort of rumors?" Olivia suppressed her sigh.

No sooner had she and Will returned from Greywell's than she had found Charlotte waiting for her. Olivia's head was already buzzing with Graham Lawford's stern admonishment about letting strangers, strange *Americans,* into her home, and the potential for social disaster it could wreak. Now her good friend and confidante had appeared, proving Graham right. Society would inevitably learn about Will and want to dig up everything it could about him. Charlotte's presence was proof that the word about him was out. There would be no hiding anymore.

It had been pure naïveté, or perhaps hubris, to think that Olivia could do anything without society taking notice. She wasn't that important a figure, but the world she came from was so small, and its confines so narrow, that any behavior that fell outside of sanction came under immediate scrutiny.

"Well . . ." Charlotte began nervously, casting a quick glance at Will.

"You may speak freely, Charlotte," Olivia said.

Her friend grimaced in discomfort. "The talk is that you have a Texas cowboy staying with you."

"Colorado, ma'am," Will drawled. Charlotte dragged her gaze back to him. "I'm from Colorado, not Texas."

"Despite what gossip says, there is a difference," Olivia said wearily. "Denver is more than nine hundred miles from San Antonio."

Charlotte, who had little idea where either of those cities were located, was well-bred enough to pretend she did. "Naturally. But one always hears of cowboys from Texas. It's where they come from."

"Well, ma'am," Will said politely, "there's cowboys from all over. Texas, Kansas, Missouri, and," he added, glancing at Olivia with a quick smile, "Colorado." He strode into the salon, filling the feminine, chinoiserie-stuffed room with his overtly masculine presence.

Without meaning to, Olivia returned the smile. Something about Will did that to her, made her forget herself. Then she remembered that they were not alone, and closely watched, so she hurriedly smoothed out her expression. She took a seat in a low-armed ladies' chair opposite her friend on the divan.

Will stood behind her, almost protective, his hands braced on the back of her chair. She felt rather than saw his nearness, the warmth of his hands close to her neck and the real sense of him standing guard, alert, against whatever threat Charlotte might offer. Olivia was grateful for that, even as she saw Charlotte's eyes move back and forth between her and Will, considering.

"Mr. Coffin is in England attempting to locate his family," Olivia explained. Mordon brought in the tea cart and Olivia poured Charlotte a cup. She offered tea to Will, but he muttered something about self-respecting cowboys drinking tree bark water.

"I see," Charlotte said, taking a sip of tea, though she could not completely hide her puzzlement.

"And I'm helpin' her at the brewery," Will said, and Olivia felt the vibration of his deep voice through the elaborate scrollwork of her oak chair.

"I did not know that," Charlotte said. Her smooth ivory brow wrinkled unhappily. "Unfortunately, Olivia, most of what is being said about you and Mr. Coffin is pure conjecture. And I am afraid that leaves too much room for speculation."

"What sort of speculation?" Olivia asked, growing alarmed.

Again, her friend's eyes danced uncomfortably back to Will. "I . . ." she began, then stopped, blushing.

Olivia understood that Charlotte was unaccustomed to speaking frankly with gentlemen in the room. Rising from her chair, Olivia stood next to Will and placed a hand on his sleeve. Both of their gazes fixed on the sight for half a heartbeat, before she said quietly, "A lady's salon can be a tedious place for a gentleman."

Fortunately, he caught her meaning immediately. "Call me if you need anythin'," he said softly to Olivia. Then, louder, to Charlotte, "A pleasure meetin' you, ma'am." He tipped an invisible Stetson, then sauntered from the room. Olivia noticed that he was slightly bowlegged, a legacy of years on horseback. He must look wonderful on the back of a horse, Olivia thought. Perhaps they could go riding together if time permitted.

"Oh, dear." Charlotte's worried voice penetrated her musings. Olivia turned her gaze to her friend. "This doesn't bode well."

Olivia returned to her seat but found she had no appetite for tea or cakes. She picked petulantly at the ribbon trimming of her skirts, feeling strangely cross and out of sorts, like a child denied an answer to a question. "You may talk candidly, Charlotte."

Relieved that Will had finally left the room, her friend relaxed and launched into her tale. "I actually received a morning call in the *morning*, from Frances Hadlow," she continued. "Of course I had the butler tell her that I was not at home, but she sent up word that she had urgent news about you. I became alarmed. So I broke the rules and had her come up." Her voice full of genuine concern, she said, "Frances spoke of a wild American staying at your home, and all sorts of strange to-doings. I thought she was talking nonsense, but now I see she wasn't." Concern was plain on Charlotte's face. "What *is* going on here, Olivia?"

Olivia decided to tell her friend the truth. Charlotte already knew a bit about George Pryce's attempts to seize the brewery, and it was a measure of Pryce's power that not even Charlotte or her husband Frederick, with a seat in the House of Commons, could help Olivia. Though Charlotte might be the recipient of gossip, she was not known for spreading it.

As concisely as possible, Olivia told Charlotte everything that had transpired over the past few days: the thugs attacking her, Will's rescue, her offer to Will, the trouble with the deliveries—all of it. She omitted the strange attraction that kept pulling her and Will toward each other, however. By the end, Charlotte's eyes were as round as beer steins, and her tea was cold.

"What a life you lead, Olivia," Charlotte breathed. "It's like something out of a penny dreadful."

Olivia couldn't help but laugh at the apt comparison, since it was her love of cheap literature that helped bring her and Will together. "I admit that coming out of mourning has been more adventurous than I had anticipated."

"But are you safe, my dear?" Charlotte asked, leaning forward and taking her hand. "Are you well?"

"I am. Surprisingly well. Actually," she admitted, "I find all this adventure to be rather exciting."

Charlotte curled her free hand into a fist. "If only we could expose that rotten George Pryce!"

"It's quite hopeless," Olivia said. But she did not feel resigned. "Will and I shall find a way to beat him, though. Don't worry."

At Olivia's words, Charlotte gazed at her with apprehension. Olivia realized too late that she had spoken of him informally. "Who *is* this Will Coffin?" Charlotte asked, anxious.

"I already told you: an American looking for his family. He is able to assist me with Pryce, and I can help him locate his relatives."

"He isn't one of those whiskey-loving cowboys who shoot down chandeliers and ride their horses through ballrooms, is he?"

Olivia chuckled. "Yes, and his spurs inflict dreadful damage to the Persian rugs. He spits tobacco juice in the Ming vases and lassoes the roast."

But Charlotte wasn't laughing. "I'm serious, Olivia. What kind of man is he?"

"He's. . . ." Olivia sat back, thoughtful. She let her eyes wander aimlessly around the room as she called a vision of Will into her mind. Even thinking about him caused warmth to pool in her belly.

"He's honest," she finally said, her gaze turned inward, "and hardworking. Thoughtful. More than you would think. Very intelligent. He's quite strong, and not just physically. Within, this fortitude. It's remarkable. And there's something about him, a wistfulness, a searching. But no self-pity." She shook her head. "He's extraordinary."

The long silence from Charlotte made Olivia finally collect herself. Straightening in her chair, she looked over at her friend, and the expression on Charlotte's face made her ask with alarm, "What is it?"

"Olivia," Charlotte said, naked concern in her stare, "be cautious."

"Will is a gentleman," Olivia protested. Something else she had omitted from her earlier story was the kiss they had shared, and she decided now would not be a good time to mention it. "He doesn't come from our world, but his behavior is honorable."

"It isn't Will Coffin that worries me." Charlotte rose and, coming to stand beside her friend, gave Olivia's shoulder a gentle squeeze. "It's you. You will break your own heart if you aren't careful."

"Mordon told me I would find you here."

Will looked at Olivia over the back of a chestnut gelding. He continued to run the currycomb over the horse's flanks, even though Olivia's coachman kept all four of her horses in top shape, making his work unnecessary. Instead of answering her, Will kept his focus on grooming the gelding. She watched him in silence from across the stable. The only sounds came from the horse, sometimes snorting and stamping in approval and shifting in the hay strewn on the floor.

After Olivia had sent him packing from the salon, or whatever she called that room filled with dust-catchers, Will knew he couldn't go back up to his room and sit like a horse out to pasture. He'd never had a place all to himself that was so big before, with its huge brass bed and a whole water closet all to himself—no outhouse for a lady's home—but even with its high ceilings and tall windows, Will's room felt too closed in, too small. Aside from the two weeks at sea, he'd never spent much time indoors, and all this moseying from roof to roof had made him itchy, so he'd gone to the one place he could loosen up.

"You must miss being on horseback," Olivia said, her husky voice breaking the silence.

"Cowboys don't take kindly to walkin'," he answered. "That's for dudes and townfolk."

"And riding in carriages?"

"Only the cook in the chuck wagon did that."

She was quiet for a moment. "Did you sell your horse before coming to England?"

"Never had one of my own," he answered. "The outfit supplied 'em for the trails or the ranch."

"But you brought your own saddle."

He ran his hand along the smooth curve of the horse's neck. "A saddle's somethin' special, a man's private property. The one thing that shows his pride, his success, where's he's been and where he's goin'." He finally looked back at her, to see her gazing at him thoughtfully. "When a man gives up punchin' cattle, he sells his saddle."

"It's a beautiful saddle," she said. "I hope you don't sell it quite yet."

Feeling oddly disagreeable, Will continued to groom the trim, gleaming horse, trying to lose himself in the familiar action. But he kept seeing Graham Lawford's undisguised suspicion and Charlotte Gough's fretting, reminding him that he was mighty far from anything familiar. But that was what he was in England to do—find that sense of family, somehow. It was only Olivia's presence that made the whole lot bearable.

"Charlotte wanted to apologize for her poor manners earlier," Olivia said, coming closer. She didn't seem to mind the dirt of the stable, crossing over the hay and clumps of feed to stand just on the other side of the horse.

"Nothin' to apologize for," Will replied instinctively.

"She was uneasy and forgot herself," Olivia explained. She began to run her fingers through the horse's black mane, and Will found himself fascinated by the sight of her slim, pale fingers weaving in and out of the darkness.

"Words don't much bother me," Will said.

"You may not dine at the Reform Club, but you deserve courtesy and respect." She sighed. "Which is more than rumor will allow. Sometimes I think we parvenus are more protective of the social pecking order than the nobility. I suppose it's born out of fear."

She had the most surprising mind, and fingers as pretty as music. "Fear of what?"

"Insufficiency, I suppose," she said. She frowned as she worked out a knot in the horse's mane. "That somehow we aren't as good as those whose manners we ape. So we beat down anyone in our path, anyone who is different or who doesn't precisely adhere to codes of behavior."

"Like cowboys."

"Or women who run breweries." Olivia braced her arms on the horse's back and looked at Will. The filtered light through the open stable doors turned her skin pearly and her eyes smoky amethyst. "Charlotte invited you and me to her house for a small dinner party tonight," she said suddenly. "It's short notice, but she thinks that the longer you stay mysterious, the more speculation will arise."

"Trottin' me out to meet the *mishpokheh?*"

She smiled. "Something like that. And having you in public will send a message to George Pryce, show that we won't be cowed by him." Then her smile faded and she asked, concerned, "I accepted her invitation, but if it makes you too uncomfortable, I can easily send our regrets."

Will wasn't that wild about spending the evening with a bunch of folks like Graham Lawford, all of them watching him like a prized steer in a pen and waiting to see what the rube might do wrong. But he wanted to hash up Pryce's schemes. And Will could see that, despite what she said, going to this cookout meant a lot to Olivia. He didn't want to disappoint her.

"Okay," he said at last. "I'll put on my best bib and tucker and we can stick it in everyone's eye."

Olivia reached over and took Will's hand, and it amazed him how such a soft hand as hers could burn him like a brand. "Thank you, Will. I think you might actually enjoy yourself. Stranger things have happened. But," she added, a line appearing between her eyebrows, "what exactly constitutes your 'best bib and tucker'?"

"You've already seen it," Will replied, "Though I got a clean bandanna I ain't worn yet."

"I think," Olivia said with a little grimace, "it's time we headed to Saville Row."

Olivia's only experience with men's clothing arose from her trips to outfit David, and so she and Will headed to Roddam & Sons of Saville Row, Gentlemen's Fine Furnishings and Haberdashery, former clothier of Sir David Xavier. It was a lasting tribute to the shop's fine craftsmanship that David had been attired in a formal black wool suit when he had been buried.

Olivia had not been inside the shop in more than

five years, but one of its attractions was its sense of tradition and continuity, so nothing at all had changed during her absence. Not the tall, glass-fronted cases displaying top-quality kidskin gloves and folded silk cravats. Not the walls covered in deep green jacquard and hung with gilt-framed hunting scenes. And not the instant solicitousness of the clerks, who immediately stepped forward the moment Will and Olivia walked inside the chiming door, offering their most enthusiastic welcomes.

"Lady Xavier, it's been so long—"

"So good to see you again, Lady Xavier—"

"How may we assist you today?"

Will looked around with alarm at the swarming salesclerks, their hair gleaming with hundreds of coats of macassar oil, shinier than their tapered shoes, their suits models of sartorial perfection, all of them so refined, such ideals of polished gentility. Yet none of them paid him any mind. His clothing, rough, ready-made and well-worn, clearly indicated that Will Coffin was not the sort of customer with whom Roddam & Sons did business. So the clerks focused all their consideration on Olivia, a regular, respected and well-paying customer.

"I need a suit of evening clothes for my friend, Mr. Coffin," she said, directing their attention to Will. "And it needs to be ready by this evening."

The salesclerks didn't know what to make of this. They stepped back, blinking at one another. Some of the other customers in the shop, a few whom Olivia recognized, began to look over at the commotion, or rather, at the lack of commotion.

"Is there a problem, gentlemen?" she asked in her best finishing school voice.

"None at all, Lady Xavier," a voice said, and the little swarm of clerks parted to admit Gilbert Roddam, the grandson of the founder of the shop and its present owner. "My assistants are merely assessing the sartorial needs and dimensions of Mr. Coffin." Peering at Will through his pince-nez, Roddam said with an ingratiating smile, "You are most unusually tall, sir. It will be a challenge and a pleasure to outfit you."

"Can you have the suit ready by this evening?" Olivia asked.

"The cost will, unfortunately, be greater," Roddam said with a sad shake of his head, "but certainly it can be accomplished."

"Just send the bill to me," she said, which was how she always conducted business.

"I'm payin'," Will insisted.

Both Olivia and Roddam looked at him in surprise. "It will be quite expensive," she said. "Roddam's is one of the most exclusive men's shops in London."

Gilbert Roddam beamed.

Will was adamant. "I ain't gonna have you buyin' me clothes."

"But—"

His look was steely, determined. "Last time someone bought my duds for me, I was still learnin' my letters," he said, so low that only she could hear.

She stared up into his eyes, icy blue and resolute, and could see what this meant to him. "Of course," she said after a moment. He gave her a little nod of approval and turned to Roddam.

"Awright," he drawled, "what do I gotta do to get a suit around here?"

"Right this way, sir," Roddam said, gesturing toward the fitting room in the back. Olivia pressed a gloved hand to her mouth as she watched the ridiculous spectacle of rangy Will, wearing his Stetson and duster, surrounded by smaller, dapper men being lead away. Will sensed how ludicrous it must have appeared, too, because he sent her a wink before disappearing behind the swinging wooden doors.

A clerk offered her some refreshment, which she declined. Passing the time, she wandered up and down the aisles of the shop, gazing at the displays of waistcoats, watch chains, collars and hats of every shape and color. Naturally, undergarments were not displayed, lest anyone of delicate sensibility come into the shop, but Olivia found herself wondering what kind of underwear Will wore. Were they the same kind of linen drawers that David favored? Or perhaps red flannel? Or maybe he wore no underclothing at all.

Olivia pretended interest in a case of hunting gaiters in order to hide her flaming face.

Surrounded as she was by the relics of her husband, she felt David's disapproval all around her, embodied in the fine gloves, bolts of suiting fabric and wool felt hats. Here she was, standing in the shop he used to frequent and thinking of another man. Another *younger* man, so far beneath her socially even our servants found his presence alarming.

Absorbed as she was in this disheartening thought, she did not hear the bell on the door ring as it opened to admit a new customer. And she was not aware of anyone approaching her until they stood directly behind her.

"What are *you* doing here?" a voice hissed.

Whirling around, Olivia found herself looking up

at the outraged face of George Pryce. In his gleaming silk top hat and fur-collared Chesterfield coat, he was the outward model of aristocratic sophistication. She had not seen him in person since their meeting two months earlier, and the sight of the man who had been causing her so much grief made her blood seethe. If only she could wallop him in the face as she longed to do.

"My business is my own," she snapped back. "*All* of my businesses are my own," she added meaningfully.

Pryce sneered. "Well spoken for a bourgeois Bayswater adventurer."

"Poorly said for a vainglorious, grasping Mayfair princeling," Olivia shot back. She wondered if she could swing one of the mannequins at him.

He took a threatening step closer but seemed to recollect where he was and stopped himself. Olivia noticed that a few clerks and customers were glancing in their direction. Forcing himself to smile, Pryce said through his teeth, "You may as well cease your fight, *Mrs.* Xavier. It is impossible to say no to me. And eventually I will win. Either you can sell me the brewery now or face your ruin."

"I don't much care for those choices," Olivia replied coldly.

"You're lucky you even have a choice," Pryce muttered. "But you won't for much longer."

"These threats bore me," she said, turning away and feigning interest in a foulard cravat.

Pryce seized her shoulder to spin her around. His face had turned an alarming shade of red and his eyes bulged slightly. "Nobody turns their back on George Pryce," he snarled.

And then he was lying on his back, clutching his

nose and howling. Will stood over him, his hand curled into a fist, wearing a half-assembled suit. Real menace, frightening in its intensity, poured out of him as he loomed over Pryce.

"Don't touch her," Will growled.

Clerks, patrons and even tailors clustered around them as the once-quiet shop filled with excited, nervous chatter. Someone helped Pryce to his feet and handed him a handkerchief, which he held to his bloodied nose.

"What is going on here?" demanded Gilbert Roddam, coming forward. Seeing the spots of blood on the handkerchief, Roddam paled. "Fisticuffs? At Roddam and Sons?"

"I want this man arrested!" Pryce insisted.

"I'm gonna make you so ugly, even your momma won't love you anymore," Will threatened, taking a step forward.

Pryce immediately scuttled back, and Olivia placed a restraining hand on Will's raised fist. There was no doubt that, if Olivia let him, Will would kill Pryce with only his fists, and gladly. "Will, don't," she said, low and quick. "That isn't the answer."

"Summon the police at once!" Pryce commanded.

"Yes, do," Olivia answered. "I am sure they would be interested to hear about you laying hands on me."

"I did no such thing," Pryce shot back.

"Are you calling me a liar, Mr. Pryce?"

Gasps of shock ricocheted through the assembled crowd. Nothing could be worse than publicly insulting a lady, and Pryce knew that Olivia had called his bluff. He would rather endure a fist to the face than suffer damage to his reputation. He looked away, muttering.

"Can you finish Mr. Coffin's evening clothes with what you have?" she asked Roddam.

"We have noted all his measurements," he said, confused, "but Lady Xavier—"

"Have it sent to my address as soon as it is finished. Thank you." In a flash, Will changed out of the half-completed suit and into his former duds. And then he and Olivia were in her carriage, speeding back to Princes Square.

"Why didn't you let me whip that blowhard?" Will asked hotly.

"That's just what he wants," Olivia answered. "A direct, personal attack. There's no way we could defend ourselves if we assaulted him. He's too powerful."

Grumbling, Will said, "But it woulda been so much fun."

"There is nothing I would love to do more than thrash George Pryce," Olivia said, smiling ruefully. "But we're going to have to find a better way to defeat him. Less satisfying, perhaps, but better. And Will . . ." she added quietly. He looked up at her. "Thank you."

"That suit was the darnedest set of duds I ever seen. Who wears that stuff?"

Thoughtful, melancholy, Olivia said, "It isn't finished yet." To herself, she added, *And neither are we.*

Chapter Eight

*Prospect sounds interesting stop cowboy a first
stop want half payment up front stop leaving
Liverpool on ten o'clock stop Maddox*

Olivia looked up and down the row of faces lining the
dinner table. She had known them for many years:
Charlotte, whom she had met abroad in school; Charlotte's husband, Frederick; as well as eight others,
Frederick's business associates, their wives, one
bishop, a *Times* journalist well-known for his cover-
age of theater, his niece and a female advocate for
women's higher education. A lively group, adept in
conversation, one step below the aristocracy and conscious of that step. Familiar, all of them.

But none of their faces interested Olivia so much as
Will's, at the far end of the table, sitting between Mrs.
Paula Creed and Miss Juliette Southchurch. Both
ladies' eyes were fastened on him as though he were
one of the Elgin marbles come to life. And who could
blame them? He was an impressive sight. In his spot-

less evening clothes, his hair well combed and his
face freshly shaved, Will looked like an advertisement
for health tonic—the kind of tonic that promised its
drinker the ideal of virile masculinity. He was ele-
gantly attired, but even with his starched white shirt,
white tie and black coat, there was an undercurrent
of wildness in him, something undomesticated and
feral, that drew everyone's gazes to him.

But women especially. Glancing quickly around the
table, Olivia saw Charlotte and every other female
guest staring with undisguised fascination at Will.
Olivia wondered whether they were waiting for him
to make another error in etiquette.

"That isn't the correct fork, Mr. Coffin," one guest
had reprimanded him gently earlier.

But Will had only grinned, supremely unconcerned.
"It don't make a difference. It's all goin' down my gul-
let, one way or the other." Later, he poked at some
food on his plate. "What the great hey are these?"

"Croquettes," someone answered.

"They look like prairie oysters," Will said, spearing
one with his fork.

"What are those?"

Will gave the table a wink. "That ain't a topic for
mixed company." Some tittering followed, but these
small lapses only added to his appeal.

It wasn't his manners that drew everyone in. From
the beginning of the dinner, somehow Will managed
to dwarf every man in the room without even saying a
word. Yet he wasn't silent for long. No one could resist peppering the cowboy with questions.

"Is it true," Paula Creed was asking, "that you've
seen red savages? And that they go about," she giggled, "*naked?*"

131

"I've known plenty of Indians, ma'am," Will answered. "Some of 'em are what you might call savage, but a good number just want to be left in peace. As for bein' naked," he continued with a smile, gesturing toward her low décolletage with his fork, "I believe you're wearin' less than most squaws."

This sent Paula into another round of giggles, with Juliette and the other women joining in. Olivia, however, wasn't laughing. She gazed down at her plate where her *canard à la rouennaise* lay largely untouched. She knew that by keeping Will as far from her as possible, Charlotte was ensuring that there could be no speculation about Olivia and Will's relationship. Yet Olivia had the strangest sensation that, relegated as she was to the other end of the table, she was in exile from his bright warmth. Her bare arms and deep neckline felt chilled despite the overheated room.

"Your Mr. Coffin is quite, ah, colorful," Edward Baffin, the journalist, said beside her. "I had no idea Americans could be so charming."

Olivia turned her attention to her dinner companion and made herself smile brightly. "Indeed, he is," she agreed. She told herself that her unease was on Will's behalf, feeling anxiety for him. But she knew that wasn't the truth. She had been to hundreds of dinner parties just like this one. They were part of a world she knew exceptionally well.

Tonight she tried to see things through Will's eyes and found it all rather hollow: the endless ceremony, the silent footmen behind the guests' chairs, the parade of dishes so numerous and extravagant that no one, not even twelve people, could possibly eat them all. The things she used to enjoy seemed frivolous, an empty but calculated display that had no correspondence to reality.

Or maybe, she corrected herself, hearing Will's deep laughter, it wasn't Will's eyes she was seeing this dinner party through but her own, for the first time. But she was growing sullen and withdrawn at Charlotte's table, which would never do. She forced herself to make conversation with the woman opposite her.

"I am most curious about your views on women's education, Mrs. Davis," she said.

Lenore Davis, middle-aged but animated, said with conviction, "Universities like Girton are a step in the right direction, but its future is far from secure without proper funding."

"Why do we need ladies' colleges at all?" demanded the bishop. "To teach them mathematics, science and Greek? Women have no use for such knowledge."

"They have as much need for knowledge as men," Olivia countered. "I myself longed to go to university, but my parents insisted I attend a school of accomplishment, and so I have been forced to teach myself anything of value."

"Everything women need to know can be taught to them by their mothers and governesses," the bishop insisted. "The raising of children, the comfort of their husbands, household management. Why fill their heads with facts that have no application? Why make them wish for things they cannot, and should not, have?"

"Such as their own businesses?" Olivia asked pointedly.

"Naturally," the bishop answered, but then realized that Olivia owned a business herself and purpled slightly, stammering.

Mrs. Davis and Olivia exchanged exasperated glances that communicated their opinion of the good bishop. "Women have the same faculties as men, and yet they are left to languish in complete ignorance," Mrs. Davis returned. "They know as much, if not less, than their own children."

"What do you think of the subject of women's education, Mr. Coffin?" Frederick Gough asked. Eleven pairs of eyes turned to Will, who set down his wine glass and stared back warily.

Oh, dear, thought Olivia. Perhaps she could find a way to distract everyone so he wouldn't have to answer.

But Will spoke before she could do anything.

"I think women need to know as much as men," he answered after a moment. "Back home, women gotta know how to farm the land, treat sickness, shoot a gun and learn the children. They need to be three times as smart as men 'cause they got twice as much to do."

"How dreadful!" Paula Creed exclaimed, holding her napkin to her mouth. "So much *work*."

"It's hard living, sure," Will answered, "but I'd rather have my woman working by my side than sittin' at home, bein' bored and tryin' to think of some way to kill time."

His woman. Olivia felt the warmth of that phrase suffuse her face. But who would that woman ultimately be? Olivia didn't like her, whomever Will settled on.

"Wouldn't you pick bein' useful to doin' nothin' all day?" Will asked Paula.

Which, of course, was exactly what Paula and all her friends did—fill their days with shopping, endless social calls and petty charities, all activities to distract them from the fact that they had accomplished nothing. When David had been alive, Olivia had been one of their ranks. She had paid calls, embroidered too many slippers and pillowcases, gone to breakfasts, teas, regattas and hundreds of other social events where she said the same thing to the same people over and over again. It was exactly the life she was supposed to lead, and her societal activity delighted David. She was a perfect well-bred woman, a model wife, fashionable and futile. And she had been quietly, oppressively miserable.

Taking over the brewery had changed all that. Olivia was now more a stranger in Charlotte's elegant dining room than she was in the Greywell's racking room, where they stored kegs of beer. Yet her position as a society widow was never quite forgotten at Greywell's. She wondered when she would feel completely at ease, whole. Certainly not while George Pryce continued to make her life miserable.

"So you are in favor of women's education," Frederick concluded.

"Bein' ignorant is plain dangerous where I come from. But that don't stop most people from bein' dangerous."

There were smiles and chuckles from the group. Olivia felt herself relax slightly. Will could make most any awkward situation enjoyable.

"What is your opinion of formal education?" Edward Baffin asked.

Will's brow creased as he thought. "Nothin' worth learnin' can be taught," he said finally.

"Didn't Oscar Wilde say that?" Juliette asked, clearly astonished.

"Yes, ma'am, I believe he did."

Olivia was just as shocked as the rest of the party,

but unlike everyone else, tried to keep her surprise hidden.

"What does an American cattle driver know about Oscar Wilde?" one of Frederick's business associates asked.

As questions went, that one was rather rude, but Will took no offense. "I saw him speak last year at the Tabor Grand Opera House in Leadville, Colorado."

"Wilde gave a lecture tour in America," Olivia recalled.

Will nodded. "He went to Denver, and then to Leadville, which is a mighty wild mining town in the Rockies."

"I can't imagine what that great lover of beauty thought of such a place," Paula exclaimed.

Grinning, Will said, "He had himself a hog-killin' time. Went down into the Matchless Mine and drank all night with the miners. Kept his liquor, too. He could really stand the gaff. And he said that the Rockies were the most beautiful part of the West," he added proudly.

Excited chatter filled the paneled dining room. No one was certain what amazed them more—that the famous leader of the Aesthetes would enjoy drinking with grizzled miners or that a cowboy might have any interest in pronouncements on the Gothic and beautiful. Olivia found herself too astonished to stop staring at Will. He continued to confound her, slipping away from easy definitions into something more complicated, more intricate. And, oh, how he pleased her in his manifold forms.

Will looked over to her with humor glimmering in his crystalline blue eyes. An answering blush rose up from deep within her. He had never seen her before in formal evening dress, and his gaze flickered over her exposed shoulders and chest, warmly approving, intimate. Yet it was more than the revealing gown she wore that made her blush.

He had taken up residence in her consciousness, a physical, palpable inhabitation that she found herself welcoming, though she knew she should push him away.

But she liked having him there. The fatigue that burdened her—running Greywell's and fighting Pryce, all while maintaining her social position—lifted when he was nearby. In Will, she had found someone who could be both a friend and a partner, who needed no explanations and accepted her as she was. Such an unusual man.

As she moved her gaze away from him to her hands, folded in her lap, she felt, for the first time in a long while, no longer alone.

Will stood and watched as the women rose, rustling in their gowns, and began to leave the dining room. Olivia had explained to him earlier that at the end of the meal the women of the party always left to sit in the drawing room and amuse themselves while the men were allowed the freedom to smoke and talk of subjects perhaps not well suited to delicate ears.

He didn't mind most of the ladies leaving—with the exception of Mrs. Davis, most of the women he'd met tonight were sheltered, silly and interested in him as some kind of trick pony. Considering what Lenore Davis said about the poor state of women's education, it was no wonder they had so little to talk about besides clothes, parties and the merits of their own children. At least the women back home had a better sense of life beyond their own little pastures. So the roundup toward the drawing room didn't bother him too much.

But Will did mind that Olivia had to leave with the other women. He'd barely been able to talk with her all night because she'd been sitting four chairs down. Will had found, over the course of the long meal, that he'd wanted to say so many things to her, trifling comments about the guests or the conversation that he knew would make her smile. She hadn't laughed at all tonight. In fact, she'd looked downright blue.

And now she was leaving.

"See you gentlemen soon," Charlotte promised, linking her arm with Olivia's. He watched them go and couldn't help thinking that he'd rather have dined on Olivia tonight instead of the dozens of plates of food he couldn't name. The grub was all right, but she was a sight more appetizing. Her slim, creamy shoulders curved above the low dip of her rose-colored silk gown, and he wanted so badly to move his palm along that exposed skin it made his eyes sting. He hated her bustle, though. How could a man know a woman's shape when giant mesas of fabric looped and billowed out behind her? And tarnation, he wanted to know her shape.

Olivia cast a quick look over her shoulder at Will before the door closed behind her and the rest of the females. He straightened. Could she hear what he was thinking? He could have sworn that earlier in the evening, after he'd talked about Oscar Wilde, he and Olivia had looked at each other down the table and practically spoken to each other without uttering a syllable. That hadn't ever happened to him before, not with a woman, not with anyone.

"Freedom, eh, boys?" Frederick Gough said with a chuckle. All the other men in the room agreed loudly, so Will made himself laugh as though he were like-minded. He didn't feel very free, not in this stiff, itchy suit. He could barely move his arms. Clearly, gents didn't do a lot of cattle roping in their fancy duds.

Taking their seats again, some men began reaching for, and lighting, the cigars and cigarettes offered by one of the servants. Will only smoked cigarettes he rolled himself, but he picked a fine-looking cigar and, after clipping and lighting it, drew its rich smoke into his mouth. A bottle holding some variety of spirits began to make its way around the table.

"Don't mistake me, gentlemen," Gough said, drawing on his own cigar, "I love my wife and her company, but there are some things a man simply cannot say to a woman."

"I never talk of business to my Elizabeth," someone said. "Nor of sport, nor politics."

"What do you talk about with her?" Will asked. He poured himself a glass of dark wine and took a drink. It tasted sweet and heavy.

Elizabeth's husband thoughtfully studied his glass. With a wry smile, he said, "She asks me how my day was; I say, fine, she tells me the children are well and then we go upstairs later and she lifts her nightgown."

Everyone, even the church man, laughed at this, and again, Will made himself join in, though he didn't feel mighty jolly. He wondered if Olivia's husband had spoken about her like this, and if he and she had talked together at all. It seemed like, outside of thoroughly coarse subjects, he and Olivia could talk about most anything. But she was different from just about every other woman Will knew, and that stirred him.

"So tell us, Coffin," the reporter asked, "what are women in the Wild West like?"

"There're all kinds of women," Will answered, circumspect. "Wives, teachers, farmers."

"But what about the *wild* ones?" one of Gough's associates asked, leaning forward. "The demimondaine?"

Will glanced around at the men's eager faces. Seemed like everyone in England wanted to know about the scarlet side of life out West. "We got plenty o' them," he said. "Every town, no matter the size, has a cathouse. There ain't too many women west of the Mississippi, so we gotta make do with what we got."

Again, knowing chuckles. "I say," Gough's associate drawled softly, "Tiverton and I are going over to St. Johns Wood later tonight. Gough's a spoilsport, but perhaps you'd like to join us?"

"What's in St. Johns Wood?" Will asked.

Most of the men exchanged meaningful looks. "The young ladies we protect. They usually have some friends stop by, as well, when we come for visits."

"They don't sing duets at the piano, I'm guessin'," Will said.

The men burst out laughing. "That's not the instrument these hussies play," Tiverton snorted. "But, by God, they should open their own conservatory!"

"Come join us, Coffin. We promise these girls can offer you a finer ride than any mustang. They're quite experienced."

Will didn't hesitate before answering, "No, thanks."

Leaning back in his chair, the reporter asked with a smirk, "Lady Xavier have you on a short leash, Coffin? Not that I would mind being on her leash. Running that brewery of hers, she's bound to be a little more . . . knowledgeable than most ladies."

If he had been in any bunkhouse back home, he would have jumped up and cleaned the reporter's clock, but Will didn't think lighting into the people of Olivia's social circle would help her preserve her reputation. So, clamping down on his temper, he said evenly, "She don't got me on any kind of leash. I just don't feel like that kinda company."

"You're being a spoilsport, Coffin," Tiverton chided him.

"I don't cotton to treatin' women like jackstraws, droppin' one and pickin' up another," Will drawled. "'Specially if one of them's my wife."

Everyone glared at each other across the table, the mood of camaraderie stretched thin.

"Perhaps when you get some free time, Coffin, you can take a look at my stable," Gough said appeasingly. "I purchased a few fine horses from Tatterstall's, and I would be appreciative of an experienced horseman's opinion."

Gough was a good host, steering the conversation toward something Will could speak on at length without wanting to bushwhack anyone. The men around the table began to settle down, smoothing their feathers, and soon everyone but Will was gabbing away without much thought about what had just happened.

He wasn't sure he much cared for England. People here seemed to say one thing and then do another, wearing different masks and keeping their intentions hidden. Plain dealing was the most respected way to conduct yourself where Will came from, whether it had to do with business or life at home. He wondered, if he ever found his kinfolk, what kind of people they would be. Like the people tonight, starched, moneyed and double-dealing? Or maybe he came from the silent men who stood behind the guests' chairs and cleared away the dishes. Will wasn't the first man from the West to have no sense of his own history, but he was taking a big gamble trying to find it.

Would it matter to Olivia, when the truth was revealed?

"Let's join the ladies, gentlemen," Gough eventually suggested, and Will gratefully got to his feet and followed the men upstairs to the drawing room. On his way, he caught sight of himself in a mirror and felt as though he were staring at a stranger. In his expensive, custom-made evening clothes, he looked like he was trying to pretend he was a cattle baron or one of Denver's swaggering millionaires. He liked the suit fine—it was the nicest set of duds he'd ever owned, and by far the costliest—but it felt like a costume.

Yet wearing this costume was the only way he could fit into Olivia's world.

He was frowning by the time he got to the drawing room, thinking about this, but his frown disappeared immediately when he spied Olivia. She was sitting with Charlotte and Lenore Davis, talking seriously. She happened to glance up as he entered the room and suddenly stopped talking. The smile she gave him could have kept him warm on the longest winter night in the Rockies. He knew those nights well, when the snow just kept coming down and the wind shrieked and hollered through the mountain passes as though it were a living thing being murdered. Holed up in some bunkhouse somewhere, Will had often wished he'd had a woman to keep him company. Not just for bodily pleasures, but to have her comforting presence near him. Someone he could while away the dark hours with—talking, reading aloud or even just sitting without saying anything at all. Of course, back then he hadn't been able to think of a single woman he'd want to spend that much time with. But here was Olivia, whose smile shimmered through him like sunlight on snow.

"Did you enjoy yourself with the men?" she asked when he came to stand beside her.

"Passably," he answered.

"I hope I prepared you enough," she said, rising. "But I simply don't know what men talk about when they're alone."

Will had no intention of telling her exactly what had been spoken, so he said vaguely, "Stupifyin' stuff. Talk of some fellers named Gladstone and Parnell." A servant offered him a cup of coffee from a silver tray, and he took it. Strange. People handing him things, dishing up his food, even helping him put on his clothes earlier tonight as if he were some giant baby who couldn't manage the jobs on his own.

He and Olivia stood off to the side of the room, watching the husbands reunite with their wives and the visible change in their behavior. Everywhere there was pretty painted china and expensive, glittering objects, women in bright silk dresses laughing and the polished sheen of a comfortable, decorative existence. Most cattle barons aspired to this kind of life, wishing and buying their way toward a European pedigree, but it all seemed flat and stale to Will.

"This how you usually spend your nights?" he asked Olivia quietly.

"I used to," she answered. "When David was alive, he wanted to host many dinner parties. They were good for business. But since his death . . ." Her voice trailed away as she observed the knotty dance of manners being executed in the Goughs' drawing room. "I find my appetite for such diversions to be waning considerably."

"I don't like makin' the women leave the room after supper," Will said. When she looked at him questioningly, he continued, "When I get married, I don't want my wife runnin' away. I want her an' me to be able to talk about whatever we want, right in front of each other."

"So, you plan on getting married?" Will thought he heard her voice grow tight, but he couldn't be sure. He glanced over at her, and she was studying her own cup of coffee as though it held the answer to a riddle.

"Someday," he answered. He tried picturing his future bride, a woman he hadn't met yet but knew he would want, and came up with nothing. She'd always been a notion, not a real person. Will thought quickly of the girl in New York, of sitting on a park bench the following morning while tugging on his boots and knowing that he didn't have the taste for meaningless romps in the barn. But what was the alternative? Marriage. To an unknown wife.

Instead of picturing this wife, he followed the lovely curve of Olivia's neck, the dark masses of her hair pinned into soft whorls and interwoven with silk roses, and the neat scrollwork of her ear. "Someday," he repeated, "but not yet. I got other plans until then."

Chapter Nine

The evening, to the degree that Charlotte's plans were concerned, had been a success. The guests had enjoyed Will's company considerably and found his profession of cattle herding to be refreshingly rustic, charmingly authentic, a safe novelty that could not damage their insular world. The truth—he was assisting Olivia at the brewery while searching for his relatives—was peculiar enough to provoke little comment. Word was sure to reach George Pryce that Olivia was not running away with her tail between her legs and had Will at her back in case anything grew dodgy.

So Will and Olivia ought to have been quite pleased with the course of the night's activities as they entered her home on Princes Square. Yet neither of them acted very pleased. In fact, their mood, as they gave Mordon their hats and wraps, was nearly funereal.

"Are you planning on retiring?" Olivia asked, lingering in the foyer.

Will shook his head. "Feelin' a bit antsy, so maybe I'll mosey over to that library of yours and find me somethin' to read."

She looked at him in the gaslight, piercingly handsome and young in his stark evening clothes. Roddam & Sons had done an excellent job in their tailoring—the suit fit Will amazingly well, emphasizing the broadness of his shoulders, his height and the leanness of his musculature—yet he still seemed ill at ease in his finery. Perhaps if she hadn't come to know him as well as she did, she would not have seen his discomfort. But she could sense a feeling of displacement emanating from him.

And she was supposed to say good night and climb the stairs, letting him sit alone in her library. Her mind turned back to the conversation she had had with Charlotte once the ladies had left the dining room. Her hostess had taken her aside as the other female guests made their way to the first floor.

"Will seems to be doing quite well," Charlotte had said quietly.

"He has a natural ability to make friends," Olivia answered. "I know I count myself as one of them."

In the glow of the gaslamps, Charlotte had looked almost mournful. "Remember my warning, Olivia. I see the way you look at each other. It is unmistakable."

Olivia hadn't been able to contradict Charlotte, as much as she wanted to. Lord, was she so transparent? Were *they*?

"Taking him as a lover would be socially devastating," Charlotte had continued.

"Perhaps I want more from him than just an affair," Olivia had replied.

"I like Mr. Coffin very much," Charlotte said. "I

know you do not want to believe this, and I wish I did not have to say so, but an affair is all that your attraction can ever amount to. There is simply no possibility it could lead to anything more permanent. But even then, the damage to your reputation would be irreparable." She sighed and smoothed Olivia's hair, an old gesture of comfort. "Come," Charlotte said, looping her arm through Olivia's and leading her upstairs, "the guests are waiting."

With Charlotte's words echoing in her head, Olivia knew full well what she ought to do—go to bed immediately, and alone.

"Do you feel like a bit of music?" she heard herself ask suddenly.

Will's unusually somber face broke into a grin. "Sure do," he said.

Taking up a lamp, Olivia led him to the music room on the ground floor. Unlike the rest of the house, here Olivia had been given free rein in her decorative tastes. It was furnished much more simply than the other rooms. The walls were papered in floral designs from William Morris, and the furniture was carved by country craftsmen in a plain style that David had never liked. He had called it crude, but she loved the refined understatement of woodwork without embellishment. There were a few sofas and chairs scattered throughout the small room, even a piano at the far end.

She had not shown the room to Will earlier; it was a rather personal place, decorated as it was in a style uniquely her own. Perhaps he would have found such a simple room strange compared to the rest of the elegant townhouse. Few people of her acquaintance knew about the music room. That had been a deliberate decision on her part. Now she knew that if anyone could appreciate such a place, it would be Will. She looked at him, almost shyly, to see his response.

"I'll be jiggered," Will breathed in open admiration as Olivia, relieved and pleased, set the lamp down on the piano. He gently ran his hands over the dark satiny surface of the lid. Such a contrast between the refined musical instrument, imported and continental, intended for elegant little spaces, and Will, lanky, rugged, meant for a landscape as open and rough as he was. Yet there was something in his delight of the piano that was fitting, his unexpected appreciation for the beautiful.

"It comes from Vienna," she explained, delighted with his pleasure. "Shall I play for you?"

"Yes, ma'am," Will agreed immediately, coming around to pull out the bench for her.

She sat, adjusting the rustling fabric of her bustle and skirts, before skimming the tops of the piano keys lightly with her fingers. Early in her marriage, she would play for David after dinner, and he would sit in one of the armchairs, listening to her and watching. Then he began bringing his newspapers with him into the music room, and eventually she stopped playing. How long had it been since she'd played for anyone besides herself? Years. Many years.

But she could feel Will's interest as he leaned against the piano. She practiced a few scales to warm up her fingers before beginning with some Chopin, Nocturne in C minor, a piece she had learned at school. The room filled with the precise, refined notes, and after she felt comfortable in the routine of the piece, she chanced a look at Will's face.

He was staring at her hands, intent, watching the

positioning of her fingers as they moved over the keys. His eyebrows had drawn down in concentration and she almost believed that he was memorizing the piece as she played. But that was impossible.

She tried to keep her fingers from becoming clumsy under his scrutiny, yet she was acutely conscious of his focus. Her hands, her arms, felt exposed—naked, almost—beneath his attentive eyes, though she wore a heavy diamond bracelet on one wrist. A flush began to spread across her chest and up into her face. Her hands did stumble then, and she placed them in her lap.

"I'm sorry," she murmured. "It's been a while since I've had an audience."

Whatever spell had fallen across Will broke instantly and he smiled warmly, leaning an elbow on the piano. "That was surely the most beautiful thing I've ever heard, Liv. Can't you keep playin'? If me watchin' bothers you, I can stare at the potted plant. See?" He demonstrated by gaping at the fern sitting in the étagère as though it were a horseless carriage.

Olivia laughed. "You can watch me if you like," she said, rearranging her hands over the keys. She began to play one of Beethoven's piano sonatas, letting herself enjoy the music as well as having an appreciative audience.

She didn't want to admit how much she basked in his attention, how having him watch her as he did now, with his forearms braced on the lid of the piano and his gaze on her alone, filled her with unaccountable gratification. He was handsome, yes, and what woman did not enjoy being the object of a good-looking man's interest? But it was more than that. She felt so much more comfortable with Will now than she had at Charlotte's dinner party. In fact, she felt freer, more herself, than she had been in a goodly while.

She poured that feeling into the piano, letting the music express what she knew words could not. From Beethoven she ran into a Mozart piano sonata in G major, finding herself smiling and nodding over the keys, bent over them in a way her piano instructor would never have approved, though it felt so good.

When the Mozart came to an end, she rested her hands on the keys.

"Have I bored you yet?" she asked, only partly in jest.

But Will looked serious. He reached down and laid his hands over hers. She felt the heat of his skin. "I could stand here all night and listen to you," he said with a shake of his head. "Between the music and the woman, I'm up to my Stetson in beauty."

She found herself blushing again, as flustered as if she were still in boarding school. All knowledge of music fled under the onslaught of his natural charm, which was that much more remarkable because it was uncontrived, spontaneous. When he took his hands away, she missed his touch acutely.

"D'you mind," Will said, after a pause, "if I give it a whirl?"

Olivia glanced up, eyebrows arched in surprise. "The piano?"

He looked boyishly flustered, the faintest hint of red blossoming along the high planes of his cheekbones and along the bridge of his nose. "Naw, forget it. I'm bein' stupid."

"No, no," she said quickly, rising so quickly that she nearly knocked over the bench. "Please." She gestured to the seat.

With a slight self-conscious grimace, Will came

around the piano and sat down. He tugged free the tails of his evening coat and let them drape down to the floor. Interlacing his fingers, he stretched his arms out in front, and Olivia heard a popping from his knuckles. When she made a face, he smiled, sheepish. "Sorry. The boys in the bunkhouse used to say my crackin' knuckles could be heard from the Dakota Badlands to the Gulf of Mexico."

For a few moments, he studied the keys, as though reading the map of a foreign country. And then, without flourish, he began to play.

It was a simple, rollicking tune, boisterous, with a pace suitable for galloping across the floor, and Olivia began to laugh with the exuberant joy of it. There was nothing elegant or refined about the tune, but it was, to her mind, as wild and Western as the man who played it.

"You are a veritable font of talents," she said to him as he played.

"Yes, ma'am," he agreed with a wink and a grin. As he moved into the next song, a lilting country ballad, he said, "There ain't much work in the winter for cowpunchers, so I played piano in saloons and sometimes for the theatrical troupes that'd come through town. Y'know, melodramas." And here he played a comically exaggerated, threatening tune befitting a mustache-twirling villain as he wiggled his eyebrows. Olivia laughed again.

"How you amaze me, Will Coffin," she said, admiring and humbled that one man could be so protean.

"This is surely finer than any of the beat-up wooden boxes I played in Leadville." He smiled and continued to play. "Take a seat, Liv. I ain't used to having stand-up audiences."

Instead of pulling up a chair, as she ought to, Olivia found herself sitting next to Will on the bench. If he was surprised, he didn't show it, but Olivia astonished herself. Even through the yards of silk in her skirt, she felt his legs underneath the piano, working the pedals, and high-leaping currents set off inside her chest when his arm would brush against her as he moved along the keyboard.

"This here tune's called 'My Grandfather's Clock,'" he explained as he played a fast, comic song. "The boys always got a big kick outta this one. I won't frighten you to death with my singin'. Usually there were girls who sang."

Olivia had a fairly good idea what kind of girls those singers were, but she decided not to comment. Will played another quick, silly tune.

"This one's 'Oh, Dem Golden Slippers,'" he said. "After a few rounds, everybody gets up and does a little cakewalk dance to it. 'Cept me, since I gotta play."

"What is that one called?" Olivia asked after he trotted out the next funny song.

He grinned at her. "'Smick, Smack, Smuck.'"

"How racy." She laughed. "I should slap your face."

"Wait 'til you hear the words," he said with a leer. Then he played a slower, sadder piece, gently longing and melodic.

"Whenever the miners or cowboys got homesick, they all asked for this one, 'I'll Take You Home Again, Kathleen,'" Will said. "Especially the Irish fellers."

But nothing prepared her for the tune he played next. It was deceptively simple, low and keen, with rolling notes that blended together to form an undulating current of heartbreaking wistfulness that pierced straight to Olivia's heart. For this song, Will was bent deep in concentration over the keys, almost frowning, as this music, fierce and slow, billowed forth from what had at one time been a perfectly ordinary piano but had somehow, under Will's fingers, been transformed into the reverberations of Olivia's own heart.

There was silence as the song ended. Olivia blinked back tears she did not know had gathered in her eyes. "What," she said, then cleared her throat, "what was the name of that song?"

"I don't know," Will said quietly. "I haven't thought of a name for it yet."

She couldn't help it. She gaped. "*You* wrote that?"

He looked at her and nodded. "Can't read music, though. It's just somethin' I've been workin' out in my head for a while. Sounds pretty good on this fine piano of yours."

"It isn't the piano," Olivia said. They sat close together, turned into each other, so that the distance separating them was narrow. Her gaze moved over his face. She continued to be amazed that one man could possess such masculine beauty, and she saw such profundity in the tropical warmth of his blue eyes, she nearly drowned. "It's you. You've created the most beautiful music I have ever heard, Will. And you had that inside of you . . . I don't . . . ." Her eyes automatically lowered to his mouth. "I don't know what to make of you."

"I'm just a man, Liv," he said, his voice husky. The keen handsomeness of his face grew sharper with unmistakable desire, as his own gaze traveled along her face, down her neck, over the bare expanse of her shoulders and chest. And wherever his eyes moved, she felt her skin heat in response.

"I know . . ." she breathed, but then her breath deserted her as he leaned closer, bringing his rough, hot palm up to cup the back of her neck.

The heat of his hand traveled all the way down into the liquid core of her, and she nearly gasped aloud at the contact. She let him draw her closer, or she leaned in herself—she couldn't tell where his will and her own began—but she knew with certainty that she had to feel his mouth. He tilted her head to accommodate him and then she felt his lips move against hers.

There was, perhaps, half a second of tentative exploration before he growled with certainty and opened his mouth, moved himself into her, and they both became fevered, straining into each other, commingling tongues and inhaling each other's breath in quick, hungry gulps. She gripped his biceps tightly, his muscles bunching through layers of linen, wool and the skin of her own hands. He threaded his fingers into her hair, gently massaging her scalp, and his other hand came around to cup just beneath her breast.

She hated that her corset kept a rigid wall of bone and fabric between them. God, why was she wearing so many clothes? When every part of her body needed to feel what her mouth was feeling, the febrile coalescence of her flesh with Will's. Such a hot explosion between them, as though it had been building for hundreds of years, finally given release.

Had it only been last night that they had kissed for the first time? It couldn't be possible. Several lifetimes had passed in the space of a night and a day.

He groaned and shifted them around so she could sit on his lap. She brought her arms up and around his shoulders—there was no padding in his coat, the breadth of the jacket was purely him—and pressed against the unyielding mass of his chest. Desire threatened to overwhelm her, but she had moved past caring. Her world had been reduced to Will, his mouth, his hands, his muttered benedictions as he tried to gather her in all at once.

She didn't mind at all when, swearing, Will reached under the front of her bodice to touch her. The nimble fingers she had watched moments before on the piano keys now played down the soft skin of her breast to find the hardened tip of her nipple. She arched up, rocked with acute, devouring pleasure, trying to offer herself up to him, to these feelings, and as she did, her elbows hit the piano keys.

A sharp, jarring burst of unmusical noise sent Will stumbling backward, knocking over the piano bench. Olivia actually had to catch herself on the front of the piano to keep from toppling forward. She hoisted herself up as she watched Will struggle to collect himself. He was panting, as though he had run a long distance, and she could tell from the tenting of his woolen trousers that he was as aroused as she. He looked around wildly, like a feral animal herded indoors.

"Will—" Olivia began. She reached for him.

"I . . ." he said, dragging his hands through his hair. "I gotta get a drink."

And then she heard the sharp raps of his boot heels on the floor, followed by the sound of the front door opening and slamming shut.

He was out on the street before he knew it, walking under the haze of streetlights, as fogged as the night that surrounded him. Will had no idea where he was going, but he kept heading south, until he hit a huge expanse of land. This was the place Olivia called Hyde Park, but he hadn't had a chance to see it until now. No one seemed to be out except himself, and he moved through this giant stretch of green, trying to take some comfort in its open spaces.

He came to the bank of a kind of river and watched the movement of the wind on the water. How long he stood there, he didn't know. His mind was wrapped in flannel and the aching heaviness in his groin made much thought beyond watching the river impossible. He barely felt the chill of the October night. His blood was still thick and hot with the feel and taste of Olivia.

"Evenin', sir," a voice said behind him.

Will turned quickly and faced some kind of lawman, dressed in a dark blue uniform with a helmet that looked like half a loaf of bread.

"Evenin'," Will returned cautiously. He wondered if he was going to get arrested for trespassing or loitering.

"A bit late for a stroll in the park, eh, sir? With no coat or hat?"

Looking down, Will realized that he had run off without anything more than the fancy clothes on his back. "I was in a hurry," he said.

"You ain't from these parts, are you, sir?" the policeman inquired. "D'ye need directions?"

"Where can a feller get a decent drink in this town?" Will asked.

"Well," the lawman said thoughtfully, "there's the Friar, and the Three Tuns. They're both pretty posh."

"I mean a place where a workin' man can bend an elbow," Will explained. He gestured to the evening clothes. "This ain't my usual gear."

The policeman's stern face broke into a grin. "Oh,

you want McNeil's. That's near Covent Garden."
Pulling out a watch from his jacket, the policeman
consulted its face and said, "In fact, I'm off duty now.
I can take you there. A pint at McNeil's sounds like
just the thing."

"Thanks," Will said. They started walking east.
"You're someone to ride the river with."

The policeman chuckled. "I don't know what that
means, but I'll take it as a compliment. I'm Ernie, by
the way, Ernie Portbury."

"Will Coffin."

"You from Texas?"

"Colorado."

Portbury sighed, disappointed. "Too bad. I always
wanted to meet me a real Texas cowboy."

Fortunately, Portbury was chatty enough for the
both of them, since Will didn't feel much like talking.
The policeman led them through streets genteel and
otherwise, crowded and empty, until they came to one
street, pure working class, *his* class, where music and
laughter were coming out of a saloon. Portbury
pushed open the door, his hand guiding Will ahead,
and they were met by a raucous chorus of "Ernie!"
from the people inside.

Will knew that Portbury had steered him in the
right direction. Unlike the pub he'd visited with
Olivia the day before, there weren't many amenities
at McNeil's. Just a long bar with a footrail, a framed
license, an upright piano where someone banged out
a tune accompanied by a fiddle and rows of tables
where men and women were gabbing happily over
their tall glasses of beer. A print of the royal family, or
so Will supposed the group of sour-faced stiffs to be,
hung behind the bar, well-dusted. Aside from the few

tips of the hat toward England, Will recognized Mc-Neil's as the British counterpart to the countless saloons and taprooms he'd been in back home.

"Who's your swell friend, Ernie?" the barkeep asked as they stepped up.

"This is Will Coffin, all the way from Texas," Portbury announced proudly as he set down his hat.

Will didn't bother to correct Portbury, but shook hands with the barkeep. He fished out some coins from his pocket and slapped them on the worn bar. "A pint for my new friend, and one for me, too," he said.

Portbury grinned. "You're a good chap, Coffin."

Two glasses appeared in front of them. Will took a hesitant sip. It was warm, but eventually he grew used to the temperature. "This is the boss," he said, surprised.

"It's Greywell's," the barkeep said. "We just started sellin' it. Folks seem to like it a great deal."

He'd never tasted the beer from Olivia's brewery before. It was mighty fine, and he could tell that she put a lot of pride into her work. No wonder she refused to let Pryce take it away from her.

Will smiled into his glass, thinking that he should tell Olivia later about Greywell's popularity. Then his smile faded as he wondered what, exactly, he was supposed to say to her at all the next time he saw her. He'd been steps away from shucking her clothes off and taking her right on top of the piano. The memory made his jaw tighten. One of her servants could have walked in and seen everything, and he knew that gossip flew faster and hotter than a Nebraska summer. Word would be all over town about how Lady Xavier had been slumming with a cowboy, and her reputation wouldn't be worth a plug nickel. Having met her fancy friends earlier that night, he didn't doubt they'd grab on to any scandal and rattle it, and Olivia, to pieces. The disgrace would cost her the brewery, too. Pryce wouldn't dilly-dally about snatching it away from her when she was down.

But he couldn't apologize, since he wasn't sorry for kissing her. Damn, if he knew that kissing Lady Olivia Xavier was going to be that good, he wouldn't have waited nearly as long as he had. He couldn't remember the last time just kissing a woman had sent his blood shooting to the moon, but Olivia had sent him all the way to Jupiter and back.

More people came over to Portbury and playfully demanded that they be introduced to Will. He found himself shaking hands with several men and women, someone named Blarney Bill, and Jinks, and the girls Kitty and Dinah, their hands as rough as his own, their accents twangy and unrefined, their clothes clean but well-used. People with jobs. His kind of people.

He grinned and laughed and accepted their jokes about America, thinking that for the first time since he'd come to England, he felt at ease, comfortable. He wondered whether his kin were the sort to come to this kind of saloon. But he kept thinking of Olivia, who never came to a place like this even though she made their beer, and who kissed like she had a wild-fire burning inside her.

"Have a dance with me, ducks," Kitty shouted over the din.

He wasn't inclined to dance with her, even though she was pretty and wholesome, but Will was enough of a gentleman to say, "I'd be delighted, ma'am."

Kitty giggled and took up a position in his arms in

the middle of the floor, where several other couples were stomping in a kind of reel. He'd been to some dances in his time and was able to move the game Miss Kitty around the floor passably well. She grinned up at him, blond curls bouncing in her eyes, and waved at her friends shouting encouragements from the bar.

They had been dancing for several minutes when Kitty asked, so low he thought he'd misheard, "So who's the lucky lady?"

"Beg pardon, ma'am?" he asked.

"You've been smiling this whole time, but you're about a hundred miles away," she explained without recrimination. "Usually when a bloke's got a look like yours on his face, he's thinking of a lady. Who is she?"

"Somebody I can't have," he said after a moment.

"Why not? Any bird with a pinch of brains would want a brawny chap like you." She gave him a looking-over that could have stripped bark off an oak.

Will smiled at the compliment, but he could feel the hollowness of the gesture. "I ain't what you'd call on her level," he explained.

"You dress like one of 'em, though," Kitty pointed out. "And look mighty grand, if I may say."

"Just a costume," he said with a shake of his head. "I'm 'bout as common as a feller can get."

"And she's high-born, right?" When Will didn't answer, Kitty's look became much more knowing. "'Course," she said wryly. "We lower classes got to keep our place. Don't try to rise too high or we'll get beat down."

Will was still silent, but the truth of her words hit him hard. Everyone in England knew how things worked. The rich and powerful kept to their own, and the workers stayed well out of their way, or else they would both face the consequences. Even if he did try to pursue something with Olivia, eventually he was going to leave, return to the country and world he knew best, and she would stay behind to face the shame that would inevitably follow. Whether she regretted her actions or not, her class would make her suffer. Pryce would ruin her.

"Don't look too down at the mouth, ducks," Kitty chided. "You got a room full of friends and good music on the piano. Whatever happens tomorrow, just forget yourself tonight."

"Right," he said, winking. "Forget." And he swung her around the room to prove her point, making Kitty shriek with glee. But Will knew that even if he could forget himself, he could never forget Olivia.

Chapter Ten

George Pryce drummed his fingers on the wooden table while casting furtive glances over his shoulder to make sure no one spotted him at this exceedingly unfashionable Shoreditch fish and chip shop.

"Expecting someone?" Maddox drawled from across the table. No one knew his Christian name; he was called Maddox and answered to nothing else. Pryce had tried to ferret out more information about him when one of his more disreputable associates mentioned that Maddox was the man to call when all others had failed. Whoever this man was, he kept his background well hidden. Pryce wanted it that way—he didn't need anyone tying his name, or his family's, to the underworld's clean-up man.

"Nobody," he answered quickly. "I want to be sure that no one I know spots me here with you."

Maddox smirked from beneath his mustache. He looked like some of the middleweight pugilists who sparred in the basement of some gentlemen's clubs, not a large man, but built of solid muscle and able to inflict damage. He had a white scar cutting across one eyebrow—evidence of the kind of dangerous life he led. "I doubt anybody of your acquaintance frequents chip shops. That's why I picked this location for our meeting. I give my punters privacy." He popped a hot chip into his mouth. "Sure you don't want one, gov'nor?"

Pryce shuddered at the greasy paper covered in fried potatoes. "I only eat *pomme frites,*" he sniffed.

With a shrug, Maddox added more malt vinegar to his chips. "Suit yourself. You're paying."

Eager to have this meeting over with, Pryce said, "You know all the details of my situation. Can you help me?"

"You've been playing kids' games too long," Maddox said. "If you want to do things right, you do it my way." He leaned across the table and fixed Pryce with his black eyes. "You understand me, gov'nor?"

Pryce swallowed, then nodded. He'd set another part of his plan in motion yesterday, but he knew that it was only a delaying tactic. Lady Xavier would find some way to wriggle out of his grasp, and he wanted to settle the matter for good.

"I understand," he finally said. "What do you intend to do?"

"I did some reading on the train from Liverpool," Maddox said, reaching into his coat pocket. He threw a few cheap paperback novels onto the table. As Pryce bent closer to examine them, Maddox explained, "Books by someone named Ned Buntline. He writes all about men like that American who's been giving you trouble. Cowboys," he added, mocking.

"I'm paying you to get rid of him and that woman, not read," Pryce muttered.

Maddox folded his arms across his chest and looked bored. "Listen, gov'nor, before I strike, I need to know my enemies: how they think, the way their minds work. So I do a bit of research, get my strategy."

"So?" Pryce demanded. "Have you learned anything?"

After picking through the pile of now soggy chips, Maddox found one to his satisfaction and gave it a thorough soaking in vinegar before biting down on it. "I've learned a lot," he finally answered, chewing. "I've learned that men like me, we're called hired guns. And we always get the job done."

Even after a night of drinking, Will was an early riser. Years on the drive had taught him to be up at first light, no matter how tired, hung over or uneasy he was. Right now, he was all three. He'd somehow managed to get back to Olivia's place at around three in the morning and, after shucking his expensive suit, he'd collapsed in bed, head reeling from a night of heavy drinking and thoughts of her.

So when he roused himself at seven—pretty late by trail standards—scratched his beard off, thrown on his usual clothes and lumbered downstairs, he'd expected either to find Olivia calmly sipping her tea in the breakfast room or still in bed. But she was neither.

"She's gone to Greywell's, sir," Mordon told him as he poured himself a cup of strong black coffee in the empty breakfast room.

"Why so early?" he asked, his voice like a rusted bucket.

"I believe there was a spot of disorder at the brewery, sir. Shall I fix you a plate of breakfast?"

"No, thanks," Will said, troubled. He bolted back

his coffee, gratefully letting it scald its way down his throat and into his stomach. "I gotta get down there." If there was any trouble, and it concerned Olivia, he wanted to be involved. The more he thought about what George Pryce could do to her, the more enraged and edgy he became. If only he'd been able to mop the floor with that lousy son of a bitch yesterday.

But, damn it, why had Olivia run off without him? He was staying with her because she wanted his help with Greywell's, but this morning she'd already hit the trail with him snoring in bed like a hibernating bear.

The thought steamed him. Will kept his word. When he said he would do something, he did it. And that meant lending a hand when there was trouble at the brewery. Was she so rattled by what had happened last night that she'd left him out in the cold? Did she think he wouldn't want to help?

Before Will realized it, Mordon had handed him his Stetson and duster and was putting him into a cab. The sound of the horse's hooves clattering on the pavement made him wince, but he took the opportunity to let the coffee work its magic. He needed a level head for the day, but anger was getting the better of him. Did Olivia really think, even after last night, he wouldn't want to do his job? Her opinion of him must be lower than a shoat wallowing in a muddy ditch.

Huntworth, the brewery's manager, met him as he stomped through the main entrance. The little keg of a man looked all in a stew.

"Where's Oli—Lady Xavier?"

"In the office," Huntworth said before hurrying away.

He found her bent over one of the desks, her head braced in her hands as she poured over a large book, with several clerks running around holding telegrams. At the sound of his boots on the floorboards, she looked up, and he saw dark rings under her eyes. Some of his anger dried up, seeing her so troubled, but not all of it. He was supposed to shoulder that trouble for her, not sit in the audience like a yokel.

"Why didn't you get me up?" he growled. "I'm here to do my job."

She shook her head. "There's nothing you can do. Pryce has found a way to disrupt my business without resorting to physical intimidation."

"I ain't just about swingin' my fists," he said.

She gave a tired smile, but it was short lived. "I know. But this is something I don't think even you can fix." Turning back to the book in front of her, she rubbed one hand over her pale face.

His vexation ebbed, leaving him a bit lost. Even if he couldn't quite solve the problem, he hated being left out. But he had bigger worries than his own hurt pride.

Will hated to see the tension and worry in her slim shoulders. He wished he could shoulder that weight. He'd bear it himself, if she'd let him. But between the room full of clerks and the scene last night, he didn't think saying so would be much appreciated right now. He stood next to her and saw she was reading some kind of listing or directory.

"What happened?" he asked.

"He bought out my hops distributor," Olivia said, furious. "And hops are one of the most important elements in brewing. They give the beer its aroma, its bitterness. Without hops, I'm ruined."

"Get another distributor."

"I'm trying." She pointed to the book spread out before her. "I've got a listing of hops growers and have been trying to contact them since five this morning. But almost all of them have sold their crops to other brewers—or Pryce. And then there's the matter of finding the right *kind* of hops. Greywell's has been using Fuggles for the past few years."

The name Fuggles would have made Will laugh under normal circumstances, but things were just too tense. "Lemme help," Will said. "I can do more than just rope steers."

For a moment, he thought she would refuse, leave him out again. Then, with a weary nod of her head, she said, "Thank you," and pushed back from the desk. As she stood, Will made himself take a few steps back, because if he didn't, he'd surely want to wrap her up in his arms and press comforting kisses to the top of her head. Given the state of everything, he didn't think she would appreciate that.

Each day grew more complicated than the last. She knew she and Will had to clear the air between them, straighten out exactly what to make of their attraction—meaning, nothing could be made of it and they both had to understand that. But he seemed to know that already, since he'd fled her home and hadn't come back until very late. She knew exactly the hour of his return, since she'd lain awake listening for him. Where had he gone? In whose company had he spent his time? Judging by the grim expression on his face, it didn't seem as if he had enjoyed himself, but she couldn't suppress the stab of jealousy that hit her unexpectedly. Perhaps she had been cowardly, leaving him behind that morning, but she hadn't been able to sort herself out after a sleepless night. And Pryce's latest assault against her threw everything into chaos.

She didn't have room in her life for these feelings. She hadn't for a long while. All Olivia had been able to do was keep her head above water. Yet Will occupied so much space in her thoughts, she could barely focus on the tasks at hand. He had awakened her from a long slumber, but to what reality? Certainly he was better than any dream she might have, but so much more complicated.

They spent all day and well into the evening trying to find a hops farmer with a large enough crop. Telegram after telegram went out and was received. The process was unendurably slow. She began to think that telephones weren't such a bad idea after all.

Olivia found herself amazed at Will's tenacity at something that wasn't purely physical. Just like herself, Huntworth and the other men who ran the office at Greywell's, he pored over telegrams and directories with a single-minded resolve that had her thinking he might have the makings of a businessman.

After Mr. Huntworth had brought in luncheon and then a cold supper, Olivia finally looked up from her work and announced, "I found someone."

Everyone gathered around as she paraphrased a telegram. "There's a farmer in Kent who has a full harvest of Fuggles and he's willing to sell if I come down tomorrow with a bank draft. His family has an old grudge against the Earl of Hessay, so he wouldn't sell to Pryce." Even the staid clerks broke into cheers, while Will gave a cowboy whoop. Olivia couldn't hide her immense relief: another crisis averted.

But as she and Will rode to her house in the carriage, he said suddenly, "I don't like it."

Olivia blinked. She didn't know what he was referring to.

"How come all the farmers we wired had nothin'," Will continued, "but this one feller has exactly what we need?" He frowned. "Seems mighty shady."

"What choice do I have?" Olivia asked. "I need those hops."

"Then I'm comin' with you," Will announced.

"Very well," she agreed, and she saw with a flicker of amusement that Will had been preparing for a fight.

"Okay, then," he said, still argumentative. He folded his arms across his broad chest.

"About this morning . . ." she began. He eyed her guardedly. She was responsible for making him so wary, and it saddened her. Though he was smart and alert, Will lived his life openly, and she hated that she'd made him circumspect.

"I could say that I knew you had come in late and I didn't want to wake you," she continued. "And I could say that there wasn't much for you to do at the brewery, since it was business-related, but none of that would be true."

Rather than look at the hard, unforgiving lines of his handsome face, she stared out the window at the passing streets. "The truth is, Will, that I'm confused by what's going on between us, and I don't know what to do. So if I stumble along my way, I hope you'll be patient with me."

"Liv," his deep voice said from across the carriage, "I ain't gonna hurt you."

"I know," she said immediately, believing it. She continued to look out the window for a long time, at London rolling by, as though she could find some solution in the shopfronts and townhouses that lined the streets.

A faint snore brought her head around. He had fallen asleep. Light from the streetlamps flickered across his face, and she saw, despite the relative defenselessness of his position, a continued wariness. He was younger than she, it was true, but he'd grown up much faster than she had, in a world where every day brought untold dangers. What must that be like, she wondered, knowing that at any moment, even the smallest threat could be your undoing? There was so much more to him than the silly novels she read could ever tell her.

"I wonder if I will hurt myself," she murmured, but she silenced herself as he shifted in his seat. She wanted to reach out and brush a lock of sandy hair from his face, but she kept her hands balled in her lap. They were both exhausted, their defenses down. Who knew where contact would lead. But tomorrow they would travel to Kent, and tomorrow they would finally face the beguilement between them, which they had barely touched tonight, and lay it to rest.

"Where're the mountains?" Will asked. He looked out the window of the hansom cab at the flat, cultivated land of Kent. With the driver riding behind them, she and Will were afforded an uninterrupted view of the country. "I didn't see any on the train ride, and there sure ain't any here."

"In Wales and Scotland," Olivia answered. "England is too genteel for mountains. Very undignified."

He smiled, but the smile faded quickly as he gazed around. They were riding from the train station to the hops farmer, and surrounding them was what some referred to as the garden of England—rich, fertile, thoroughly domestic.

"I've been wonderin' what England looked liked outside the city," Will said with a frown, "and it's all walled-up farmland. I've ridden fences longer than London, no company 'cept the grassland and the clouds. Ain't there nothin' wild in this country?"

"Aside from you, no."

He shot her a dry look, and she smiled sweetly, then sobered. "Perhaps that is what your father and mother were searching for, why they left England," she suggested. "A place that wasn't enclosed. Where they could live without boundaries."

"Sure are too many of those in England," Will said, gazing out the open front of the cab, and she understood they weren't talking about farmland anymore.

"Will—" Olivia began.

"I wish I'd met you in Denver, Liv," he said fiercely, turning to her. The cab's interior was rather small, and he filled it more with his presence than his size. She felt the warmth of his body in the confined space and the heat of his eyes. "I could've courted you proper. I could've had half a chance to win you. Back home, if I wanted somethin' I took it, and nobody told me otherwise. If they had, I'da sent 'em hollerin' for the hills. But nobody was fool enough to tell me no."

"Will—" She felt her heart contract.

"But here, I gotta slink around like a whipped mule." He shook his head. "It ain't right. If a man wants a woman, he should be able to act, and lemme tell you, Liv," he continued, his look so ferociously hot she felt it burn through all the layers of her wool coat and traveling dress to mark her flesh, "I want you. Like I never wanted anybody before. It scares me a little, how much I'm thirstin' for you."

They were riding together in a hansom cab down

the lane of a small Kentish town, and yet there seemed to be only this, her and Will. "No one has ever said anything like that to me before," she managed, her chest tight, her breasts heavy.

Cupping the side of her face with his leather-gloved hand, Will's mouth twisted slightly, bitterly. "I'm tryin' to do the right thing by you, Liv. Even if it rips me apart to do it."

She pressed her cheek into his glove, which had taken on the heat of his skin, and held his wrist. "I know," she said, her throat aching. "Me, too. I just wish the right thing didn't make me feel so awful."

He pulled his hand away, and she looked confusedly at him. "I can't touch you and not want more," he said.

Will tried to press his large body into the farther corner of the cab, a nearly impossible task. "Those things look like dunce caps for Paul Bunyon," he said, abruptly changing the subject.

She followed his pointed finger to several conical roofs pointing up through the treetops. "They're called bells," she explained. It was almost intolerable to pull herself away from him, force their conversation back into exchanges of pleasantries and information, but he was right. They couldn't continue as they had without disaster following. "They're special roofs used in oast houses, where hops are dried. When you dry hops, the moisture escapes through the bells. You see them all over Kent."

He nodded, but she could see that he wasn't taking in any of what she was saying. She barely heard herself. All she was aware of was a powerful longing deep in her belly that could not be appeased. She'd never felt this way before, not for any of the young men who'd courted her during her season, not even for David. At best, she and her late husband had possessed a comfortable affection for one another—nothing like the devastating need that tore through her whenever she was near Will or thought about him.

It was an agonizing relief when the cab pulled up outside the hops farm. She gave the driver a handful of coins to have him wait until the meeting was over so he could take them back to the train station. Will helped her down as the farmer rushed out to meet them. Giving a polite bow to Olivia and exchanging a more cautious, curious handshake with Will, the man led them inside to examine his harvest.

Though she had brought a bank draft for the specified amount, the process of negotiating took much longer than she had anticipated. Apparently, the farmer hadn't quite made up his mind, and they spent a goodly amount of time haggling over the price. Olivia saw that Will was growing impatient with the whole process, so she suggested that he examine some of the farmer's horses, which were corralled nearby.

Some time later, she wandered outside to find him, arms braced on the fence, watching a few sorrel mares grazing. His look was almost wistful, seeing the lovely arched necks of the horses bent to the ground, the sheen of their glossy hides and their fine, strong legs promising freedom to whomever rode them.

"His wife is fixing luncheon for us," she explained at his questioning glance. "This may take a while longer."

Will chewed on a blade of grass and shook his head. "I don't like it. It's like he's stallin' or somethin'. We should go."

"I need these hops."

"Fine," he said. "But I'm on the lookout for anything cross-eyed."

After they finished their luncheon, an agreement was reached. Following that was the matter of arranging transport. By the time everything was settled, dusk was draping itself across the countryside. The farmer waved them off and shut the door to his house, and Will helped her back into the waiting hansom.

As she was climbing aboard, Olivia had a brief feeling that the cab driver looked different. She had thought that the man who drove them out had worn long sideburns; this fellow had a mustache. But she tried to dismiss her apprehension. After all, she had not gotten a very good look at the driver, since he'd been behind them most of the time. She stepped into the cab, getting ready to settle herself in for the ride to the station, when she heard Will say behind her, "Whoa, Liv, this driver ain't—"

Suddenly the driver's whip gave a sharp crack, and the cab sped forward, throwing her into the carriage, the door swinging open and leaving Will behind.

"Driver, stop!" she shouted, struggling to raise herself up onto the seat.

But the man didn't listen.

She banged on the roof of the cab. "Stop immediately," she demanded as the countryside raced past. They were not on the road back to the station.

"Shut up," a voice behind her snarled, "or I'll turn this whip on you."

Great God, she had been kidnapped.

Chapter Eleven

For less than a second, Will just stared after the cab as it raced away, the door hanging open like a broken wing and the heel of Olivia's little boot visible on the floor. But he was already moving before he could blink his eyes. He acted without thought, switching into a state of mind where everything was pure reflex and instinct.

He ran back to the corral where the horses grazed and grabbed a bridle hanging on the fence post. One of the mares was too startled by his sudden approach to move as he quickly slipped the bridle over its head. He made a quick mental note of the differences between the English bridle and the American ones he was used to before swinging himself up onto the bare back of the horse and kicking it into a gallop. They cleared the fence in a smooth jump and took off down the road in pursuit of the cab.

Under other circumstances, Will would have relished being back on a horse again. It felt natural—more natural than being on foot—and he loved using the horse as an extension of himself to eat up the land beneath them. But these weren't ideal circumstances for appreciating life in the saddle, and he focused all his attention on catching up with the cab, where, God help him, Olivia was trapped.

They bolted down the road, trees and fences whipping by. He hunched over the neck of the horse, urging it onward. He could hear Olivia shouting at the driver to stop. She didn't sound panicked—more nettled than anything—and he saw her try to reach up through the open door to hit the driver. But the driver knocked her hand down hard, causing her to yelp and fall back, and Will's blood, already riled, turned hotter than a branding iron. He spurred his horse hard.

The driver looked over his shoulder. Will could barely make out his features in the coming night, but he saw the cold determination on his face. Will'd known something about that mudsill wasn't quite on the level, but he hadn't done anything about it. Now he had to clean his plow and get Olivia to safety.

He knew who'd sent this mean hombre: Pryce. The son of a bitch had gone from bad to worse.

Then Will heard and felt the unmistakable zing of a bullet whizzing past him. Another pop, another bullet, and he ducked low to avoid the gunfire. *Damn it.* His horse spooked a little, but he kept firm hands on the reins and moved it in a zigzag pattern across the road to dodge the bullets. Will didn't fear gunfire— he'd been around it all his life—but no one in England had ever used it except him, until now. And that meant one thing: Pryce's man meant to end the war between them—at the cost of Olivia's life, and likely his own.

Well, damn him if he thought Will would roll over

and die. He planned to fight until he couldn't fight anymore to keep Olivia safe. But he had to fight smart. He let his horse fall back a little, giving Pryce's man the idea that he'd been scared off, letting him get comfortable. But he still followed when the cab veered off the road and into a wooded area, bouncing over a rutted, barely marked path. Ducking under low branches and skirting around trees, Will raced through unfamiliar territory, the pounding of the horse's hooves in time with his own racing heart.

When he saw the driver relax a touch, Will kicked his horse hard. It shot forward until it was alongside the cab. He was glad to see the cab was low and small, the driver's seat just a little higher than the horse's ears. The driver aimed his gun at Will and fired, but Will knocked the man's arm just as the pistol went off, sending the bullet off course. He felt a burn in his upper arm; he'd been grazed. Will was about to strike again when he saw Olivia's head poke up from the window.

"Get back down, damn it!" he shouted at her.

But she had other plans. As the driver tried to steady his gun, she grabbed his hand and held it tight, her face resolute and her eyes narrowed.

"Let go!" the driver bellowed, trying to shake her free. She wouldn't release him, but she couldn't pry his fingers off the pistol, either. So Will watched, stunned, as she sank her sharp little teeth into the back of his hand. Screaming, Pryce's man dropped the gun, and it disappeared behind them in the darkness.

But the driver was enraged. He pulled his hand free and sent it across her face, throwing her back and nearly flinging her from the cab. She hadn't had the presence of mind to grab the frame of the open window. Her boot heels scraped against the floor of the cab, trying to gain purchase, but the wheels clattered over rocks and branches and sent the speeding hansom bouncing. Olivia dangled over the ground beneath her, gripping hard. Any second, she could fall and be crushed by the cab, or slam against a tree.

Will wanted so badly to knock the driver's teeth down his throat, smash his face in until he couldn't breathe anymore, kill the bastard who'd hit Olivia. But he had to make a choice: go for the driver or get Olivia to safety.

So he gave Pryce's man one hard punch to the ribs to wind him, and then brought his horse up next to Olivia, who struggled to draw herself upright.

"Get on," Will yelled, reaching his arm out for her.

She judged the distance between his galloping horse and the hurtling cab with an expression of uncertainty.

"Trust me," he said. And then she let him put his arm around her waist as she looped her own arms around his neck. Thank the Lord she was a slim thing. He pulled her up and out of the cab, then across the withers of the horse so she rested against his chest.

The cab sped forward as Will drew the horse away.

"What are you doing?" she cried. "We should go after him!"

"I got two of us ridin' bareback," Will said, determined, "chasin' after someone on a carriage who may have another gun." He shook his head. "Nope. I ain't gonna risk you."

"Don't worry about me," she insisted. "That man should be caught."

Will slowed the horse to a canter. He heard the cab clattering away in the distance.

"He'll be back," he said grimly. The horse trotted,

then walked and finally stopped. "His work ain't finished. But next time I'll be ready for him. And as for you," he added, sudden fury in his voice as he turned his head to face her, "what the hell were you thinkin'? Grabbin' his gun like that?"

"He was *shooting* at you, Will," she said hotly. Even in the evening darkness, he saw the bright, resolute spark in her eyes. "I couldn't let him do that without trying to help."

"Next time don't worry about me," he said. "Take care of yourself."

"Don't be an idiot," she snapped. "I was worried about you."

He might have appreciated that last statement a hell of a lot more if they had been someplace else. He might have gotten a whole heap of enjoyment from having her pressed so close against him, her arms around his shoulders, her face and delicious lips so near his own, except for a few, minor problems.

"Where the hell are we?" he asked, looking around.

She also gazed around. They were in the middle of some kind of forest or woods, surrounded by trees Will didn't recognize, amid the sounds of animals he had never heard. Dusk was over, and night had fallen.

Olivia began to laugh. At first, just a small chuckle; then it began to spread through her until her body shook and sent vibrations through his own.

"We've managed to find the last wild place in Kent," she finally managed to gasp through her laughter. There was the faintest note of delayed fear in her laughter, a realization that she had escaped great danger. "And we're lost."

Will didn't feel like laughing at all. They were out in the wilderness, the world of drawing rooms and polite dinner parties far away. Olivia's slim body pressed against his own and her arms wound about his neck. She was so close, he was engulfed in a warm female scent of perfume and skin, and thank God, she was safe.

But, really, how safe was she?

Pryce's man might have been gone, but the brittle cage of society that had kept Will at bay was gone too. He didn't know whether he could trust himself around her without it. He was out in rough country, as he'd longed to be ever since his arrival in London, and now that his wish had been granted, he'd damned himself.

"We gotta get back," Will said for the hundredth time.

Olivia, tired, hungry and sore from a bustle not designed for bareback riding, tried not to sigh. They'd been riding through the dark woods for more than an hour and were no closer to finding their way back to civilization than they had been at the beginning of their misadventure. Yet Will was determined to get them at least to the hops farmer's home, if not back to the train station, that night.

"I'm tryin' to track our way," he muttered, "but I don't know this land, and it's blacker than the devil's coffee out here."

"Maybe we should stop," Olivia ventured.

She could have sworn she heard something akin to panic in his voice. "Can't stop," he insisted. "Gotta get back."

But Olivia had had enough. "Please put me down," she said. When he made no move to do so, she let go of his neck and painfully eased her way to the ground. Bracing her hands at the small of her back, she stretched. "I can't go any farther, Will. Not on horseback."

He also slid down and held the reins. "Then we'll walk."

"And wander around in the dark? That's even more foolish than riding."

"I don't know what the hell you expect me to do," he snapped.

She frowned. Will had a temper, but she didn't quite understand why he was unleashing it on her. He must be as tired and hungry as she. "Let's rest a while. We can wait for dawn and then find our way back."

"You wanna sit out here?" he asked, disbelief plain in his voice. "In the dust?"

"I didn't realize cowboys were so circumspect about dirt."

"It ain't me I'm worried about."

"Good, because I'm not worried about me, either." When he didn't answer, and she could feel rather than see his uncertainty, she continued, "I'll be fine. In fact, it's rather exciting. I've never camped out under the stars before."

"Sleepin' under a roof is better," Will said, tense. "Warmer."

"Then we can build a fire." She tried to smile encouragingly, even though she didn't feel particularly encouraged herself. "Maybe we could think of this as an adventure," she suggested, trying to convince herself as much as him.

"I got shot at and you were shanghaied," he said dryly. "That's enough adventure for one day."

True. Olivia had spent years reading about exciting chases, gun battles and kidnappings, and she'd

181

longed to one day have a life half as exciting as that of the artless Lorna Jane. Yet when she'd read those stories, all danger was transitory, nonthreatening. Lorna Jane was the heroine. She could never be seriously hurt or killed. It was the implicit promise of every novel.

Olivia wasn't living in a book. There was no guaranteed happy ending, no assurance that she would remain safe and unhurt. She or Will could have died today. The thought made her stomach flip and her mouth dry.

But she was too tired to go on. If she didn't sit down and rest her bruised behind, she'd likely make a fool of herself by starting to cry. It had been one of the longest and most terrifying days she had ever known. "Please," she said simply.

She heard his muttered curse. "All right," he said at last. "But at first light, we're headin' out."

Olivia tried to recall what she could from the Buffalo Bill novels as she prepared their campsite. While Will tethered the horse, she picked up leaves and twigs from a small clearing. Genteel ladies never slept outdoors, except, perhaps, on safari, but even then they were in tents, on cots or beds, attended by numerous servants, with as many civilized comforts as their bearers could carry.

And now she was out in the wild, the noise and sights of London distant, breathing fresh air. She'd never spent this much time outdoors before. The idea was both exciting and frightening. The world she inhabited was so small, so limited, she'd experienced very little in her thirty-two years, including sleeping outside.

She took a bit of comfort knowing that Will was an

experienced hand where outdoor life was concerned. He finished tying up the horse and was preparing a fire. Olivia watched as he gathered the kindling, stacked it and produced a small box of matches from one of the numerous pockets of his waistcoat. She'd half-hoped he would light the fire by striking flints or rubbing sticks together, but it made sense that a cowboy wouldn't rely on such unpredictable techniques. With a scrape and a hiss, the match caught, illuminating the lean planes of his face for a moment. He didn't look as though he enjoyed the prospect of an al fresco evening as much as she. As the kindling caught and began to burn, the light turning him gold and hard, Olivia supposed it was because he'd endured out-of-doors existence his whole life and didn't relish the idea of leaving behind his soft bed in London. Neither did she, come to think of it.

What would David make of this scene? His wife, gently reared and trained to a life of domestic ornamentation, about to sit on the uncovered earth across from a wild American. She doubted he could even imagine it, would laugh at the prospect's impossibility. Yet, she reminded herself, he likely didn't think she could run Greywell's, either.

Gingerly, she tried to sit on the ground but found that her bustle made it nearly impossible to get comfortable.

"Turn your back, please," she said.

"What?" Will looked up from his crouched contemplation of the fire.

"I have to remove my bustle and I can't do it in the dark, nor can I with you staring at me," she explained. No matter her attraction to him, she could not ignore years of training and strip off her bustle right in front of him.

Grumbling something about ridiculous females, Will scooted around. He even took his hat and lowered it over his eyes. "There. That make you happy?"

"Beyond words," she said sardonically. Then she began the unenviable process of untying her bustle underneath layers and layers of skirts and petticoats, all without removing any other articles of clothing and without the assistance of her maid, Sarah. She tried not to grunt and strain at the task, but it was impossible to do silently.

"Birthin' cattle back there?" Will asked.

She shot his back a dark look. "Being a woman is not for the faint of heart," she said. She continued to work the bustle free. "I'd like to see the House of Lords try to conduct business while wearing corsets and bustles. They would surely enact a law banning the dreadful things. There!" At last, the contraption came free, sliding down to lay like an empty cage at her feet. Even this smaller bustle, designed for traveling, could not be endured for a long period of time, and she quickly placed it behind a tree to spare Will having to stare at it. The back of her dress now dragged, weighted down with loops of material ordinarily supported by the bustle's frame, and she was sure she looked ridiculous, but she was so much more comfortable. If only she could remove her corset . . .

"You can turn around now," she said, and Will did so, appearing cross and ill-humored. She sat down again, tucking her legs off to one side, facing him across the fire. He continued to crouch, as though ready to flee at any moment.

"Pryce sent that driver," Will said abruptly.

The cold feeling that had been threatening to over-

GET UP TO
4 FREE BOOKS!

You can have the best romance delivered to your door for less than what you'd pay in a bookstore or online. Sign up for one of our book clubs today, and we'll send you **FREE* BOOKS** just for trying it out...**with no obligation to buy, ever!**

HISTORICAL ROMANCE BOOK CLUB

Travel from the Scottish Highlands to the American West, the decadent ballrooms of Regency England to Viking ships. Your shipments will include authors such as CONNIE MASON, SANDRA HILL, CASSIE EDWARDS, JENNIFER ASHLEY, LEIGH GREENWOOD, and many, many more.

LOVE SPELL BOOK CLUB

Bring a little magic into your life with the romances of Love Spell—fun contemporaries, paranormals, time-travels, futuristics, and more. Your shipments will include authors such as LYNSAY SANDS, CJ BARRY, COLLEEN THOMPSON, NINA BANGS, MARJORIE LIU and more.

As a book club member you also receive the following special benefits:

- **30% OFF all orders through our website & telecenter!**
- **Exclusive access to special discounts!**
- **Convenient home delivery and 10 day examination period to return any books you don't want to keep.**

There is no minimum number of books to buy, and you may cancel membership at any time. See back to sign up!

*Please include $2.00 for shipping and handling.

YES! ☐

Sign me up for the **Historical Romance Book Club** and send my TWO FREE BOOKS! If I choose to stay in the club, I will pay only $8.50* each month, a savings of $5.48!

YES! ☐

Sign me up for the **Love Spell Book Club** and send my TWO FREE BOOKS! If I choose to stay in the club, I will pay only $8.50* each month, a savings of $5.48!

NAME: _____

ADDRESS: _____

_____

TELEPHONE: _____

E-MAIL: _____

☐ **I WANT TO PAY BY CREDIT CARD.**

☐ VISA   ☐ MasterCard.   ☐ DISCOVER

ACCOUNT #: _____

EXPIRATION DATE: _____

SIGNATURE: _____

Send this card along with $2.00 shipping & handling for each club you wish to join, to:

Romance Book Clubs
20 Academy Street
Norwalk, CT 06850-4032

Or fax (must include credit card information!) to: 610.995.9274.
You can also sign up online at www.dorchesterpub.com.

*Plus $2.00 for shipping. Offer open to residents of the U.S. and Canada only.
Canadian residents please call 1.800.481.9191 for pricing information.

If under 18, a parent or guardian must sign. Terms, prices and conditions subject to change. Subscription subject
to acceptance. Dorchester Publishing reserves the right to reject any order or cancel any subscription.

JOIN NOW!

whelm her took sudden possession of her bones. "I never believed he would go this far."

"He's gone, all right," Will said. His voice took an edge, like the blade of a knife. "It ain't just about the brewery anymore. Hirin' that gun a' his proves it."

"What do we do now?"

"Stop playin' nice."

She shuddered, wondering just what that entailed. "Lord, I am completely out of my league," she said quietly. "I went to finishing school. I learned how to waltz and throw dinner parties. Taking on the brewery was the biggest challenge of my life. Now I have men trying to ruin and kidnap me. And shooting at you. I am completely at a loss."

Will's eyes met hers over the fire. His jaw was taut, and there was no softness about him at all. "No one's gonna hurt you." There was no doubt in his voice; it was a simple statement of fact. Despite her fear, Olivia felt that Will would protect her even at the cost of his own life.

She couldn't think about that now.

"You're hurt!" she cried, spotting a black trail on the sleeve of his coat, the mark of a bullet.

He glanced down. "Naw. Just a powder burn."

"Oughtn't you dress it?"

"Got no bandages," he said with a shrug.

Scowling at his indifference to his own injury, she pulled her skirt up slightly and tore a strip of fabric from her white cotton petticoat. "Let me," she said, starting to rise, but he stopped her.

"I'll do it," he said gruffly, reaching across the fire and taking the makeshift bandage from her. It seemed to Olivia that he went to great pains to keep from touching her. She sat back and watched him push up the sleeve of his coat, then roll up his shirtsleeve to expose his forearm.

She didn't know what was most striking—the sculpted muscle of his arm, dusted with golden hair, or the red welt that the mercenary's bullet had left on Will's skin. He wound the strip of fabric around his injury, deft and practiced.

"You've done that before," she noted.

He didn't look up at her as he continued to dress the abrasion. "Gotta do your own doctorin' on the trail. But we still lose men every time."

Olivia shuddered to think that Will could have been one of those accepted casualties. "From bullets?"

"Nope. Mostly gettin' kicked and thrown by horses or stepped on by cattle. Sometimes floods or rivers wash 'em away. An' all kinds of other stuff. Bad water. Snake bite. Fevers."

It sounded awful, precarious. "I wonder you needed guns at all."

He looked up from under the brim of his hat. "We used 'em to scare off rustlers."

"Just to scare them?"

His face grew distant, his expression hard. "Sometimes we got one."

Softly, she asked, "What happened, Will?"

He stared into the fire, his arm forgotten. "I was takin' watch one night and caught some fellers tryin' to rustle our cattle. So I let off a few rounds, tryin' to drive 'em away. They started to take off, but one thought he'd be a real bandito and shoot back. I fired at 'im, an' he went down." Will frowned, then looked up at her, and she saw the pain he bore. "Takin' a

186

man's life ain't easy, Liv. It ain't like they say in them books you read. It marks a man."

"I'm sorry," she said.

"I ain't," he answered. "I did my job. Stealin' cattle or horses is a killin' offense. But that don't make it feel good."

"Could you . . . could you kill again?"

"If I had to." As he stared at her, his gaze and voice were level. "If there was somethin' worth protectin'."

She was both chilled and reassured by the idea. She did not like the idea of Will ending someone's life, yet she knew she could always rely on him.

The night was growing colder, as October was wont to do, and she found that her smart little traveling dress and matching jacket didn't quite fit the bill for camping. Absently, she rubbed her arms.

In a swift motion, Will stood and came around the fire to drape his duster around her shoulders. He ignored her objections and stalked silently back to the other side of the fire. Olivia felt engulfed by the lingering heat of his body and the rich scent of his skin permeating the coat's fabric. Unconsciously, she closed her eyes and pressed her cheek into the collar of the duster, inhaling deeply, as she pulled it closer around her. It was wonderful, as though she was surrounded by Will, wrapped in him like a secret. A little sigh of pleasure escaped from her lips.

"Jesus, Liv," Will growled, breaking her reverie. She opened her eyes to see him through the flames, his eyes sharp and piercing. "Don't do that to a man."

"I . . ." Her voice trailed off. What could she say? That she wanted him despite her best intentions? That no man had ever risked as much for her as he had? That she hadn't realized how lonely her life had been before him, and she dreaded what it would be like once he'd gone?

He had awakened feelings in her that had lain dormant for many years, since even before David had died. She wasn't oppressed with weariness when he was nearby—shouldering the burden of her business, her social obligations, the intimidation of George Pryce. All this became bearable because of Will. No, she couldn't say any of these things, though they were all true.

"I wish you'd sit and make yourself comfortable," she said instead. "You're making me nervous," she added.

With obvious reluctance, Will sat, cross-legged. He unrolled his shirtsleeve to cover his bandaged arm. Then he pulled out a knife, picked up a nearby stick and began to whittle. Olivia looked at the knife. It had a strange coffin-shaped handle.

"Is that—?"

Will nodded tersely. "Yeah. The bowie knife Jake found with me." He turned it over in his hand, considering. "I've had to replace the handle and the brass pins a few times, but I always kept it. The only thing my parents left me, 'sides the letter."

"A whole legacy right in your palm," Olivia breathed. "Amazing."

He didn't answer, but continued to work at the stick. It was clear that he didn't have any purpose to his whittling besides giving his hands something to do. No sooner did he pare one stick down than he reached for another and another, tossing his handiwork into the fire. She watched him for a long while, fascinated by his large, capable hands with their long, deft fingers, the square, blunt nails and the broad span of his palms, the hands of a man who had worked his whole life. She pictured those hands on her, remembering the feel of them on her skin, rough and hot, and she barely stifled a moan. The five years she had spent without a man in her bed seemed like the beat of a hummingbird's wings compared to the week she had known Will and desired him.

She had to distract herself; otherwise she would leap over the fire and force herself on him.

"Tell me about Colorado," she said, breaking the stillness.

He looked up at her, the firelight turning his eyes aquamarine. "I miss it," he said softly. "That was always the best part about finishing a drive—comin' home to the mountains."

"They must be so beautiful," she said wistfully.

For the first time in what seemed like days, Will broke into a genuine smile, heartbreaking in its gorgeousness. "They sure are. Tall as giants, capped in snow. Ridin' through 'em, you feel like you're at the top of the world, everythin' beneath you, and if you just reached high enough, you could shake hands with God."

Warming to his topic, he continued, "In the winter, they're like castles carved of ice, white and glittering like diamonds when the sun is out. And in the summer . . ." His voice trailed off as he turned to inner landscapes.

"In the summer?" she prompted, wanting to go there with him.

"In the summer, the valleys look like green velvet cups full of gems—every kind and color of flower you can think of, spillin' over, climbin' over anythin' that'll stand still. Blue penstemons, scarlet paint-brush, purple fringed gentians. Up on the mountains, there's phlox, wild iris, harebell. You'd hardly believe that a few months earlier, everythin' was covered in snow."

"I'd love to see it," she said quietly, and she meant it.

He stared at her for a long time, the only sounds coming from the pops of the fire and the rustling animals in the underbrush. She couldn't read him, the firelight turning his face into something too handsome, too hard, to interpret. So strange, when moments earlier he'd been speaking of his home with such feeling, such transparency.

"Some folks think it's too tough," he said finally. "Too rugged. A body's got to be made of strong stuff to survive in Colorado."

"I may take to sleeping outdoors, you know," she said, half in jest as she gestured to the dark woods that surrounded them. "I'm beginning to think I'm strong enough."

A ghost of a smile crept into the corner of his mouth. "I think you are, too, Liv. Stronger than you give yourself credit for."

As compliments went, this one floored her. To have Will, who'd endured the toughest life had to offer, consider *her* strong was simply amazing. For several moments, she couldn't speak. "Maybe," she said, regaining her voice, "I'll come visit you someday in Colorado and see those wildflowers."

The smile remained, but it was rueful. "Yeah," he said with a dip of his head, "maybe someday."

But they both knew she would never make it. There was a great deal of distance, physical and otherwise, that separated Colorado from England, distance that she could not navigate. A silence fell upon them both as they contemplated this. Olivia stared at the ashes forming in the fire, and Will looked up at the sky.

"I didn't think there were stars in England," he said, his head tipped back. "It's good to see 'em again, like old friends waitin' for you at the saloon."

"I'm sure they're glad to see you, too." She took a stick and nudged some of the burnt kindling, sending a tiny cascade of sparks down to the ground.

Still gazing heavenward, Will asked, "How'd your husband die?"

The question caught her by surprise. He hadn't asked much about David until now. "He collapsed at work and never regained consciousness," she said. She stared abstractedly at the stick in her hand, then snapped it in two and threw it into the fire. "The doctor said his heart wasn't very strong. It just . . . gave out. David's death came so quickly, I didn't really believe it until almost a month later."

Finally, Will looked back down. "Do you miss him?"

"I did," she answered, more honestly than she had ever spoken of David before. "He was so funny, so droll, the way he saw things just slightly askew. He could make me laugh sometimes with only a look."

Will, strangely subdued, nodded.

"But," she continued, "he hadn't made me laugh in a long time. I found myself missing him even while he was alive, missing our marriage and what it had once been."

"Liv—"

She blinked hard. "Could you tell me about Denver? And Leadville?"

He frowned, confused.

"I want to hear more about where you come from,"

she said. "And . . . I don't want to talk about the past anymore."

Thankfully, he nodded in understanding. Will was a natural storyteller, comfortable talking and spinning yarns. He continued to speak, describing the wild, brash cities and towns he'd lived in, the outrageous people who also called them home and the tenacity they needed to keep rising above adversity. His voice was deep and gravelly, smooth as whiskey, and just as warming.

Olivia found herself rapt in him, watching his face, the small, concise gestures of his hands. She lay down on her side, cushioning her head on her outstretched arm, with his duster pulled over her. Soon, the clouds of sorrow, weariness and fear unwound themselves around her heart and were replaced with something she was unfamiliar with—happiness. To be away from London with Will, hearing him talk of his home, covered in his coat, warmed by the fire and his presence. An unusual gift. One she would not refuse.

Despite lying on the hard ground and her lack of dinner, Olivia soon found herself drifting off to sleep. She was exhausted. The past few days had worn her out completely. And she felt so safe with Will nearby. She gladly escaped into slumber.

When she awoke some time later, the fire had gone out and the night was very, very dark. A nocturnal hunter flew overhead. Somewhere out there, Pryce plotted her destruction, and his mercenary was ready to do whatever it took to eliminate her. The world was huge and black, threatening to swallow her. Her corset pinched.

"Will?" she asked, her voice very small.

"Yeah?" He didn't sound as though he had been asleep.

"I'm cold."

"Want me to light the fire again?"

"Could you . . . lie next to me?"

The longest pause Olivia had ever heard followed. She thought perhaps he had gone to sleep. But then, "Yep."

She heard his weight shift and the rustle of leaves. His shadow crossed the inky sky. And then he was stretching his long body out behind hers, pulling up the duster to cover them both as he fitted himself alongside her. For a moment, he wrestled with his body, trying to get it positioned right, until, at last, he seemed to surrender and draped his arm across her waist.

If she had thought to sleep, she knew now it would be impossible. But how much better, she thought, feeling the hard, muscled length of him settle into her softer curves, his breath on her neck that was answered by every inch of her skin, the welcome weight of his hand pressed into her ribs, how much better to suffer this all night long than to pass the time in oblivion. As she had all her life, until that moment.

Chapter Twelve

The thought was plain in Will's mind, as clear as if he had spoken out loud: *That's it. I'm in hell.*

Because what other way was there to describe what was happening right now? Lost in the boondocks, lying on the ground and pressed up tight against the one female he wanted more than any other but couldn't have. Will remembered hearing of that one feller in Greek mythology named Tantalus from a traveling theatrical show called *The Agony of Hades.* Old Tantalus was being tormented for eternity with a hunger he couldn't satisfy and a thirst he couldn't quench—food and drink just out of reach. And here, beside Will now, was the grandest banquet he'd ever known, the feast of Lady Olivia Xavier. But even with his napkin tied around his neck and his plate in hand, he was being turned away.

She shifted, sighing a little, trying to get comfortable. As she did, he could feel the movement of her body, the breath coursing through her, the arrangement of her long legs, slender arms and all that skin he wanted to touch. Over and over until he'd learned her body as well as he knew the mountains of his home. His hand rested as lightly as it could on her waist, but he was prevented from feeling her by the stiff cage of her corset. He hated corsets. Who wanted a woman who couldn't breathe, couldn't move, and all for the sake of a too-narrow waist? Besides, Will had a feeling Olivia didn't need much corseting. She was as slender as a doe, and just as quick.

Sometime during the day she'd lost her bonnet, and now the back of her neck was bare to him, a few inches from his mouth. Even in the dark, he could see the pale glimmer of that skin, the downy wisps of dark hair that curled and were swept up into an unraveling bun. Will took a deep breath to settle himself, but by doing so, a tiny lock of her hair was drawn into his mouth. Silky strands played across his tongue as he gently savored her, wanting to pull her all the way in, take her completely.

He was having the damnedest time remembering why they were staying away from each other. Will had been up against some of the toughest hurdles nature could throw in a man's path—floods, droughts, avalanches, winds so sharp they cut tears out of his eyes. Here was the most mouthwatering woman he had ever known lying right beside him, wanting him as much as he wanted her. All the shrill voices screaming that they couldn't be together were miles away in the city, trapped behind brick walls and wrought-iron fences. The fools who never said what they meant, whose women were sheltered and whose men lead two lives. What the hell did they know about what was right and what was wrong? Not a damned thing.

He bent his head closer and ran his tongue up the nape of her neck, tracing the arc and tasting her skin—warm and floral, succulent.

Olivia moaned. She tilted her head forward, offering herself, exposing more to his searching mouth.

He brought his lips to the shell of her ear and the juncture of her jaw and neck, exploring, learning. She was so soft, so ripe and fragrant. He sucked her earlobe into his mouth and gently nipped at it with the very edges of his teeth.

She moaned again and pushed herself against him. Through the heavy folds of her dress, he felt the lush curve of her bottom press into him. And damn, she had to know what he was about, because he was as hard and upright as a saddle horn, ready to take the grip of her hand or any other part of her.

"Liv," he groaned along the bend of her neck, "if you want me to stop, you gotta tell me now."

"If you stop," she said, husky and low, "I'll go mad." She turned to face him.

He wasn't in hell anymore. He'd call it heaven, but he didn't think angels felt what he was feeling. Because she was kissing him and he was kissing her, and he'd never, ever, in his whole life felt anything like what he was feeling now. Their tongues moved together, their mouths opened, and she overwhelmed him. She had so much to give, but she took from him, too. And he wanted her to. He wanted her to take as much as she wanted, and keep on taking until he had nothing left to offer.

She pressed against his chest while his hands moved up and down the narrow span of her back, gripping her hard with palms spread wide. And then her fingers were everywhere, deftly working at his vest and unbuttoning his shirt. The cold night air stung him while the burning embers of her fingers touched him and he sucked in his breath at the feel of her on his skin, the way he'd wanted her for it seemed like the whole of his life.

He needed to touch her, too. But her damned dress was covered in hooks and buttons and a hundred other kinds of fastenings. Plus the corset underneath. And the immense number of underclothes. But unless they stopped what they were doing and spent the next thirty minutes carefully undressing her, there would be no way to touch her completely—and he couldn't wait any longer.

Will began to bunch up her dress in his arms as his hand reached for, and found, the slender form of her calf. He growled. He had pictured her legs so many times in his mind and now that he could actually feel them, shapely and covered in silk stockings, he nearly exploded. She mewled into his mouth as her hands continued to spread across his chest, moving to his stomach, which quivered like a stallion's. He slid his hand farther up her leg, past the delicious bend of her knee, under the ruffled hem of her drawers, past the garter, finally reaching, sweet Lord, the bare skin of her thigh.

She jumped, then panted into the curve of his neck, "Yes."

He felt a surge of pure possessiveness burn through him. He wanted to brand himself into her, his skin against hers.

His hand moved over the satin of her thigh and higher. He palmed the surprising roundness of her buttock, more pert and full than he would have expected to find on such a slender woman. She had the kind of behind men dreamed about, like a split peach, firm, and he stroked it proprietarily.

But her fingers, God, also explored. They moved over his stomach and then lower. Groaning, he felt her dexterous hand cup him, tracing the outline of his shaft, which reared up under her attention. He couldn't think, couldn't place himself past the sensation of her touching him through the fabric of his trousers.

He didn't think he could last much longer. No, he knew he couldn't. Not without feeling her, too. Not without touching her as intimately as he could.

Will's hand shifted, sliding over her thigh again until he found the juncture of her legs, her sex, slick and furnace-hot. Dampness soaked through her drawers. Her body jolted again, but she pressed herself closer to him as she set up a stroking motion of her own, up and down, as his fingers worked to find and then entered her opening.

Olivia jerked and vibrated like a bow releasing an arrow. She cried out into his mouth, and he felt her contract around him as her own hand stilled. For some time, she was like that, drawn taut, leaning into his hand, as a multitude of small earthquakes shook her.

"Will," she gasped, "Will Will Will."

Yet even as the final tremors subsided, she was fumbling with the buttons on the front of his britches, pulling at them until they popped open. His eyes rolled back as her bare hand wrapped around him.

"Don't make me wait for you any longer," she breathed.

"No, ma'am," he growled.

With a sharp, tearing tug, Will removed her drawers. He hooked one hand behind her knee and brought it up, settling his legs between hers. His other hand gripped her waist tightly. One deep thrust and then he was inside her.

Paradise.

Olivia wasn't a virgin, but she was tight, so damned tight that he saw stars. Those same stars flooded him as he moved, slowly at first, finding their rhythm together. An unbelievable sliding, a slight hitch and catch each time. And she moved with him, her arms around his shoulders, words that weren't words flowing from her mouth.

He'd wanted her naked, but having them both almost fully dressed sent his blood into a stampede. Surrounded by clothing but joined together as intimately, as profoundly as possible. And the sweet hotness of her, surrounding him but filling him, too, with herself.

Will rolled over onto his back, taking her with him. Despite the dark, he felt her surprise as she straddled him.

"I've never . . . done *this* before," she managed to gasp. "But," she added, adjusting her hips, "I like it."

"I like it, too," he rasped. Which was as much as an understatement as calling the Grand Canyon a ditch. He held her hips as she braced her hands on his chest and moved experimentally. He nearly came then, feeling her discover her pleasure, learning what made her feel good and the power she had to make it possible. But soon she knew exactly what she wanted and how to get it. Leisurely at first, and then with more and more speed, she rode him, throwing her head back and holding his hands against her. He felt as wild as a bronc under her, but he wasn't trying to throw her; he wanted her on top of him forever.

Forever came a little faster than he expected. She tightened, arching, and her release triggered his own. His whole body became condensed to one small point that burst outward like a meteor shower. It seemed to go on eternally, his pouring himself into her welcoming body, a kind of pleasure he'd never experienced, never dreamed he would know.

She tumbled down onto his chest with a little, "Oof" of release, limp and languid. Spread out over him in a tumble of skirts and legs and arms, Olivia made the sweetest blanket.

"Will," she murmured, running her fingers through his hair and down the bridge of his nose, "so beautiful. Such a beautiful man."

He wrapped his arms around her, holding her as tight as he could without crushing her, wishing that everything could stop now. That there wouldn't have to be a tomorrow. Everything would fall away and there would be only this, he and Olivia, still joined together, the stars spread overhead that saw without judgment, two people intertwined in the most profound communion.

A falling star shot by, and he made his wish. But he knew that it could never come to pass. He'd only been granted a brief taste of what could be; then tomorrow would come. No wish could prevent the dawn.

She must have slept, because the next thing she knew, Will was gently nudging her awake. He was true to his word to head out at dawn—the sky was just beginning to pearl with daylight. Olivia unwound her arms from his neck; she had been lying across him as he stretched out on his back. In the gray light, his face close to her own, she saw the shadows of stubble darkening his jaw and upper lip, and her hand went up to rub its roughness.

But he caught her hand before she could touch him. "We gotta go," he said, hoarse and deep.

Olivia slid her palm from his grip and sat up. She brushed at the leaves clinging to her skirts and the top of her dress, dislodging only a few. Abstractedly, she reached up to try to repin her hair, though it was a losing battle without a mirror or maid to assist her. As she did so, Will stood and shook out his duster, then replaced his hat and gloves. She could not help watching as he buttoned his open shirt and vest, catching a glimpse of the bare chest and skin she had felt last night.

When she was fifteen, she and some of her giggling schoolmates had visited a museum, and she had been dared to touch one of the Greek statues of an athlete. Will's body reminded her of that statue, the flawlessly defined muscles, the hard-contoured plane of his stomach, the absolute symmetry and precision of his physique, but where the statue had been cold marble, Will was warm flesh, and that made him even more perfect. She still felt his skin underneath her hands, even as she tugged on her own gloves, the echo of his bodily presence finally touched and experienced.

Will reached out to help her to her feet, but both their hands were gloved, and there was too much fabric and leather in the way to feel him again except the guidance of his fingers. Their eyes caught and held.

"I wish we could stay out here and not go back," she said. Her own voice was thick with morning and exhaustion.

"We can't," he answered.

"I know."

He went to get the horse, placidly grazing on the remains of autumn grasses. She thought about retrieving her bustle and decided to leave it behind. Putting it back on seemed like too much of a bother, and besides, why should she care? Things like bustles became silly and inconsequential in light of last night.

Will helped her up onto the horse and then swung up himself. "I think we should head east," he said.

Olivia nodded. "I put myself in your hands." She realized, too late, the many implications of that statement. She had been, literally, in his hand, and she shivered recalling that pleasure. Astonishing that a cowboy, a man who made his living using the strength of his hands, had been so gentle and yet so assertive in uncovering the source of her ecstasy. And he had found it, better than she had ever on her own.

They slowly picked their way through the forest as Will scouted a trail back to the road and civilization. He kept one arm around her waist while he held the reins in his other hand. Tension stretched between them, and the contrast between the intimacy of the night before and this awful morning nearly split Olivia in two.

"What happened between us felt too good to call it a mistake," she said finally. It was easier because he sat behind her, and she stared ahead at the Kentish woods as she spoke. She felt Will stiffen behind her. "But things will be different in London." Even saying the name of the city made her sit up straighter, as though invisible eyes were observing her posture.

"I know." His voice was flat and hard. "It's gonna kill me, havin' you so close, knowin' how good it is between us. And not bein' able to do anything about it." He swore softly. "It's like cuttin' my own heart out with my Bowie knife."

Olivia's throat tightened. "I hate this."

"Yeah. Me, too. But I gotta stay away from you, Liv. I don't trust myself around you."

His words made her heart both sink and lighten. She understood well the temptation he offered, especially now that she knew what their passion could become. Yet no man had ever desired her so much that they could not restrain themselves, and the knowledge that she could make such a strong, physically potent man as Will lose control gave her a peculiar pleasure. Here was a uniquely feminine power she did not know she possessed.

"What about right now?" she asked. She indicated their bodies nearly, but not quite, touching as they rode the horse.

A tiny smile quirked in the corner of his mouth. She wanted to press her own mouth to that spot. "Darlin', I'm too tired and hungry to do much besides sit upright, let alone pull you offa this horse and seduce you."

She didn't think it would take much effort on his part to seduce her, since she was most of the way there already. But if he could keep his desire in check, she could, too. And so they continued through the woods in silence. Every fall of the horse's hooves brought them closer to London, closer to the jeweled cage of society and away from the brief freedom of the woods. Olivia couldn't help letting her mind wander back to last night and even further back, into her past.

Most girls were kept ignorant of what transpired between men and women in the bedroom. Olivia had been somewhat lucky in that one of the girls at her boarding school had stolen a few of her brother's racy novels and they were circulated secretively. In the pages of those anonymously written books, Olivia learned about a whole world of erotic experiences that she longed to have for herself. When the time came for her to marry, she was excited, eager to put into practice that which she had read about.

After a few months of austere lovemaking, Olivia had shyly suggested to David that they attempt a few of the postures she had read about in school. He had been horrified by the suggestion. Such actions were limited to loose women and debauched men, and as a respectable married couple, they were neither of those things. Further, he questioned the morality of the school she had attended. So she grew used to their routine, but never found the carnal inferno she had been anticipating. On nights when David did not visit her bedroom, she gave herself pleasure, but it was not as satisfying as sharing it with another person.

What a revelation Will was! The way he touched her, the way he made her feel—those French novels barely did justice to the experience. A whole world had been opened to her.

And then closed just as quickly. She and Will could never give in to their desire again. What liberty they had tasted in the Kentish wilderness had to be ruthlessly shoved aside, buried beneath the strict codes of propriety that governed every aspect of her life. It seemed an impossible task. How could anyone look at her and not know what she had experienced, and with whom? Most of what had made last night so unforgettable was the fact that it was *Will* inside her, around her. She couldn't think of any other man she wanted that way.

"Here's the road," Will said, and in a remarkably short time they were cantering back toward the hops farmer's home. Olivia couldn't decide whether she was glad to see the pointed bells of the oast house or if she felt like weeping. Civilization and its constraints lay in their path. Olivia made herself sit upright, her body not touching Will's, as she slipped on the tight garments of propriety.

As they rode up, the farmer came running out with a dog at his heels. He looked relieved to see them, but before he could speak, Will swung down from the horse and grabbed the man's shirtfront.

"What part did you play in all this?" Will demanded, giving the farmer a shake.

Frightened, the man answered, "Nothing." Will only shook him harder, causing the dog to bark in alarm, but with a look and snarl from Will, the dog slunk away. "All right!" the farmer cried. "I was told to keep you here as long as I could."

"And?"

"And that's all! I swear! I didn't know about the cab driver until I found a man knocked out in my barn and a horse missing. You have to believe me," the farmer insisted, turning pleading eyes to Olivia.

"I still want your hops harvest," she said coolly. She could hear in her own voice the strict elocution lessons she had been given, the enforced gentility. She sounded so different than she had in the woods. But which was her real voice? "At half the original price."

The man nodded readily, and Will let him go, and he went stumbling back. She slid down from the horse and attempted to adjust her dirty, wrinkled dress.

"My wife will fix you breakfast if you like," the farmer offered.

Olivia discreetly pressed a hand to her growling stomach, recalling that it had been many hours since her last meal, and that she had exerted herself quite a bit since then. But she also knew that she and Will had to return to London as quickly as possible to see after her brewery. Lord only knew what George Pryce was planning next. With the introduction of this new mercenary, one who fired a gun and had no scruples to kidnap a woman, she understood that the fight had gone past simply acquiring Greywell's and was now about destroying her. She shuddered thinking what this man might have done with her if Will had not rescued her.

And she was even more appalled thinking what he might do with the knowledge that she and Will had given in to temptation.

"We need a ride back to the train station. Have your wife pack up a basket and take us into town on your wagon," she said.

The natural authority in her voice contradicted her bedraggled appearance, and with a ready nod, the farmer ran inside to shout directions to his wife. Oh, she could be a fine lady, all right, Olivia thought sardonically. Even after a night of fiery lovemaking in the wilderness.

She turned to Will, who was tethering the horse to a fence. His hat was low over his eyes, but the square line of his jaw above the collar of his duster drew her gaze. A man with no history, no place but the one he made for himself, hard but capable of abundant tenderness—all combined to make one man, Will Coffin.

Her transitory cowboy. Destined to slip through her fingers. She missed him already.

Maddox left George Pryce at a music hall, sitting by himself as the piano crashed and the girls danced to comic songs. He smiled to himself as he stepped into the busy street. There was something so damned amusing about seeing that swell toff rubbing elbows with the hoi polloi—that's why Maddox kept arranging their meetings at lower-class establishments. Let the bastard see how the other half lived, get him good and uncomfortable.

He liked to keep his clients uncomfortable. It helped preserve a sense of balance, of power, and it made them more amenable to his demands. Pryce had been angry that the American had managed to elude Maddox's bullets, and even angrier that Lady Xavier wasn't either dead or trussed up in a shack somewhere. But Maddox knew this was only the first round. He needed to feel out the terrain, understand who or what he was up against.

And though the American and the woman had gotten away, Maddox knew he'd learned quite a bit. The American had a weakness, and all weaknesses needed to be exploited.

Sidestepping a fast-moving cart, Maddox continued his walk. He had to make a few purchases this afternoon before heading south of the river to Wandsworth. To Greywell's.

Chapter Thirteen

The fuss that met them at the brewery could have woken a bone orchard. Will and Olivia came straight from Victoria Station, and no sooner had they gotten down from the cab than two dozen Greywell's hands came running out to shout at them.

"We're all right," Olivia assured them, as calm as Sunday morning. Aside from her missing bustle, she looked neat and tidy. No one would ever guess that she'd spent the night on the ground, or just what she'd been doing on the ground, and with whom.

Will was both relieved and disappointed. Making love with Olivia had been unlike anything he'd ever experienced before—he hadn't felt like grabbing his boots and sneaking off the way he usually did after a night of female company. Waking up next to her had been one of the best moments of his well-traveled life, but it hadn't lasted long. It couldn't. She was a lady with everything to lose, and he was just a cow-puncher. For a few hours last night none of that had mattered. Now it did. And it hurt like hell.

"Lady Xavier," Huntworth cried, shouldering his way to the front of the group, "everyone was so worried when you and Mr. Coffin didn't return last night. I was on the verge of notifying Scotland Yard."

"Mr. Coffin kept me safe," Olivia said with a reassuring nod. "Please tell me what happened in my absence." She began to walk inside, with the brewery employees all following like ducklings, and Huntworth chattering and reading off his ever-present clipboard. Will walked behind them, scanning the yard for suspicious characters.

Goddamn this country. He'd never felt so fenced in. Here he was, having spent the most amazing night of his life with the most wonderful woman he'd ever known, and they both had to pretend it had never happened. But what were his other options? Walk into Greywell's, bold as brass, his arm around Olivia's waist to signify that they'd become lovers?

And that's all they had been to each other. He'd be damned foolish to think otherwise. Back home, Will stayed away from ranchers' daughters. He knew he wasn't a good prospect; he was just a hired hand, not even the trail boss. He didn't have the ambition ranchers' daughters wanted, and he drifted around too much. The girls he sparked with were fast, town-dwelling women who weren't looking for husbands. And there were always the soiled doves, willing to satisfy a man's more basic needs without asking for more than the going rate. For a long time, Will had been satisfied with this arrangement.

Sometimes he envied the boys in the bunkhouse who got letters from sweethearts. But soon enough those letters began to make demands—when was the wedding, how big was their spread going to be, what about churching and schooling the children? If the sweethearts stayed true, eventually the cowpuncher sold his saddle and went off to take his bride and leave the freedom of the trail behind. That loss of independence was something Will never coveted from his fallen compañeros.

He moved into the brewery. Olivia was carefully examining the equipment with Huntworth. They checked the dials on some tanks and made notes. She was completely focused, shutting out everything but the health of her business, including, he noted grimly, himself.

That was good. She had to be able to walk away, protect herself. There would come a time when he'd have to leave, and it wouldn't do either of them any good if she mooned and pined for him.

But would it kill her to look even a little bothered by it?

He felt a little bump against his leg. Looking down, he saw a large orange tabby cat rubbing its face along his trousers. Probably the Greywell mouser; judging by the size of the cat, he'd caught whole herds of mice.

"Howdy, feller," Will said, hefting the cat in his arms. He scratched under its chin and was rewarded with a rolling purr. "Did you miss Liv, too?"

The cat wasn't talking but was content to lay in Will's arms. Will had never had any kind of pet—never stayed in one place long enough for it to make sense—but over the past few years on the trail, he'd started to grow restless with his wandering ways. He hadn't known what he wanted, what would make his nerves stop jangling like spurs. He'd thought maybe he needed a wife, but the idea of being shackled to one woman the rest of his life made him itch. The same with having a spread of his own. Nothing felt right. Nothing could pin him down.

And then Jake had died. It took his old friend's death to finally make Will take out the burnt letter and find his family.

"*Folg mich.* Don't be like me, Will," Jake had said just before the end. "Don't let yourself blow around like an *oysvorf.*"

"I'm not an outcast," Will had answered.

"*Zei nit kain golem.* You make yourself one. But you're too much of a *mensch* to become a forgotten *bocher* like me." Then the coughing, which eventually killed old Jake, had taken over, and it was a long time before he spoke again. "Find something, someone, to anchor you," he eventually gasped. "*Farshtaist?* Otherwise you're just the lost *boychick* I found in the mountains."

He'd died not long after that. And Will had spent the whole seasick voyage across the Atlantic thinking about what Jake had said. It still made him smile, even now, that Jake kept referring to Will as a *boychick*, a little boy, even though Will had grown to be taller than Jake by half a head. But the rest of Jake's words haunted him.

Will thoughtfully pet the orange tabby, whose eyes had closed happily. Lost. Was he lost? He'd thought he'd come to England to find the anchor Jake had wanted for him, yet he'd never felt more at sea than he did right now.

Damn, Will swore, he wasn't used to living in his head like this, and it was downright nettlesome.

"So you've met our fearless mouser," Olivia said, coming to stand beside him. She ran one hand through the cat's striped fur, sending the animal into new heights of ecstacy. "He prefers sleeping under the warm mashing tanks to killing rodents."

Will looked at her. She really was the loveliest woman he'd ever known, but the past few days had left her face pale and drawn. Her violet eyes were ringed with the bruises of exhaustion, color had leeched out of her lips and she seemed to sway a little as she stood before him.

"Everythin' seem up to scratch?" he asked. He wanted to get her home so she could sleep.

Olivia nodded. "Mr. Huntworth and I couldn't find anything damaged or tampered with, but I'm hiring some extra men to stand watch." She sighed, and Will felt it in his bones. "I just don't know what Pryce is going to do next. I wish there were some way to take action against him instead of reacting all the time."

"I'll think of somethin'," Will said.

She gave him a watery smile. "*We* will think of something. In the meantime, we had better go home before Mordon sets up his own search party, complete with hounds and torches."

Why did that sound so good to him, the words *go home*?

Once they returned to Princes Square, Will was going to insist that Olivia go straight up to her room and get some rest, but they were met at the door by a furious Graham Lawford.

"Where the hell have you been?" he demanded.

"It's good to see you, too, Graham," Olivia murmured, slipping past him into the entryway of her house.

Will didn't cotton to the possessive tone in Lawford's voice. "She's fine," he growled. Ignoring the butler patiently waiting to take his hat and coat, Will stood toe to toe with Lawford, silently daring the man to take just one swing. Will wanted to clean somebody's clock, since he hadn't been able to get the son of a bitch who'd kidnapped Olivia, and this pompous horse's ass would nicely fit the bill.

"Where's her bustle?" Lawford snarled right back, low.

"Right up your—"

"Enough!" Olivia stepped between them, her hands raised to beat them back. Will and Lawford each took one pace back, like roosters readying for the next strike in the cockpit. "I am bone weary and do not feel like officiating a pugilistic bout in the foyer of my home. Unless either of you wants to be thrown out into the street, I suggest that you both cease hostilities. Now."

Lawford grumbled as much as Will, but they didn't argue with Olivia. Instead, glaring at each other, they followed her upstairs into the drawing room. A servant brought in some tea and sandwiches, and though Will was hungry enough to eat rancid bear meat, he didn't want to let his guard down around Lawford and the sandwiches went untouched. He stood by the window, watching the street, as Olivia quickly told Lawford what had happened the day before—leaving out the part about Will and she making love in the forest.

Will stuck his hands in his pockets. Even with Lawford eyeballing him, hot as a three-dollar pistol, Will's mind went back to last night. He could still feel Olivia around him, hear the little husky gasps she made as they moved together, taste the warm musk of her skin. He stared at the street as though he could tear it apart with his eyes alone, trying to corral those thoughts. Trouble was, his memories were as wild and rowdy as mustangs, kicking at anything that tried to fence them in.

"God *damn* it," Lawford cursed loudly behind him.

Glancing over his shoulder, Will saw Lawford stalking back and forth, his dark face tight with rage. Olivia, more resigned, sat and sipped from her cup of tea.

"I could *kill* George Pryce," Lawford continued. "I should have him arrested."

"On what charge?" Olivia asked. "We have no evidence linking him to what happened yesterday. I'm sure that the farmer would be paid handsomely to lie."

"Or he'd be picked off before he could say anything," Will added grimly.

Olivia paled, but nodded. "The man who tried to abduct me shot at Will."

Lawford cocked a disbelieving eyebrow at Will. "He looks fine to me."

Riled that Lawford would even question him, Will rolled up the sleeve of his coat to reveal the bandage on his arm. A faint rusty bloodstain had seeped through the fabric.

But Lawford still didn't look impressed. "It's just a scratch," he scoffed. He pulled up the leg of his trousers and pushed down his sock, exposing a long white scar on his calf. "Got this from a Zulu chieftain's spear."

Will tugged at the collar of his shirt and pointed to an old injury along his collarbone. "Apache arrow," he challenged. "Had to pull it out myself."

Lawford started to remove his jacket. "Let me show you the souvenir I picked up in Kashmir."

"You two are insane," Olivia cried, interrupting

them. She glanced back and forth at Will and Lawford, appalled. "Have you forgotten what we are discussing here? The possibility of murder."

Both Will and Lawford readjusted their clothing sheepishly. But Will felt for the first time that maybe this Lawford feller wasn't such a stiff.

"Tell me again about this man," Lawford said.

"Dark. Mustache," Will answered. "A touch smaller than me but looked like a bruiser. He knew what he was doin' with that shootin' iron."

"He had a Liverpudlian accent," Olivia added.

Will didn't know what that was exactly, though the hired gun had sounded different from the people he'd met so far in England, even the lowlifes. "There's a gap in his left eyebrow, like an old boxin' scar."

Lawford looked black. "He matches the description of a man my people have been tracking for a long time. An underworld professional by the name of Maddox. Cold, dangerous, willing to do anything for money. He's smuggled opium, sold guns to Fenians and murdered several men." Lawford cursed under his breath when Olivia turned even more white.

"And now he's on Pryce's payroll," she breathed.

"With all the power at my disposal, I can't get to that bastard," Lawford said.

"Will and I are thinking of something," Olivia said, and damn if he didn't light up inside like a prairie sunrise hearing those words.

Lawford looked at him, hard and piercing, so Will kept the brim of his hat low over his eyes. Olivia had told him it was considered rude to wear your hat indoors in England, but he didn't care much for politeness right now. Will had a good poker face. He knew this because he could out-bluff most boys in the bunkhouse, and even some of the ace gamblers in town. So he used that stony face on Lawford, urging the man to call his bluff.

The clock ticked a few times and Lawford finally looked back at Olivia, clearly put out, as ready for a fight as Will.

Will was glad Lawford was in Olivia's corner, since he had the feeling the solicitor could be a fierce customer and a worse enemy. Even though he'd proved that Lawford could stand punishment, Will would be glad to see the last of him.

"Well, Graham," Olivia said, rising, "I appreciate your concern and I do hate to be uncivil, but I must seek the solace of my bed to try to catch up on some lost sleep. I have a feeling that the next few days are going to be even more trying than the last."

"Before you go," Graham said, stopping her, "I should let you know the reason I came to your house in the first place. This concerns you, Coffin," he added, glancing at Will. "We may have found your family."

Will tensed. "Is that a bluff or d'you mean it for real?" He didn't want this Lawford fooling him.

The man looked as serious as Will felt. "It's true. Another day or two and my men will have a name and address for you. It took some doing, but we managed it. Because Olivia asked," he added.

"Will, that's wonderful," Olivia said, coming quickly to give his arm a squeeze.

But he barely felt the touch of her hand. He was so close, close to finding out who he really was and where he came from. And once he knew that, he would know where he was headed. Wouldn't he?

Will thought he would be happy when he neared

the end of his search, but mostly he felt numb. He couldn't get himself to feel anything. What the hell was going on? He was aware of Olivia and Lawford watching him, gauging his reaction, so he made himself smile. "Yeah," he said, "that's bang-up."

Olivia woke, hearing the large clock in the hallway strike midnight. The candle on her bedside table had burned quite low, leaving her bedroom mostly draped in shadow. The fire, too, was almost out. Olivia didn't want to wake the maid, so she got out of bed and rekindled the fire herself. Out from under the covers, with the flames in the grate struggling to come alive, the room was quite chilly. She slipped on her wrapper and sat near the hearth to warm herself.

After Graham had left, saying he would be back sometime in the next few days, Olivia and Will had eaten a strangely quiet luncheon. She had thought the news that they were closing in on his next of kin would have made Will happy, but instead, he had fallen into an uncharacteristically grim silence. She would have asked him why he was so gloomy, but the stony expression on his face seemed to preclude any conversation. So, after nibbling on a cucumber sandwich, and saying good afternoon to Will, who barely seemed to listen, Olivia dragged herself up to her bedroom. Her maid had just managed to strip off Olivia's clothes and gotten her into a hot bath.

Olivia had actually fallen asleep in the bath, but thankfully Sarah managed to find her before she accidentally drowned herself. After brushing out her hair and changing into a white cambric nightgown, she'd finally managed to climb into bed. It was a little strange, since the afternoon was at its height, and normally Olivia was either at the brewery or paying calls at this hour, but the heavy drapes were pulled to shut out the light. She had been asleep before Sarah left the room.

Now, however, Olivia found herself completely awake in the middle of the night. What could she do? Perhaps she could try to sleep again, but that seemed unlikely. All her account books for the brewery were downstairs in the study, and she didn't fancy running through the house clad only in her nightgown.

Staring into the now lively fire, Olivia wondered whether Will was also awake. Most likely not. Still, she longed to see him, talk to him. The day had been horrible, an exercise in polite torment, with her not being able even to touch him after a night spent so intimately. Now, with the house asleep around her and the dark of night spread across the city, Olivia felt very alone. Alone after she and Will had been so close, intertwined on the forest floor like vines. Her eyes began to drift shut as she recalled how he had touched her, the way he made her feel and how she had discovered what gave her pleasure, too.

She forced herself to stand up and walk to her bookshelf. At this rate, she would be running to Will's room and pounding on his door within the next minute, demanding that he make love to her. But she couldn't. He was being far nobler than she—denying himself because of her, because the repercussions could destroy her reputation, whilst he could simply move on and leave scandal behind.

So, sleepless, restless, she had to distract herself somehow. She scanned some of the book spines, reading their titles, and then pushed a row aside to reveal stacks of paper-covered novels: her flimsy treasures.

Olivia picked up one book, *Ambush at Sage Canyon; or, The Desperado's Return*. It would do, despite the fact that she had read it three times already. The accounts of stagecoach holdups and last minute rescues would comfort her.

Setting herself in the chair by the fire, she opened the book and stared, unseeing, at the pages. After reading the same paragraph three times without remembering a single word, Olivia slapped it down on a little table, frustrated and disgusted with herself.

Thinking about it now, Olivia realized she had faced and overcome a number of obstacles without fear. Transforming herself from a silent owner to involved and vocal partner in the running of Greywell's was the most significant. She had taken the risk, despite the costs, because Greywell's was something she wanted.

Then why was she hiding in her room like a coward when the only man she had wanted in many years was so close? Soon Will was going to find his family. And then, it was likely he would return to America and settle down. Get married. Have children. She and Will had such a brief time together—and she was squandering it on uncertainty and fear. David's sudden death had taught her that a person's journey on this earth was brief. She didn't want to walk down this path alone. Not now.

In the years since David had died, Olivia had been living in two worlds, not fully part of either. She was both a society widow and a business owner, and she was always acutely conscious of this split. She wanted to be whole, the way she felt when she was with Will. Defined, certain, undivided.

With sudden resolve, Olivia got to her feet. She was

219

tired of being an amalgam of different worlds. By attempting to appease the two conflicting forces in her life, all she had gained was uncertainty in both. Will brought her into focus, clarified the ambiguous. When they were together, Olivia escaped her doubts. She could be everything and compromise nothing. Finally.

She stepped into a pair of low-heeled slippers, then, before she could let hesitation swamp her, walked to her bedroom door and opened it quickly.

Will stood on the other side.

Barefoot, dressed in trousers, braces and an unbuttoned shirt, he looked as surprised to see her as she him. For several seconds they simply stared at each other. Then he stepped forward and, possessed by a strange instinct, she moved backward until they were both inside. Keeping his eyes locked with hers, he shut the door behind him.

Her bedroom, which moments earlier gaped like a chasm in long shadows, now seemed exceptionally small. The fire popped in the grate. She became aware of his exposed chest, the delineations of muscle that shaped his pectorals, his ribbed abdomen. He had the body of a laborer, hardened by work.

Olivia glanced up to see him watching her, the cool blue of his eyes heated by the fire—and hunger. A ferocious devouring.

She tried to think of something witty to say, clever and dry, to regain her composure, but all sensible thought fled. Energy, feral and dangerous, poured from him, a wild and profound disquiet that almost frightened her even as she found herself drawn to him.

"I can't stay away," he said, a raspy growl.

"I don't want you to," she answered.

He inhaled sharply. "You know what you're sayin'?"

Olivia had never felt more certain of anything before. She nodded. "I've had enough of words."

Eyes still fastened to hers, Will reached behind himself and locked the door. The sound of the tumbler sliding into place was the sound of her own resolve. She was not going back.

Chapter Fourteen

She didn't want to be civilized, and they weren't.

Will and Olivia crashed together, not getting much farther than a few steps into her bedroom, a rough little jolt as their bodies and mouths met. She thrust her fingers into his hair, pulling his head down to hers, while one of his large, agile hands cupped her behind as the other strummed along her neck. Their lips were all over, inside each others' mouths, a hot and liquid ferocity of feeding.

Only one day had passed between last night and this, but a lifetime, too, and they meant to make up for it.

When his hand left her neck she was sorry; then she wasn't sorry at all as she felt the heat of his palm through the fabric of her gown, on her breast. He groaned into her mouth. She arched into him. Before now, there had been so many layers of clothing. But not anymore.

Then he bent his head and licked the tip of her breast through the cloth. She felt the effect of his tongue everywhere—her other breast, between her legs, the ends of her fingers. Like the most exquisite electrocution. She cradled him to her. The white cotton gown became transparent through his ministrations, and she could see the dusky pink of her nipple through the fabric. He saw, too, and with fingers far more dexterous than she would have believed, he undid the row of buttons down the front of the gown and peeled the material back, uncovering her breasts.

"So beautiful," he said hoarsely. "As beautiful as . . ." He frowned, trying to think of the appropriate simile. "As beautiful as you," he finally said.

"Will—" But she couldn't speak anymore as his hands touched her breasts, skin to skin, and a sudden fever shot through her. Her knees buckled.

Will caught her. Scooping her up easily, he began to walk with her, her slippers falling to the floor. She thought he would take her to the bed, large and welcoming, but instead he set her down on top of a waist-high table next to a sofa. China bric-a-brac was cleared with a sweep of his arm and went bouncing to the oriental carpet. Dimly, she recalled that the last time they had made love, she and Will had been in his element, the outdoors. But now they were in her world, the cultured confines of her room, and it jarred her a little. But then those thoughts barely registered in her mind. Instead, she focused on Will, who stood between her legs, holding her arms, kissing her past coherence. She didn't care whose world they were in, as long as they were together.

She gave a small squeak of surprise as his fingers gripped the cheeks of her behind and scooted her to the very edge of the table. Her legs dangled down, her toes just brushing the soft pile of the rug.

"What—?" she wondered brokenly as he disappeared. He had dropped to his knees, kneeling in front of her. Again, his quick hands moved, pushing up the hem of her nightgown. Between her uncovered chest and now her bare legs and, God, between her legs, Olivia was mostly revealed to Will. She had a flash of memory—David had never seen her with the lights on, never seen her nakedness, nor she his. And he had never, ever knelt as if in prayer between her legs as Will was doing now.

The expression on his face as he gazed at her dark triangle of hair was a cross between reverence and pure, bodily desire.

"The sweetest peach," he murmured.

At least Olivia had secretly read those contraband, provocative books in school; otherwise she would have had no idea what he was planning. But even so—

"Will!" she could not help crying as he lowered his head again. His hands held the outside of her thighs. And his mouth found her, a different kind of kiss, more private, more full. She gripped the edge of the table as a scream climbed through her. She briefly worried the servants might hear, but then all rational thought fled under Will's exquisite onslaught. She couldn't have silenced herself if she wanted to. No, it was impossible. How could he make her feel this? She didn't even know what to call what she was feeling because it was everything, it was her, it was Will, and her body couldn't know such intoxicating pleasure. She'd never thought she had the capacity, but she was bursting with it, replete.

Then she hooked her legs behind him as tremors overtook her, the fine, diamond seizures moving through her body.

These had barely subsided before she felt him lifting her gown completely, over her shoulders, stripping her in a fluid motion as he stood. The nightgown joined the china dustcatchers on the floor. He was shrugging out of his braces and tossing aside his own shirt right after that.

Evidence of his desire was written across the gleaming sculpture of his muscles. He was immaculately crafted, an ideal of form and function, yet living and hungry. For her. Impossible, but real.

She hooked her fingers into the waistband of his trousers and brought him closer. As they came together for another tropical kiss, she undid the buttons of his fly. And then there he was, in her hand, hard and pulsing with life, with need. She stroked him.

"God*damn*," he growled. She loved to see the way her touch affected him, the look almost of pain that tightened his handsome face, knotted his jaw. Here was a man who felt his lust and reveled in it. The pagan pleasure of his own body, and hers. The uncertainties and disunities that plagued her were gone now in the conviction of desire.

Olivia wanted to touch him again, but he was busy getting his legs out of his trousers. They were flung across the room by a sharp kick, and now they were both naked. Her hand wrapped around his shaft as their mouths intermingled; his fingers located and shaped the slickness between her legs. She was shivering, shuddering, overcome, as she continued to sit at the edge of the table. His fingers pulled her open, just a little, just enough to accommodate, while his other hand came around to support her and hold her upright. But she could feel the tremors in his arms and down through his hands.

His hips surged forward and she moved to meet him, and they were locked together. Will inside her. She around him. They cried out in unison, almost surprised, unbalanced by the exquisite pleasure they found together. She wrapped her arms around his shoulders. She was no longer the brewery owner or the *haute monde* widow. She was Will's, and he was hers.

They set up a rhythm. She forgot the world, forgot everything she knew of herself. She had one memory, one present, one future, and that was Will, moving inside her with a friction and cadence so acute and magnificent she nearly wept from it. And while they moved, Will growled in her ear, whiskey warm, animal and possessive.

"Darlin'," he panted, "I'm so goddamn close an' I want you there with me."

Even as he spoke her body clenched and tightened. She gripped him hard, contracting around him. She moaned, overwhelmed again, shot through with an agony of pleasure because this time she wasn't alone; he was in her and she was full, so full. He groaned her name as he gripped her, becoming rigid, and she could feel the soft, interior pulses of him emptying inside her. Such a blessed feeling. Satiated, together.

They gasped for air, their bodies slick and heaving.

"Maybe someday," she breathed, "we can make it to the bed."

He gave her a wolfish grin. "Honey, I believe that day is at hand."

In due course, they did make it to the bed. But before then, there were a lot of very interesting places to explore—a small stiff-backed sofa, a plush footstool—

and even more interesting places on Olivia that got his attention.

Will felt pickled, lit up, like the biggest lush on nickel night at the saloon. He was drunk on Olivia and couldn't get enough. Jake would have called him a *chazzer*, a pig, but Will didn't care. He'd had enough of wanting Olivia, killing himself because he couldn't have her, and now that they'd finally given in to their need for each other, he was determined to soak her up like the desert floor in rainy season.

And she was game, too, which to Will's mind was the best part. She laughed, grew serious, then frisky, as fascinated by his body as he was hers. She whispered things to him that would make the oldest sinner blush, things she'd read about and wanted to try, and Will was more than happy to oblige.

They had themselves a fine old time.

If sometimes he found himself wishing for a little more, a small piece of her heart to go with her willing body, he made himself remember that time on earth was short, his time with her even shorter, and he needed to be glad for what he got.

In a heap, they fell together onto her bed, and both took long drinks of water from the pitcher on her bedside table to cool themselves. Then, quietly, they lay cupped against each other. He couldn't recall the last time he'd stayed with a woman after they'd gotten their pleasure, but he just couldn't make himself put his clothes on and leave. His body was a mite worn out, yet he stayed because he wanted to be near her for as long as he could.

"I can't believe you don't have any sweethearts back home," she murmured.

He shrugged, neither a yes or no.

Olivia rolled over to face him, propping her head on her outstretched arm. "Hasn't there been *one* girl you courted seriously?"

"Darlin'," he drawled, "I'm lyin' here with you as naked as a cat. I don't want to talk 'bout other girls." His eyes moved over her, and he was struck again by how goddamn lucky he was to have found her, this mouthwatering willow of a woman. Slim, but lush, white and pink and made for loving.

"I don't mind," she said.

It meant something to her. She wanted to know about him, not just his life riding the range and driving cattle, but the other side, too.

"There was one girl," he finally said, "in Colorado Springs."

"Oh?" She looked both interested and a bit put out. Will could have laughed and punched himself. "Tell me about her."

"Not much to tell. We'd courted for a while, and I was thinkin' 'bout maybe askin' for her; then I hit the trail. When I got back, she'd given me the mitten and married someone else."

"I'm sorry," she said, not sounding particularly sorry at all.

Will shrugged again. "If I'd been serious, I woulda acted sooner. But I kept puttin' it off and puttin' it off. It weren't a big surprise that she'd found herself somebody better."

"Better than you?" she asked, her dark eyebrow as arched as her voice. "Impossible."

"Quiet, woman," he said, giving her behind a playful swat. She laughed and punched him in the arm.

"There were plenty a' gals who found ol' Will Coffin to be quite a catch."

Her dusky violet eyes serious, she said, "You are. Any woman would be fortunate, indeed, to win you."

Kitty, the girl he'd met the other night at McNeil's, had said almost the same thing to him, and it hadn't meant much. But hearing those words coming from Olivia was like drinking the best whiskey—warming and dizzy-making.

"You should have no problem finding a wife when you return," she continued.

Frowning, he asked, "Why this fever to get me gone an' hitched? Tryin' to tell me somethin'?"

She lowered her eyes, staring at his chest. "Trying to tell myself something," she said softly. "I have to keep reminding myself that you'll be leaving, maybe soon, and you'll find a woman more . . . suitable."

As confessions went, this one made him want to bawl and cheer at the same time. "I ain't thinkin' 'bout tomorrow or the next day," he said. "Just right now, with you. Ain't that enough?"

It seemed to be. She smiled, both sad and content, and let her eyes drift shut.

His hand ran up and down the curve of her hip, a woman's hip, full and rounded, despite her slenderness. He spread his palm over the slight swell of her firm belly.

"Liv?"

"Mm?"

"How come you ain't got children?"

Her eyes opened and an old shadow passed over her face. "Yes," she murmured, "my empty house."

"I shouldn'ta asked."

229

"You should know." She traced her fingers along his collarbone, the edge of the scar he'd gotten a long time ago, but her gaze was far away. "David and I tried for several years. Finally, I became pregnant. He was so happy, and I was, too. But five months into the pregnancy, there was a problem."

He'd seen those problems before, in the ranchers' wives, the sodbuster women having baby after baby and soiled doves who weren't cautious. Sometimes the babies didn't make it, and sometimes the women didn't. Or both mother and child were taken away in pine boxes.

"We called the doctor right away," Olivia went on, "but it was too late. I miscarried. It was . . . ugly. So much blood. And the doctor told me," she said, her voice thickening, "that I was lucky to be alive, but there would be no children."

"Aw, Liv," Will said, wiping a tear away with the pad of his thumb as it trailed down her cheek. "I'm sorry."

She nodded, then leaned into his palm as his other hand stroked the dark silk waves of her hair. "We asked for a second opinion, and a third, but the doctors all said the same thing. The miscarriage had left me barren."

He'd seen a lot of death and loss over the course of his life. A body couldn't live out West and not meet up with sorrow, but still, Olivia's fate stuck in his chest like cactus needles. She had such a warm and generous heart, just right for loving children, and to have that taken away seemed hard and cruel.

"It took almost a year for me to recover," she continued, drawing in a breath, "and David stayed out of my bed out of deference to my health. But even when

I was completely healed, he didn't visit me at night. Maybe a few times, but I could tell he wasn't particularly enthusiastic about the idea. Finally, I got the courage to ask him about it, and he said that he didn't really see the point anymore."

"What?" Will didn't think too much could surprise him, but this did. Surprise quickly turned to anger. He saw red, a sudden gut-punch of rage that hit him hard and fast.

She sat up a bit, letting her hair fall into her face as if to curtain her bitterness. "If I couldn't conceive, there was no reason to continue sharing a bed. That's what David said."

"Are you sure that heel's dead?" Will growled. "Because if he ain't, I'd like to rawhide and plant him myself."

Her smile was rueful. "I am quite sure David is no longer alive. It took me a long time to determine if I was, however."

He was so mad he could spit. "Listen to me, Liv," Will said, taking both her hands in one of his own. With his free hand, he tipped up her face so she could look him square in the eye. "That husband of yours was a beefhead, a *schmuck*."

"I don't know—"

"If he didn't realize that he was the luckiest son of a bitch in England because you were his wife, then he deserved to have the tar beat out of him. And if he didn't make love to you on account of you being unable to have babies, then it really is good that he ain't alive anymore, 'cause I surely would kill him myself."

She looked at him for a long time. "I believe you," she finally said.

Will exhaled loudly, trying to calm himself down.

He really was hopping mad. It just ticked him off mightily to think that David Xavier had been given the greatest blessing, Olivia as his wife, and thrown it away. Few men were so favored, but Xavier had wasted his gifts.

"Now, if you were my woman," Will said, a smile curving one side of his mouth, "things would have been a heap different."

She smiled, too, knowing and heated. "How different?"

"Well, for starters," he said, "every chance I got, I'd do this." And he pulled her against him, bringing their mouths together, open. He let himself pretend that he had all the time in the world to explore her, as leisurely as you please, the wet inside of her mouth, her velvet-rough cat's tongue that met his own and stirred all the way down. Even just kissing, Olivia had so much heat in her, she could burn a barn and all the fields with it. Lord knew, Will was on fire.

Then she pulled back. "Surely you wouldn't stop there," she prompted.

As games went, this one beat horseshoes by about three hundred miles. "Nope. Next, I'd do this." He gently pushed her down onto the bed so she lay on her back. Propped on his side, Will moved his hands all along her body, shaping and sculpting her, trying to learn her as well as he knew his mountainous home and the black glittering sky above. He took his time, feeling the warm satin of her skin flushed with desire, the bow of her collar, each breast, small but full and tipped dark pink, the echo of her ribs that tapered down to her smooth belly, the dark V of silky-crisp hair between her legs and the legs themselves, strong and sculpted beneath ivory flesh.

I'm praying, he thought to himself. He'd never been one for the doxology works, preferring to take his divine inspiration from what surrounded him. But lying here with Olivia, touching her reverently, he felt something shift inside him, something large and profound, as though he'd finally learned the answer to a riddle he'd been trying to solve.

But he couldn't touch her worshipfully for very long before hunger took hold.

"That can't be all," Olivia said breathlessly, as hungry as he was.

"Then I'd do this." He bent down and took possession of her mouth again as his hand went between her legs, finding her as she opened for him. And they moaned together as he stroked her, bringing wetness from the inside out. Her hips bucked, urging him to go faster, be quick, but Will wanted to go slow. He wanted to draw this out, draw her out, until time melted.

His other hand cradled her breast, then found the hard tip and rubbed. She arched, offering herself up to him. Will wanted nothing more than to bury himself in her, but he made himself stay beside her, touching her most secret places. Several times, he brought her right up to the edge, then slowed his pace as she panted.

"Do you know what I'd do next?" Olivia asked, breath shallow as she gazed up at him through short, black lashes.

"What's that, darlin'?"

"This." With surprising strength she reached up and took hold of his shoulders, then pulled him down on top of her. Her task was made easier by his complete lack of resistance. He settled immediately between her opened legs and almost chuckled as he felt her hand grasp and position him at her entrance. Then he didn't feel much like laughing as her hips rose to meet his, and with a sharp hiss of breath he slid into her. They might have been carrying on all night, but she was still glove-tight and hot.

They both became delirious, moving together, around and inside. Her heart knocked against his own. He wanted to go as far into her as he could, so deep that boundaries lost meaning and they weren't two people anymore but something else, something new entirely. So he plunged, again and again, searching, seeking. And it felt so damned good. He thought he'd surely die of it, which, to his mind, wasn't such a bad way to go.

He could feel it, as sure as sliding down the bank of a flood-swollen river to be washed away below. Olivia was becoming dangerously precious to him. Someone he was starting to believe he couldn't live without.

"Will, please," she cried into his shoulder, "I want you so much."

"Sweet Olivia," he groaned, "I'm yours. Only yours."

She tensed around him, then gripped him hard, over and over, finding fulfillment with a sharp cry. He was right behind her, released like a bullet, and he shouted her name. There was so much he wanted to say to her but couldn't, and so he let the simple shape of her name hold everything he felt. Such a small word, so elegant and refined, now weighted with his own wandering soul.

Chapter Fifteen

Urgent knocking on the bedroom door woke them both. At first, Olivia didn't know what to make of the sound. It penetrated a deep, dreamless sleep—the first she had enjoyed in a long time. Which made sense, given the fact that she had made love all night with a man at least four years her junior, a man with a boundless sexual appetite that was satisfied only when she had sleepily insisted that she was completely worn out. Olivia didn't even have time to suggest to Will that he return to his own room to prevent speculation. She was asleep before the words left her mouth.

Groggy, disoriented, she heard the insistent knocking as if lying at the bottom of a lake. Eventually, she opened her eyes and looked around. Her room was filled with bright sunlight, and it appeared as though a tornado had recently passed through it. Knick-knacks were scattered on the floor, several chairs had been overturned and there were telltale heaps of clothing strewn about. Turning her head, she saw

Will stretched out beside her in the bed, sprawled on his stomach in an attitude of oblivious satiety. The sheets were bunched around his waist, appearing snowy next to the dark bronze of his taut skin.

She could have spent at least half an hour simply looking at Will in her bed, a sleeping wolf, handsome and dangerous. The tenderness he was capable of made her breath catch in her throat just remembering it. She could almost believe at times last night that there was more between them than simple attraction—the way he had said her name, touched her, just looked at her. And her own heart had been so perilously exposed, vulnerable. She had burned for him, yes, could feel desire stirring even now, but there was that something else binding her to him in a way she wasn't prepared for.

Nor could she think about it now. There was that awful, relentless knocking.

"Please, madam," Mordon said through the door, "it is most urgent you rise. Mr. Huntworth is downstairs."

Any vestiges of lethargy were immediately shaken off. Olivia sat up in bed. "I'll be down in ten minutes," she called.

"Shall I send Sarah up to help you dress?"

Olivia glanced over at Will, whose aqua eyes were now open and regarding her alertly. They were both quite naked.

"No, I'll manage on my own," she answered.

Mordon's footsteps died away as Olivia got out of bed. Pulling on her drawers and chemise, she tried to calm her racing mind. She felt herself begin to fracture again, all sense of unity from last night lost. Mr. Huntworth never came to her house, unless . . .

"There's trouble," Will said behind her.

She whirled around and saw him stepping into his trousers. The sight of him unclothed in broad daylight made her already racing heart leap. It still astonished her that any man could be so solidly built, so well-muscled that he put classical art to shame, and that he had desired her was nothing short of miraculous.

"I'm certain Pryce or his man Maddox have struck again," she said. She contemplated her corset, and the idea of squeezing into it was unbearable. Instead, she located a starched, stiffened camisole she usually only wore at home and slipped her arms into it. Her fingers stumbled over the buttons, but she managed to get it on properly. A small bustle and two petticoats followed.

"I shoulda stayed at the brewery last night," Will said darkly. He was also dressing, putting on his shirt and hoisting his braces onto his shoulders, but she saw the way his gaze lingered on her as she ran around her bedroom in search of clothing.

"I hired extra men to do that." She selected a shirt-waist and long, gored skirt; Olivia had no time for Regent Street fashion. As she turned to her mirror, she saw that her face betrayed exactly what she had been doing last night. Her lips were swollen and red, her cheeks lightly abraded from Will's stubble, her eyes slumberous despite her agitation. Perhaps by the time she reached Greywell's it would be less noticeable. Until then, there would be no help for it. Surely the servants knew already.

Will appeared behind her in the glass as she roughly dragged a brush through her hair.

"Liv," he said softly.

She stopped in midstroke, meeting his eyes in the mirror. They were clear and serious.

237

"You want me to clear out?" he asked.

Olivia set down the brush and turned around. She knew what he was offering. Leave before word could circulate about them; absent himself from her presence if she found him embarrassing, a reminder of her iniquity. She looked at him steadily and was struck again at how Will surpassed simple definition. He was pure physicality, but he was exceptionally intelligent and perceptive, more so than any man she had ever known, and protective of her.

"I want you to stay," she answered levelly.

He smiled a little, as if he had been expecting her to say just that but not believing her all the same. "You don't have to be polite. Tell me to light a shuck and I'm gone. I'll find someplace near the brewery an' keep helpin' out there."

She placed her hand on his rough, tense jaw. "I am not being polite. I want you here."

"There'll be trouble."

"If there is any trouble, there is no place I need you more than beside me."

His grin, the one that ignited her from the inside, spread across his face and onto hers. "Darlin', anythin' you want."

They leaned into each other and kissed quickly, causing tiny flames to lick along her spine. Her adventure far surpassed anything the fictitious Lorna Jane could ever experience.

"Madam," Mordon said again at the door, "please come quickly. Mr. Huntworth is growing exceptionally agitated."

"One more minute, Mordon, and I'll be down."

Olivia watched Will tuck in his shirt as she pinned up her hair and slipped on a short-waisted jacket. She had been given an opportunity to end their affair before serious damage could be done, but she had chosen not to. She told herself it was because she needed Will close at hand to help her counter Pryce's threat, but that wasn't the complete truth.

Without trying, Will had lain claim to most of her heart, and she wanted, against reason, to give it to him, no matter the cost.

Despite the hideously early hour, George Pryce was in a wonderful mood. He couldn't help whistling to himself as he ambled back along Park Lane to his house on Upper Brook Street. He strolled around a few bakery wagons and even nodded a courteous how-do-you-do to a passing bobby, who recognized him immediately and blustered out a "Good day, Mr. Pryce," before he walked on.

Oh, it really was a fine morning. Pryce took the front steps of his house two at a time, and smiled at the astonished butler before giving him his hat, coat and gloves. He then made his way into the dining room to have a cup of coffee and read the paper, blissfully content.

His eyes scanned the sporting news, but his mind was still back with Maddox at the Notting Dale stockyards. Pryce's mood was too high to even register anger at being forced to meet his mercenary at such a filthy, stench-ridden location. But Maddox insisted that such places were the safest, since no one of Pryce's acquaintance would ever venture to such disgusting and disreputable spots.

"So it's done, then?" Pryce had asked Maddox over the awful squeals of the pigs.

Maddox nodded. "I carried out my plan exactly.

Lady Xavier won't be brewing any more beer. Greywell's is finished."

He could barely suppress his delight. "What about the American?"

Surveying the pigs being driven to market, Maddox shrugged. "I'll manage him."

Though it wasn't exactly what Pryce wanted, he was still marvelously thrilled. That happiness lasted all the way back to his Mayfair home, where, in a clean, sweet-smelling dining room, he could finally revel in his triumph. No one said no to George Pryce, and, by God, he had proven it. She would be ruined at last, and then he could finally turn his attention to something new. There had to be hundreds of prospects to claim his interest, and his mind spun thinking of novel playthings.

"What's so amusing, George?" his father asked, poking his head into the dining room. "I could hear you laughing all the way from the top of the stairs."

"Nothing, Father," he answered. He made himself calm down. "Just pleased about the cricket scores."

Frowning, Henry Pryce disappeared from the doorway. No doubt he thought his youngest son the veriest wastrel, exulting over something as inconsequential as cricket. But even his father's disapproval couldn't diminish Pryce's good humor. All he had to do now was sit back and watch the death throes of Lady Xavier's prized brewery.

"What happened?" Olivia asked as she and Will hurried into the Greywell's office. Huntworth had left to get back to the brewery on his own, and they hadn't spoken much on their way there from Princes Square. Olivia had been quiet and tense, chewing on her bottom lip and staring out the window. All the same, she had reached out across the carriage and taken his hand, squeezing it tight.

She wanted him to stay. He didn't know whether he was being blessed or cursed by this, pretending for a little while longer that they somehow had a chance together, that a gap as wide as the Rio Grande didn't separate them. All he let himself think about was that she didn't want him to leave her just yet, and that was fine enough for now.

And if she let go of his hand when the Greywell's gates come into view, that was to be expected, even though it made his chest ache a bit.

As they entered the office, Will saw immediately that one of the men she had hired to stand guard was sitting in a chair, being attended to by a doctor. The man's eye was swollen shut and he looked as though he'd spent the night at the bottom of a barrel of rotgut, knocked galley west. He held a bloodied cloth to the back of his head.

"I didn't even see 'im," the guard was saying. "I were makin' me rounds, just checked in with Frank an' gotten the all clear. And then, wham, I were knocked out cold." He grimaced. "Next thing I knew, Frank and the other boys were standin' 'round me and sayin' to get the doctor. Nobody saw nothin'."

"How is he?" Olivia asked the doctor.

The older man frowned. "He took a nasty blow to the head, could be a concussion. I'll want to observe him for the next day or two. He was lucky—the hit could have killed him if it had been just a bit to the side."

"I reckon whoever clocked him knew that," Will said.

Olivia looked at him, alarmed. "Maddox?"

241

"Yep."

"He got in, but to do what?" she asked. She turned to Huntworth. "Have you conducted a search of the premises?"

The manager nodded. "We couldn't find anything."

"We'll look again," Will said. "Maddox didn't bust in here just to clean this feller's plow."

So they broke into teams, all the employees of Greywell's, searching from one end of the brewery to the other. Almost nobody spoke, instead examining the smallest detail to catch whatever monkey-wrenching Maddox had done. It took almost two hours, during which all production had to be stopped.

"This is going to cost me a fortune in business," Olivia said to him as they stopped near the well.

"Can't take any chances," he said grimly. He put his hands on his hips, brushing his duster back.

She nodded, then stared hard at his hip. "You're armed."

Will also looked at his Colt, which he had strapped on just before they left. The polished handle gleamed in the pale light coming in from the windows. "I didn't think I'd be needin' this in England." He glanced back up at her. "You look like you're starin' at a rattler."

"And you're wearing the rattlesnake," she said. Her brow was lined as she continued to stare. "It's yours to use. If you wanted someone dead, there isn't much that can stop you now. That makes things very different."

Will pulled his duster closed. He saw himself in her eyes—he wasn't a cowpuncher anymore but a gunslinger. The kind of man who could deal out death like a hand of poker. "I know. I can feel it. I haven't worn my six-shooter in a while. It can change a man."

"I don't want you to be like Maddox," she said, troubled.

"I ain't him. I don't kill for money."

She looked stricken. "Nothing seems real, anymore. Guns, kidnapping, sabotage. These hardly seem the things of civilized London. More like . . ."

"Them dime books?"

Her smile was rueful and pained. "I thought I wanted a life like Lorna Jane's, foolish as she was."

"And now?"

"I just don't want anyone to get hurt. You, especially."

Surely he was a goner. He knew his time with Olivia would be ending, sooner than he would like, but he had to tell her, let her know that last night wasn't just about riding mattresses; something else was happening to him that he felt from the crown of his Stetson to the heels of his boots. And it was all new to him.

Before he spoke, he glanced over at the well.

"What is it?" she asked, seeing his face change.

"Somethin's shady." He walked over to the well, with Olivia following. "Looks like the cover wasn't put on right."

She frowned. "Show me."

"Look," he said, pointing, "the wooden top that covers the well ain't lined up. I seen Huntworth here, fussin' over everything, makin' sure it was all jus' so. He checks this here well about a dozen times before movin' on. And see here," he continued, holding up the lock, "somebody opened this without a key."

"How do you know?"

"Some fellers I knew in Oklahoma showed me how

243

to force a strongbox without shootin' the lock off. They used some special tools they got from a Boston housebreaker. Looks like somebody got at this lock, too, but made sure you couldn't tell without lookin' real hard."

Whitening, she said, "Oh, God, what does that mean?"

He was already running to fetch Huntworth. "He got to the well," Will growled.

The manager looked as if he might faint, but he managed to pull himself together enough to send for the chemists.

"We can have them test the water, just to be sure." Huntworth stared at the well. "Our search teams passed by the well three times and didn't see anything. But Mr. Coffin was more perceptive than any of us." He looked at Olivia. "He may have saved us from a disaster."

But Will was too keyed up to be much interested in Huntworth's praise. He, Olivia, Huntworth and just about all the workers of Greywell's waited while several men in white coats removed the cover, took samples of the water and then brought the samples into their laboratory to do some tests. Will hated standing around doing nothing, his hands clenching and unclenching at his sides. He wanted to smash the windows, throw his fists into the sides of the brewing tanks, anything besides this cooling of his heels. Worst of all was the way the waiting wore at Olivia, with Will unable to do a damned thing about it.

Needing something to do with himself, Will took out his gun, careful to keep it pointed at the ground. He turned the cylinder, checking to make certain five bullets were in place, then made sure the hammer was on an empty chamber. He wanted to be ready for whatever happened. After putting the Colt back in the holster, Will looked up and saw everyone, including Olivia, staring at him. Their faces were all stunned, as if he'd been handling fire. But Will made himself shut those faces out. If he had to take Pryce down, he had to be primed, English balkiness be damned.

They all looked up expectantly when the chemist *jefe* came out of the laboratory, but his chalky face already told them the story.

"The water has been contaminated," he said, clutching a clipboard to his chest. "A very specific set of chemicals were poured into the well, tainting it. But you can't taste the pollution. If we hadn't been alerted to the problem, we would have brewed poisoned beer and sold it to the public."

There were curses, groans and even a few sobs from the crowd.

"Can we repair it?" Olivia asked.

"It will take several months to purify the water," the chemist said. "Until then, we'll have to cease production entirely."

Someone cried, "We're ruined," and murmured agreement followed. The mood of the entire brewery was bleak. Will watched as Olivia slid into a hastily offered chair, her face ghostly pale, her eyes staring straight ahead, unseeing.

The blackest rage Will had ever felt nearly split him in two. Blind with fury, he stalked from the brewery. In a way, he reveled in it, a pure form of hate that refused to be ignored. It made him act, when he had been idle too long. The Colt on his hip felt like lightning. He was halfway to the gates of Greywell's before he heard Olivia calling to him. As he turned, she came jogging across the yard to stand beside him.

"Where are you going?" she demanded.

"I got business to take care of."

She looked almost as angry as he felt. "This isn't Dodge City, damn it," she said, not even blushing at her language.

Will didn't answer, tightening his jaw so much it almost cracked. Just then, a misty rain started to fall, turning the cobblestones slick and black. Will moved to take Olivia's arm, but she pulled away.

"You gotta get out of the rain," he said.

"I'm not going anywhere," Olivia answered, the arches of her brows drawn down furiously, "until you swear you won't kill George Pryce."

"Goddamn it!" Will shouted. "I won't let that son of a bitch live, not after what he's done to you. I can't just twiddle my thumbs and let him get away with it. If you think I'm that kinda man, then you don't know me at all."

"I know you aren't stupid, Will," Olivia said. She had run out without her hat, and her hair was now completely wet, dripping into her eyes. She didn't seem to notice. "If you so much as touch Pryce, there isn't a judge in England who won't convict you. You could be thrown into prison, or worse; you might be hanged."

"I don't care."

She gripped his sleeve and fixed his eyes with her own. In the rain, she looked both impossibly vulnerable and also unbreakable, like a storm-lashed tree. "But I do." Unconcerned who might be watching, she stepped closer, so her skirt brushed against the bottom of his trousers. "No matter what Pryce does to me, I refuse to let you throw your life away. That would hurt me far more than anything he might do."

He stared at her for a long time, this strong woman who could be rocked with hard luck yet never lose her soul. A rare one, this Lady Olivia Xavier. After a moment, he took off his hat and placed it on her head. It rode low, almost covering her eyes, but he tipped it back just enough so she could see.

"Keep the rain off your head," he said, not worried about getting wet himself. A little English drizzle was nothing.

She smiled, though it was small and rueful. "Thank you."

Will breathed out loudly, like a horse snorting his impatience. "Jesus, Liv, you don't know how hard this is for me. Sittin' around with my thumb up my behind while Pryce tears you apart. I thought I was supposed to protect you."

"You are. You do. But murdering him was never part of our agreement. There will come a time when I will need you, but until then"—she shook her head—"we'll find another way to strike back."

"While we were thinkin' of a way, Pryce took out the water supply," Will said, angry with himself. "Any more thinkin' and he'll wipe us out completely."

Olivia straightened and, wearing his Stetson, looked the picture of a tough-willed Colorado woman.

"He won't get the chance," she said. She took off his hat and set it back on his head. Her lovely face was set and determined, more so than he had ever seen it. It was an inspiring sight. "I have a plan."

The rest of the day was spent outlining Olivia's strategy to the staff of Greywell's. There were some objections, but she countered them coolly, with a steadfast calm that welled up from somewhere deep inside her. She simply refused to be cowed by George Pryce, would not accept defeat of any kind. Perhaps a few months ago she might have conceded, accepted Greywell's as a complete loss.

But Will Coffin had shown her that there were things worth fighting for. No matter what obstacles were thrown in her path, she understood that time was precious and could not be spent wringing her hands and giving in to misfortune. She would tell him this, when they had time alone. And she longed for that time alone, very badly.

But there were things to attend to first. And there wasn't much time to act. So, very clearly, she explained what she intended to do and how she meant to go about doing it. The employees of Greywell's stood around her in the large room that held the cooling tanks and listened. Gradually, the uncertain and fearful looks on their faces were replaced by tentative smiles.

"What about the cost, Lady Xavier?" Mr. Huntworth asked. "It seems dreadfully prohibitive."

"In addition to Greywell's, my late husband left me with a significant settlement that is paid quarterly," she explained. "I will discuss these plans with my solicitor and have him withdraw funds immediately."

"Will he agree to this?"

Olivia mustered her best finishing school look, the one as cold and polished as glass, but beneath that look was her Western backbone, grown in the past few weeks. "He will have no say in the matter."

Gulping, Mr. Huntworth nodded.

Will helped make the deliveries of the beer that was

potable while Olivia and the clerks busily made preparations. She instructed the Greywell's chemists to begin purifying the well immediately. There was immense activity around the brewery that lasted all day—one of the most strenuous and trying Olivia could remember. They needed everything in place as soon as possible so she could finally beat George Pryce.

As she went about her business, she would occasionally see Will across the room. His smile and wink helped her stand a bit straighter. She wasn't alone in this challenge. He was with her, and knowing that made every burden that much easier to bear.

Was it the Western code of honor that kept him working so hard at a business that wasn't even his, when he wasn't even drawing a wage or salary? She didn't think that was the only reason. From what Will had told her, not very many people out West could afford that code. Life was too difficult and unpredictable. Most looked out for themselves. Perhaps it was some kind of English integrity, bred into his blood from his parents. But no, there was no such thing as inherited decency. Then what, she asked herself, kept him here?

The honor he possessed was all his own. It didn't belong to any geographic region or way of life. Will Coffin was a good man with a strong and gallant heart, tempered with affable humor and enjoyment of life's pleasures. He didn't brood or sulk or bemoan his fate when he had been given a rough path to follow, as others might have done.

As Olivia wrote out a telegram, she heard Will talking to one of the wagon drivers, making a joke that had the other man laughing, and she realized that she truly liked Will, who he was as a man. He filled a room with his presence, but he wasn't domineering. He was both sunny and strong, sociable and trustworthy. She turned and watched him through the open office door. A few of the younger female employees, going about their work, had come by and were lingering around him, smiling, shy, flirtatious.

The jealousy that billowed inside of her died quickly when she saw Will speak politely to the girls. He was deferential, friendly, but clearly unresponsive to their overtures. Olivia could not help the exultation this provoked. He didn't want them, even though those girls were more suitable, less problematic than she was.

Any question of who Will *did* want was answered when he caught her watching him. The look he gave her was so purely intimate and carnal, moving over her face and along her body, there could be no doubt of his meaning. Her belly flipped in response and she became aware of her legs pressed together. Olivia licked her lips and Will smiled, warm and lazy, before ambling off.

For now, she reminded herself. Her adventure with Will—and that's what it was, it couldn't be more than that—would come to an end, sooner rather than later. For now, he could be her partner and her friend, help her carry the burdens she had shouldered.

It was a long day, made longer by the fact that she had to wait to be alone with Will. She struggled to focus on the papers in front of her. The sooner she finished her work, the sooner she and Will could go home together. She felt as though she stood outside a lush garden, permitted to enter it every so often and tormented when she waited to be admitted. Oh, she could get very used to having Will in her bed, in her house. Dangerous thoughts crept into her mind and refused to leave.

There was only so much they could accomplish in a day. Her plan was being set in motion, and within two days either she or George Pryce would be ruined. Her heart pounded at the gamble.

Eventually, she and Will went out to climb back into her carriage to journey across the river to Bayswater, long after night had fallen.

Will was handing her into the carriage when the unwelcome voice of Prudence Culpepper cut through the foggy night.

"Lady Xavier," Prudence said tightly, stepping up beside Olivia. A bored-looking footman stood nearby, politely staring off into the distance, and Prudence held a newspaper in her hand.

Olivia wanted to scream. She was much too exhausted to contend with her brewery's shrill and self-righteous neighbor. "Mrs. Culpepper," Olivia said wearily, "I have had a very long and tiring day and I must insist that we postpone this discussion for another time."

But Prudence was not backing down. She cast a baleful look at Will, her lips compressed until they were almost white. "What I have to say cannot wait, Lady Xavier," Prudence insisted, almost spitting the word *Lady*. She held out the newspaper. "I have read the most shocking thing about you and your American. And I find it utterly disgusting."

Will took the paper, Prudence flinching at his proximity, and handed it to Olivia. A column from the society pages had been circled. He stood at her shoulder as they read it together.

> *Considerable notice has, of late, been given to a certain Lady X, known in recent years for her unusual decision to pursue public employment following her husband's death. Though some have found her actions more disreputable than remarkable, others have hailed her decision as an advancement for women and innovators alike.*
>
> *Recently, however, Lady X has been seen keeping company with an American cowboy—not a cattle baron, dear readers, nor a burgeoning industrialist. No, Lady X's cowboy is indeed a Texan with little to claim but his spurs and saddle. One can only speculate whether our Lady X will soon change her interest from porters to porterhouses. The late Lord X would likely have something to say on the topic.*

"You're from Colorado," Olivia said to Will when they finished reading. "Everyone gets it wrong." She crumpled the newspaper and tossed it down to the pavement.

Prudence trembled with fury. "You are missing the point!" Clutching her reticule, she continued, "You think no one has noticed what has been going on between you two, but they see."

"It ain't nobody's business what Olivia does," Will snarled.

"It most certainly is," Prudence said hotly. "Inappropriate behavior will not be tolerated by decent society. And I can tell you," she added, "that lascivious behavior with an American bumpkin is inappropriate."

"How dare you?" Olivia snapped, enraged at this insult. She heard Will's sharp intake of breath beside her.

"How dare *you,* Lady Xavier?" Prudence countered. "Do you think you are so removed from the rest of us that anything you do will be shrugged off, accepted? We all have to live under the same strictures, and believing that you are somehow exempt is unbelievably arrogant. And self-destructive," she added smugly. "If you continue like this, no respectable person will acknowledge you."

"What if I don't want them to acknowledge me?" she answered stormily. "What if I don't care?"

"It isn't simply a matter of being invited to country house parties and you know it," Prudence retorted. "Like it or not, your reputation affects everything. Including your brewery."

"What?" Will asked.

"It's true," Prudence said, turning to him scornfully. "As one of very few female business owners, Lady Xavier is under intense scrutiny. Her actions are held up before the public. And no one will want to trade with a woman of low reputation. She will certainly be shunned should she be suspected of moral impropriety. I am seriously considering moving the mission in order to put as much distance between this den of iniquity and my house of moral charity."

"Are you quite finished?" Olivia said between her teeth.

"I've spoken my piece," sniffed Prudence.

"Ma'am," Will drawled, "I don't believe in talkin' disrespectful to ladies, but since you've shown that you ain't nothin' more than a gossipy hen an' not much of a lady, I'm gonna tell you to hit the trail."

Prudence gasped in horror. Without another word, she spun on her heel and marched off, her footman trailing after her.

Tremors of rage shook Olivia's body. She felt almost sick with it. But beneath the anger was dread.

Back at Princes Square, Olivia went up immediately to the drawing room. She poured herself two fingers of scotch and drank it back, feeling heat slide down her throat and into her belly. Olivia stood at the sideboard, staring at the decanters of liquor. The fire reflected in the crystal surfaces, dazzling, hypnotic. She wanted to lose herself in the contemplation of the flames, in the tiny prismatic world contained within the glass. In that world, there would be no George Pryce, no society columns, no Prudence Culpepper or the many she represented. Just perfect, clear glass and fire.

Will came up behind her. His hands went to her shoulders, and she leaned against him. So solid, so sure. She tipped her head back so her forehead rested against the underside of his jaw. She breathed deeply, taking in the warm leathery musk of his skin.

"Take me to bed," she whispered. "Make me forget."

"Liv—"

"Just a little while," she said, turning around and staring up into his desire-filled eyes. They burned down at her as she slid her arms around his waist. "It's all the time we have."

"Just a little while," he repeated, and then their mouths came together and she made herself forget time.

They were lying quietly in bed when a slip of paper slid beneath the door. Frowning, Olivia sat up. If there was an urgent message, Mordon usually knocked.

"Leave it," Will said. He tugged on her hand.

But she was too mystified to ignore the note. She quickly got out of bed and picked up the scrap of paper, unconcerned by her nudity.

"It's for you," she said, perplexed. Will's name had been written across the front. He was at her side almost immediately and she handed him the paper.

They stared at each other. After a long moment, he opened the note.

"It's a name and address," he said, reading it. He looked up at her, his expression inscrutable. "Lawford found them. He found my family."

"That's wonderful," she said. Her voice sounded far away.

The world, which she had been struggling so hard to keep at bay for the past few hours, was determined to invade this sanctuary. And neither she nor Will could stop it.

Chapter Sixteen

Will held the piece of paper and stared at it.

"This is it, huh?" he asked, not looking at Olivia. His eyes moved over the words Lawford had written in a bold, educated hand. "Search is over."

"That's right," Olivia said. Her voice sounded far off. "Over."

Where was the jubilation that was supposed to come when this moment arrived? Jake had put so much weight on Will finding his family, sure that if he was given this one thing, the days of rambling and knocking around would suddenly stop and Will would finally put down some roots. And here it was, the answer to a lifetime of questions he'd never stopped to ask.

"What does it say?" she asked.

Will handed her the note and walked away. He started putting on his clothes without thinking, his actions mindless as he tried and failed to get his mind around what this information meant.

"Benjamin Bradshaw," Olivia read aloud. "Nine Half Moon Street. London."

"That on the other side a' town?" Will asked as he buttoned his shirt. He reckoned that whoever this Ben Bradshaw was, he had to live far from Olivia, in the seedier part of London.

"No," Olivia breathed. She shrugged into a robe, then came over to him quickly and grabbed his arm. "Will—Half Moon Street is in Mayfair."

The name meant nothing to him. "Yeah?" He distractedly shoved the tails of his shirt into his britches and turned to look for his boots.

"You don't understand." Her voice almost shook as she held him tight. Her urgency made him glance up, and he was nearly confounded by the look on her face. She stared at him as though he were covered in stars. "Mayfair is the most exclusive part of London. Only the wealthiest and most esteemed families live there. People like the Rothschilds."

It was as if his mind was swamped in molasses. He couldn't make sense of what she was saying. When he didn't say anything, Olivia continued, "Don't you see—if Benjamin Bradshaw is a member of your family, and if he lives in Mayfair . . ."

"Then I'm from money," Will concluded. He rubbed his hand over his face. "I don't know, Liv. I don't *feel* rich."

She seemed genuinely happy for the first time in a long while, George Pryce and gossip-mongering newspapers forgotten. That smile of hers, which tied itself around his heart surer than any lasso, spread across her face, and she wrapped her arms around him. "Will, this is brilliant. It's the most wonderful news."

He pulled away, frowning. "You're glad I might be loaded?"

She looked dazed. "No—" Olivia backed away, holding the front of her robe closed. "But things will be so much different for you, better, perhaps, if you come from a family of influence. I was hoping"—she looked away, then looked back—"that there might be some chance for us, after all."

He understood her right off. And that charge, which he hadn't been able to find before, came galloping through him like a stampede. "We can tell all them *yentas* to shut their big bazoos," he said with a growing smile.

"Exactly," she beamed.

Will grabbed her around the waist and swung her in circles until she shrieked. "Liv, sure as shootin', them's glad tidin's." He slowed and set her feet back on the ground, staring down into her lovely, shining face. They stared at each other for a few moments as the room still gently spun around them. Her hands spread on his chest, and he could feel her against the pounding of his heart. "I mean it, Liv," he said softly. "That's the best part about all this. Soon as I can, I mean to call on you, accordin' to Hoyle."

In answer, she slid her hands up his chest and linked her fingers around his neck. She tipped back her head and he came down for a kiss, hot and full of promise. And just like that, he felt it, like holding a handful of aces or not losing a single head on a cattle drive—that sense of peace, of rightness that had been missing for so long. The sandstorm that gusted through his heart quieted, and in the stillness, there was only Olivia.

"Before we get too distracted," she said breathlessly, pulling back, "we ought to put our clothes on and go see Benjamin Bradshaw. It's nearly ten o'clock, but let's not wait until morning."

"No, ma'am."

Now that Will understood that what he had been missing had been living here at Princes Square all along, he finally felt keyed up about finding his kinfolk. A family of his own—Olivia, this Bradshaw and who knew what other relatives would be revealed to him. After he got decent, he slipped out and waited in the music room while Olivia called her maid. She wanted to make a good impression on Will's family and made herself endure the long ritual of dressing.

Will sat down at the piano and began picking out a few notes. He thought about maybe putting on his fancy suit of clothes to meet his family, but he knew he'd feel even more awkward and stiff in those duds. And he wasn't ashamed of who he was—a cowboy, and a damned good one, too. And he'd make Jake proud, to boot.

Will played "My Grandfather's Clock," thinking that maybe he'd meet his own grandfather soon. He gave the notes extra kick as plans began forming in his mind. He could stay in England, maybe raise horses in the country, since Olivia had said Englishmen were pretty wild for horseracing. He and Olivia would finally wallop George Pryce. They could run the brewery together. Get married. There wouldn't be any children, but Will wanted Olivia more than he wanted babies. He might miss Colorado, too, but it was only a place. Olivia was everything.

As futures went, his looked pretty grand. So when Olivia appeared in the doorway of the music room in an emerald green dress with a wide, open collar and snowy blouse underneath, Will jumped up from the piano bench and swooped her into an impromptu waltz around the small room, humming a tune.

She laughed, the finest sound Will knew of, as she was led through the steps.

"We might yet see you presented at court," she chimed. "You'll charm all the aristocrats."

"I ain't interested in them fancy folk," he said, slowing. "Just you. Just my kin."

"The world is changing, Will," she said with a smile. Their hands were still intertwined, her slender fingers wrapped in his rough ones. "And changing for the better. At last."

The lights were blazing in the front windows of the elegant townhouse on Half Moon Street. Olivia saw that several carriages were waiting outside, which meant that a dinner party was most likely taking place. Perhaps for privacy's sake, it would have been better if Will's family wasn't entertaining guests when their missing relative arrived, but there would be no more waiting. She and Will, eager as they were to meet his family, had spoken little during the ride over. There was too much to say and feel, an overwhelming tidal wave of emotion that choked away all words and left them to hold hands silently as they drove eastward. Olivia didn't know if it was his hand that shook or her own.

Though she wanted to leap down from the carriage as soon as it stopped, she waited patiently for the footman to open the door and offer her a hand. Once standing on the sidewalk, she nervously adjusted the bodice of her dress and gazed up at the impressive facade of the house. It wasn't much bigger than her own, but Mayfair had a certain sheen of gentility that even affluent Bayswater could never approach. Somehow, she had the strangest feeling that she had been at this address before.

"Ready?" Will asked at her side.

She nodded, covering her uncertainty with a quick, bright smile. But Will did look quite apprehensive, and heartbreakingly young, as he also stared at the front of the townhouse. He swallowed and tugged at the bandanna around his neck.

Olivia smoothed the lapels of his duster. "You look fine," she assured him. "Better than fine. Marvelous."

"Maybe they'll make me muck out their stables," he said, only half joking.

"Will," she said seriously, "they will be so happy to finally meet you. And why shouldn't they be? You're strong, intelligent, courageous and have a wonderful heart. You will make any family proud." She cupped his chin with her gloved hand. "So no more nonsense about stables. *Farshtaist?*"

The sound of Yiddish made Will's anxiety lessen, as she hoped it would. He flashed her a grin, and Olivia was confident that no one, no matter if they came from Mayfair or Montana, would be able to deny him.

"Let's quit beatin' the devil around the stump, then," he said, and took her hand to lead her up the front stairs. With a wink, he knocked smartly on the door.

An unflappable butler in formal dress greeted them. "May I assist you?" Behind him, the clink and murmurs of a dinner party sounded.

"We would like to speak with the master and mistress of this house," Olivia said. She presented the butler with her card, and, after quickly scanning it, he placed it in a waistcoat pocket.

"I am afraid that they are unavailable at the moment," the butler said, gracious but decorous. "But I will indeed inform them that you called."

"It is most urgent that we speak with them now," Olivia continued. "I am certain they would want to meet with us if they knew the consequence of our visit."

The butler would not be swayed. "Alas, madam, I am unable to assist you in this matter, but I can assure you—"

Will, who had been steadily growing more and more restless during the course of this excruciatingly polite conversation, had reached his limit. "Step aside, son," Will said, shouldering past the butler. Will's size and muscle easily overpowered the smaller man. "I got me important business inside."

Olivia quickly followed him into the middle of an immense foyer, two stories high, with a huge chandelier glimmering above. Once again, she was assailed by a powerful feeling of having been here before.

The butler's calm demeanor gave way to heated indignation. "See here, sir, this is absolutely outrageous!" A few footmen rapidly appeared, much younger and broader than the butler. "Either remove yourselves at once or I will be compelled to use force."

Olivia realized that Will had been keeping his natural rowdiness in check for a long time and was eager to let it loose. With a ferocious grin, he raised his fists in preparation for a fight. The footmen, sensing that they had a formidable combatant on their hands, braced themselves.

"Let's get a wiggle on, fellers," Will said.

"Wait!" Olivia stepped between Will and the footmen. She turned to the butler. "We would never disturb the occupants of this house if we did not think the matter was of the utmost urgency. We don't want to fight," she added with a glare at Will, then looked again at the butler. "Please tell your master and mistress that Lady Olivia Xavier begs just a moment of their time. I assume all responsibility for any disruption this may cause."

The butler still appeared doubtful, but Olivia gave him a look that wouldn't be argued with. He glanced quickly from the imperious lady to the bellicose cowboy and, deciding that he would rather face the wrath of his employers than these peculiar strangers, led them to a small retiring room off the foyer with instructions to wait. Clearly, they were not deemed worthy of the drawing room.

Olivia sat in a ladies' chair while Will paced. The room was stuffed with elaborately carved furniture and ceramics, a touch too ornate for Olivia's taste, but she made no comment about it to Will. A Gothic Renaissance clock ticked loudly, and between Will's boots going back and forth across the floor and this noise, Olivia felt as taut as a bowstring. Her heart ached for him, what he must be going through at that moment, and when he glanced her way she offered him an encouraging smile, despite her own trepidation.

He took in the room and made a face. "Not sure if I cotton to my kinfolk's spread. Little too stuffy for my likin'."

He did look out of place in the extravagant, cramped space, a rangy cowboy amid the ferns and folderol. "Perhaps you can convince them to put spittoons on the floor and mount longhorns on the wall."

"And have everyone come to dinner by ringin' the bell and yellin' 'Come and get it,'" he added.

"You could have Pug-roping contests," Olivia suggested. They were both growing giddy from tension.

"And crumpet quick-draws."

Before they could carry their hysteria any further, the door to the drawing room opened and a man and woman in full evening dress entered, looking exceptionally confused and a bit annoyed. Olivia got to her feet, frowning. They looked much too young to have a grandchild Will's age.

"Lady Xavier?" the man asked. "What exactly is this about?"

Her memory returned in an instant. She *had* been in this house before, when David had been alive, for a ball. She dropped into a curtsey. "Lord and Lady Donleveigh, I apologize for the intrusion. May I introduce my friend, Mr. Will Coffin?"

Lord Donleveigh shook hands with Will, frowning. "That American we've been hearing about?"

"Yessir," Will answered, but he looked as puzzled as the earl. "Ain't your name Ben Bradshaw?"

"Goodness, no," Lady Donleveigh exclaimed. "His name is Rupert."

A cold worry began to gnaw in Olivia's stomach. "Do either of you perhaps have a relative by the name of Benjamin Bradshaw?" she asked. "A cousin or uncle?"

The earl and countess exchanged concerned glances. "Not to my recollection," Donleveigh said cautiously. "Though my family is extensive, and so is Wilhemina's. What is this all about? You have interrupted our dinner and terrified my servants."

"I'm lookin' for my kin," Will explained, "and I was told that I'm related to someone by the name of Bradshaw who lives here." He looked at Olivia. "Maybe Lawford was wrong."

"I doubt it," she said. "With all the resources at his disposal, Graham Lawford seldom errs." Turning back to the earl, she asked, "Perhaps the last owners of this house were named Bradshaw?"

But he shook his head. "This house has been in my family for three generations. And no one has ever had that name. Now, please, leave my home immediately."

Olivia felt herself sag with defeat. She couldn't believe that Graham had been wrong, and worse, that she and Will had been so excited and confident about what the future held for them now that he was connected to Mayfair for nothing. She didn't want to risk looking at Will, fearing that she might begin to weep if she saw what she was feeling reflected in his face.

"Just a moment," the countess said, interrupting her thoughts. "That name does sound awfully familiar." And without another word, she left the room.

Hope surged inside her, and Olivia gave Will another encouraging smile, which he didn't return. Instead, he stared at the open door, his expression unreadable. But Olivia knew there were numerous well-connected guests gathered in the dining room. It was very likely that one of them might be named Bradshaw, or know who that person might be. Olivia clasped her hands tightly.

"Been hearing a lot about you as of late, Lady Xavier," Lord Donleveigh said disapprovingly. "And I must say, it isn't the done thing."

"Trust me, my lord," Olivia answered, "everything

will be worth it in the end." She barely felt his censure, wrapped up as she was in anticipation of meeting Will's family.

The earl had nothing to say in response to this, but he turned with the others to watch the door. Finally, his wife reappeared. She had a very peculiar look on her face, a look Olivia could not fully decipher.

"I have found the man you are looking for," the countess said. Olivia's heart lodged in her throat. Lady Donleveigh turned to a person hidden from view by the door and motioned him forward.

An older man, quite fit and hale for his years, stepped into view. He was wearing simple, well-made clothes and tall work boots. He glanced around the room warily, holding his cap in his hand, uncertain what was transpiring until his eyes fell on Will.

"Luke!" the man said. He stared at Will with undisguised joy. "You're alive!"

"This is Benjamin Bradshaw," Lady Donleveigh said. "Our coachman."

Somehow, they got shuffled into another room downstairs, where the servants lived and worked. They passed heaps of maids and footmen, all staring at Will with curiosity, and then Olivia with plain distrust. But none of this reached Will—he wasn't paying attention to much besides Ben Bradshaw, his *grandpa,* and Olivia. She was silent, but old Ben had plenty to say.

In a little space Ben called a pantry, they sat down at a table, and Will finally learned the names of his parents.

"Luke, he were my boy, married Hetty Overbury. She were the cook's assistant at the Saltneys' place,"

Ben explained. He kept touching Will's sleeve to make sure he was real, and sometimes stopped to wipe his eyes, which would fill. After learning that Will wasn't his lost son, but his grandson, and that poor Luke was long dead, Ben had started to cry. The mister and missus of the house looked right embarrassed and scampered away as soon as they could, but not before suggesting that their coachman take his visitors somewhere more appropriate. Then they ran back to supper like horses fleeing a burning barn.

Even as Will was bowled over by everything happening, he still noticed that the well-heeled Lord and Lady Whoever They Were wanted their servants out of view and away from their dinner guests.

"Were they married long?" Will asked. He looked at Ben's face and, yep, saw some of his own there. Peculiar.

"Just a few months," Ben said. "Luke worked with me in the stables, and one day he said he were tired of bein' another man's servant, he wanted to be his own man. 'We'll go to America, Hetty an' me, an' start over.'" Ben's eyes grew watery again. "Guess he didn't get that wish."

Will was used to his parents being dead, but he wasn't used to someone else mourning them. He glanced over at Olivia, who was staring at Ben as though not really seeing him. Her face was strangely blank.

"But tell me about yourself, lad," Ben said, collecting himself and smiling broadly. Will felt cool water dance down his spine, watching his own grin on another man's face.

Will told him about Jake, and his life in Colorado

and on the trail, trying to think what his granddad would want to hear. Ben listened, all ears, saying things like "Coo," and "Blimey."

"So you're really one of them blokes ridin' horses and shootin' guns?" he asked, amazed.

"Somethin' like that," Will said. He figured maybe later he'd set Ben straight about what cowboying was really about, but for now, it didn't matter.

"You don't hold up banks, or trains, like that Jesse James?" Ben asked sternly. "I won't abide my grandson bein' a criminal."

Will smiled a little. "Naw. Ol' Jesse was killed last year, an' I don't plan on takin' his place."

Looking relieved, Ben nodded. "That's good. But I'm glad to hear that you inherited the Bradshaw way with horses. We been coachmen and stablemasters for generations. Horses run in our blood."

Will had always felt more comfortable on the back of a horse than standing on the ground, and every trail boss was plum agog at the way he could manage the remuda of spare horses on the drive. "Maybe you're right."

"Of course I'm right," Ben said, slapping his hand on the table. "You're a Bradshaw."

"Will Bradshaw," he murmured, testing the words. It didn't feel proper; not yet, anyway. Coffin was the name Jake had given him, and he wasn't ready to cast it aside.

He and Ben both stood as Olivia rose to her feet, her skirts rustling. She still looked far away. "I'm sure you two have quite a bit of catching up to do," she said quietly, moving toward the door. "And I don't want to intrude on private family business. It was a pleasure meeting you, Mr. Bradshaw." Then she was gone.

Still standing, Ben and Will stared at each other across the table. Ben looked at a loss, which was no better than Will felt. "Hang on," Will said, and bolted after her.

He found her walking aimlessly up and down Half Moon Street, past the row of carriages waiting, even her own, and past the other flush houses that lined the blocks.

"You look poorly," he said, coming up to walk beside her.

She shook her head, but stiffly, like a puppet. "I'm perfectly well. But don't let me keep you. I'm sure you must be very happy to finally meet your grandfather. I can send the carriage back for you."

"Liv," Will said, taking her arms and turning her to face him. He was spooked by the blankness of her expression. "You walked right past your own coach. What the hell is goin' on?"

Olivia blinked and gazed at the streetlamp behind him. "Mr. Bradshaw seems like a lovely man. And you look so much alike. I don't think there can be any doubt . . ."

Understanding hit him like a bullet, and with that awareness, the last remains of hope died. "I ain't rich," he said flatly.

Olivia regained some of her alertness, but just enough to smile sadly at him. "I thought everything would be all right once you claimed your birthright. That somehow you could be the prince in exile, like a fairy tale. Foolish, I know, but when it comes to you, I have been quite foolish."

"We both have," Will said. He had forgotten, but now he saw. Truth was, he wasn't good enough for her, he couldn't have her and there would be no miraculous change to make things different. The English had a special word for fellers like him: common. Will Coffin—or Bradshaw—was plain common, and even though Olivia's title had been paid for, she was still as high above him as the tallest peak in the Rockies. She wouldn't say so, but it was true.

He couldn't be a part of her world, and he knew he couldn't ask her to come with him and join his. True, her house wasn't as grand as the one on Half Moon Street, but it was so much finer than anything he could give her. Even with Jake's money, the best Will had to offer wasn't close to what she deserved. She was no rancher's wife, killing chickens and chasing dust, showing off an upright piano from Philadelphia to the other ranchers' wives. She was a lady, and a lady ought to have better than a hardscrabble life.

He saw that she was staring over his shoulder toward the house, and he turned to follow her gaze. Outlined in the first-floor windows were several people staring at them. Lord and Lady Fancy Pants and their dinner guests, gawking at him and Olivia like some kind of dog-and-pony show. That was the way things were in this country—everybody watching, everyone minding each other's business. He wanted to tell them all to go chase themselves, but it would only make things worse for Olivia.

"You go on home, Liv," he said. He blocked her from view with his own body. The figures in the window slowly drifted away. "I'll come by later to pick up my gear."

Her eyes widened. "No—"

"Don't worry. I'll still help with Pryce."

"That's not what I meant. I don't want you to leave."

"But I gotta. Maybe Ben'll let me stay with him for a spell, 'til—"

"Until what?"

"I go home."

Olivia put her palms against his chest and bent her head so it touched the back of her hands. "Oh, Will," she said, her voice muffled, "this was not how I envisioned our story ending. In all those silly books I read, the hero and the heroine rode off into the sunset together."

"I know, darlin'," he said, and he couldn't help it, he wrapped his arms around her shoulders, trying to memorize the feel of her there to keep him company for the long, solitary years ahead. "But this ain't no book, this is real life, and sometimes life kicks us right in the seat of our britches."

Chapter Seventeen

"Is that you, Pryce, old man?"

George Pryce put down his newspaper and looked up at the well-groomed face of Graham Lawford. As usual, Lawford dressed as somberly as an undertaker—nothing but black and gray. It was a little maddening, since Pryce knew that Lawford had scads of money and could afford some of Bond Street's more lively garments. Well, if Lawford wanted to be dark and gloomy, that was his business.

"Lawford, good to see you," Pryce said without much enthusiasm as he rose just enough to shake his hand, then sat back down again. He reached for his paper, but Lawford did not pick up the dismissal.

"Haven't seen you at the club in ages," he said cheerfully. "Too busy gadding about town, eh?"

"Mmm," was all Pryce answered. He was too annoyed to notice that Lawford, who hardly exchanged nods with him on normal occasions and had the grim mien of a judge, was practically brimming with cheerful bonhomie. Pryce blamed himself for the interruption. If he wanted to be alone with the paper, he should have stayed home. But ever since Maddox had contaminated the Greywell's water supply, his mood had been especially light, and he had fancied he wanted the company of men of his own circle. Now he was beginning to regret it.

"I can see you're busy," Lawford said, finally understanding. "And I have to be off. Business, you understand."

Didn't he just? With a curt nod, Pryce picked up his newspaper again, but then damned Lawford's voice speared through the paper. "I say, Pryce, will I be seeing you tomorrow night?"

"What's that?" If there was a social event of any consequence, Pryce was always invited. This was the first he'd heard of anything for the next evening, and it rankled.

"Lady Xavier's little gala," Lawford said. "She's celebrating her third year in business at that brewery of hers, and having loads of people over to her home for some tasting. She said she just brewed fresh beer for the occasion." He frowned. "I'm surprised you didn't know about it. I recall that you were once interested in getting into brewing."

Pryce made himself shrug indolently. "I lost interest in that venture. Too plebian."

"Ah, well. My tastes must run to the baseborn, since I told her I'd come. I'm sure you'd find the whole thing a dead bore. *A bientôt.*"

Once Lawford had gone, Pryce allowed himself to smirk. He looked out at the reading room of the club, filled with large, comfortable chairs, men poring over their newspapers and puffing contentedly on cigars, safely away from annoying female company. He did love this club, loved its exclusivity, its staunch adherence to masculine decorum. And in two days the club would be filled with furious talk of how Lady Olivia Xavier had served poisoned beer to the best of high society.

Several men glanced over when a giggle escaped from Pryce. He clamped down hard on his wild impulse to laugh. But it was simply too rich.

She didn't know. Maddox had done his job perfectly, and Lady Xavier had no idea that her well had been corrupted. Pryce supposed that he ought to be concerned that many people he knew would likely drink the beer and be sickened by it, but they were wealthy and could afford prompt and effective medical care. They were in no real danger.

The only person in danger was Lady Xavier. Her ruin would be spectacular. And George Pryce had to be there to see it.

Olivia stood in the doorway to Will's room, watching him pack his few belongings into a battered duffel. He owned very little, and it took much less time than Olivia would have liked for him to completely clear out his possessions. She wished he owned mountains of things, just to keep him here a bit longer, but in all too short a time the Vetiver Chamber was merely another empty bedroom.

"That's it," Will said, closing his bag. He glanced around the room as though trying to take it all in, imprint it in his mind.

Olivia stepped to one side as two footmen came in and carried out the duffel and the Winchester rifle. One was about to pick up Will's saddle at the foot of the bed, but stopped and looked at him first.

"Go ahead," Will said. "It don't matter."

She covered her mouth with her hand as the footman tucked his arms underneath the rig and carried it out. Will didn't let anyone touch his saddle, his most prized possession, but it was a measure of how much he was hurting that even the saddle meant little to him.

Then they were alone in the room. Olivia leaned against the doorframe, bracing her hands on the jamb, as she stared at him. His face was starkly handsome in the harsh morning light, his jaw taut and his eyes blue ice. Will's mouth, usually grinning contagiously or offering untold pleasure, was hard and set. He seemed so tall and broad, so unmovable. There wasn't much about him that recalled the easygoing cowboy who had strolled into her life with fists swinging a few weeks earlier. He seemed like a man who had taken several hard blows and was that much stronger, more tough because of it.

Thanks to her.

"Will—"

"Don't." His jaw worked. "We know there ain't nothin' to say."

"I didn't want it to turn out this way." She took a few steps forward. "I wanted—"

"The impossible. We both did." He shook his head. "But we didn't have a snowball's chance in Texas."

She let her eyes move without seeing through the room. She never spent much time in the Vetiver Chamber, especially since David had died and the number of guests staying with her had dwindled to almost none. She hadn't been particularly lonely, but Will had changed all that. She had never felt more alone than she did at that moment.

"I'll understand if you hate me," she said at last. "Right now, I hate myself."

He sighed heavily, then came to stand in front of her. "I don't hate you, Liv. It's this place I can't stomach. Tellin' a body who they can and can't love."

She looked up at him sharply, and he smiled ruefully. "Yeah," he said, "I love you, Liv. It bushwhacked me, but it's gospel."

Olivia felt herself stabbed through with a hot blade. She had always longed to hear those words, and she realized she had been wanting to hear them from Will for almost as long as she had known him. There was a flare of joy inside her, ruthlessly cut by circumstance.

"Don't go," she said desperately. "You can't say that and go."

"That's why I gotta. I can't watch you get torn apart just 'cause I got feelin's for you. It ain't worth it."

"Let me decide that."

He shook his head. "Nope. This is somethin' that's outta your hands." He started to move past her, then stopped. "Liv, I'm doin' the right thing. Everythin' you told me 'bout how you'd be out in the cold if you didn't mourn your husband long enough, that'd be a hundred times worse if you took up with a no-name cowboy with nothin' but a saddle and a coachman for a granddad. And all that pain it'd cause you, it'd be on account a' me, and I just won't let that happen."

"But—" He silenced her by bending down and pressing a soft, sweet kiss on her mouth that was over much too quickly.

"I'll be back tomorrow, Liv," he promised, "to finish Pryce. Then it's adios."

Olivia couldn't move as Will left the room. She

stared at the spot where he used to be, his afterimage. She listened for the front door opening and closing and strained to hear the carriage pull away. Then, uncaring that the bedroom door was wide open and anyone could walk by and see her, Olivia sank to the floor. For the first time since David had died, she began to cry, and once she started she could not stop.

Ben took him in, after getting permission from the butler, housekeeper and, finally, the lord and lady of the house. So, after a short time of sleeping in a bed that could hold four grown men, Will lay down that night in a narrow cot in a narrow room. There was one little window that looked out onto the street—or rather, the boots and horses' hooves going back and forth on the street. Aside from Ben's bed and the one hastily put in for Will's use, the room held a washstand, a small cracked mirror, Will's saddle and two daguerreotypes, browning with age.

"That's Emma, me wife," Ben had explained, pointing to one of a sturdy woman in a neat, plain dress. "She died 'bout four years after Luke left home." His grandmother.

"And is this—?" Will had asked about the other photograph.

"Your parents. On their wedding day." Will had stared hard at the picture for a long time, finally seeing the faces of his mother and father. They didn't look quite comfortable in their fine wedding duds, and they seemed very young. Will's father, Luke Bradshaw, resembled Will so much that he almost thought it was himself in the daguerreotype.

Now he lay in bed, Ben gently snoring, and kept staring at the picture. Light from the street fell through the high window, bathing the room in an ambient glow. The shadowy ghosts of his family gazed out with unaging eyes. He tried to find some connection with them, outside of resemblance, but even now, after talking with Ben all day, Will felt as removed from Luke, Hetty and Emma as he did from the characters on the traveling stage. Ben was a good old man, and Will was growing to care for him, but there were few people who had a place in his heart. Jake, for one. And Olivia.

That day without her had been one of the worst of his life, tempered only by Ben's constant joy at seeing his lost grandson. Every goddamned minute felt like the longest, coldest winter, and he actually checked his fingers once to see if he'd gotten frostbite. While Will helped Ben out in the stable and listened to stories about his father, his mind kept rambling back to her.

He tried to picture where she would be throughout the day. At noon, she probably went to Greywell's. There was still a lot of work to be done before the gala the next night. Will would have gone, but she had sent a note saying that he needed to spend time with his grandpa, and that everything was under control for the meantime. She would see him tomorrow evening.

It had helped to work in the stable, helped blow off the steam that had been building all day. He had mucked stalls, groomed horses and polished tack, building up a fine sweat as though he could somehow burn Olivia off like a fever. Will kept telling himself that he was doing the right thing by ending their affair, but if it was the right thing, why did it hurt like a son of a bitch?

Now, lying in bed, physically beat but his mind hopping like a jackrabbit, he saw her clearly at home. It might be late, but she would be up. Maybe reading one of them dime novels she fancied. Or maybe she was fed up with cowboys and would turn to something a little more enriching. That library she had held hundreds of swell-looking books. Surely one of them had to be better than two-bit tales of cowpunchers.

The next night, they would finish the business with Pryce. Olivia had downplayed the risk she was taking, but Will knew that there was a lot at stake. If her gamble didn't pay off, she could lose Greywell's and a whole lot more. He knew that she'd eaten up a sizable amount of her money just setting things up for tomorrow. Once everything had played out, and if Pryce got what was coming to him, Will and Olivia wouldn't have any reason to see each other again.

"Jesus," Will muttered, sitting up. He put his head in his hands and stared at the floor. He felt like he'd been sucker punched. Now he knew what the boys in the bunkhouse felt when they got those letters giving them the mitten. If it was anything like what ripped through him now, it was a wonder anybody managed to get back in the saddle. Will had thought losing Jake was hard, but there was some sense in the *alter bocher*'s death. Will was ready for it. Giving up Olivia, though, blindsided him.

He knew he wouldn't be able to sleep. As quietly as he could, he got dressed in the dark and slipped out of the room. Ben had told him to use the servants' entrance, and it wasn't long before he was back out on the street. There, Will took huge gulps of air. To keep himself from running toward Princes Square, he started walking quickly east, along a path he'd taken almost a week earlier.

"Tex!" Portbury shouted when Will appeared at McNeil's. "Didn't think I'd be seeing you again." The policeman slapped Will heartily on the back. "What can I buy you?"

"Whiskey," Will said. Portbury signaled the barkeep for two glasses, but after the drinks were poured, Will added, "Leave the bottle."

As Will downed his whiskey in a single shot, Portbury eyed him uneasily. "Blimey, Will, you look like a mourner at your own funeral."

Steadily, Will refilled his glass. He offered more to Portbury, but the other man held up his hand. "Just as long as mourners get drunk, I got no problem with that." The whiskey still blazed as it went down, telling Will that he had a ways to go before he was good and numb.

"Well, mate," Portbury said with a shake of his head, "I can tell when a bloke wants nobody but the bottom of his glass. If you want me, I'll be over in the back."

He barely noticed the other man's leaving. Will hunched over the bar and steadily poured whiskey down his throat, and as the night went on, the berth around him grew wider and wider. It seemed no one wanted anything to do with the big, angry American, and everyone wisely left him alone.

Until someone grew drunk and bold.

"Oi, Yankee Doodle," a slurred voice said behind him. When Will didn't turn around, the man said again, louder, "Oi," and jabbed Will in the shoulder. He sniggered to himself.

Will smiled darkly down into the shot glass resting on the bar. He silently prayed that the drunk fool behind him would go just a little bit further.

"Nice 'at," the man continued. To get Will's attention, he reached up to flick at the brim of Will's Stetson, but Will was faster.

He whirled around and grabbed the man's wrist. "Don't touch my hat," he growled.

The man, ruddy with drink, still managed to pale a touch. He moved to shrink back, but then saw that everyone in the pub was watching. "Your 'at's as ludicrous as you are 'omely," he challenged. For good measure, he added, "An' your country's a bleedin' joke."

The crowd gasped.

"Amigo," Will said with a widening grin, "you just turned this day around." And then he let fly.

Ben found him in the stables the next morning. Will sat in a clean stall, his legs stretched out in front of him, staring out the open door into the courtyard.

"Don't the sun ever shine in this goddamned country?" Will muttered when Ben stepped into the stall. But his granddad didn't answer the question.

"Great God!" Ben cried, then lowered his voice when Will winced. "What in the saints' names happened to you?"

Will looked up at him, one eye swollen shut and dried blood in the corner of his mouth. "Just lettin' loose a bit," he said.

Ben looked both annoyed and strangely proud. "I sure hope you won that fight."

Will took off his hat and ran his fingers through his hair, then gazed at the blood on his hand as if it were someone else's. He tried to smile but couldn't. "I did." Then, softer, he added, "An' I lost, too."

"My lad," Ben said, crouching down next to Will

and placing a hand on his shoulder, "there's one thing a man needs to learn, else he'll wind up smashed to jelly long before he reaches my age."

"What's that?"

With a sad smile, the older man said, "There's no way to beat a woman out of you."

Between the Donleveighs' cook's application of beefsteak to his swollen face and a few hours of dreamless oblivion, Will looked almost presentable. He dressed for the gala in Ben's room, slipping on the expensive evening clothes that, after tonight, he doubted he would need anymore.

"Aren't you a fancy gent?" Ben asked, sitting on the bed and watching Will finish his bowtie.

Will made a face at his granddad in the mirror. "Like a barnyard rooster in peacock feathers." He scowled at his uneven bowtie, then tugged it loose to try again. One thing he hadn't mastered was the art of men's neckties. Knotting a bandanna was the only thing he knew about finishing an outfit, and he reminded himself that he liked it that way.

"Here," Ben said, standing, "let me."

Will turned and raised his chin so his granddad could work his craggy fingers at the tie. It warmed him a little, even as he felt so damned cold inside, thinking that this was exactly what granddads and grandsons were supposed to do. Maybe, if Luke had lived, he would have shown his son about neckties and shaving and how to woo a girl.

But would his dad have known what to do now? Tonight, Will was going to make sure that Olivia's plans for Pryce went off smoothly, and keep his hired gun Maddox from causing her any hurt. Will almost hoped that there'd be trouble—despite the brawl at McNeil's last night, he still had more fight in him. Even though he knew that the thing he wanted to take down couldn't be fought with fists or guns.

When everything was said and done, Will would have to tip his hat and say good-bye to Olivia. He wasn't planning on staying in England much longer after that. Knowing she was so close by but unreachable—that was the worst kind of hurt a man could stand.

"I'm not paining you, am I?" Ben asked as Will winced under his attention.

"Naw," Will answered. "Just thinkin' 'bout somethin'."

"That woman from the other night," Ben guessed, "when you first came to see me."

Will didn't answer, but stepped back and looked in the mirror once the necktie was finished. It looked a fine sight better than his attempts. But he couldn't wipe the blue look from his face. He slid his arms into his long-cut coat.

"She's gentry, isn't she?" Ben asked behind him. "I remember seeing her at one of the master's parties, with her husband."

"Husband's dead." Will pulled out his bag from under the cot and got his gunbelt. It wasn't exactly the latest in Paris duds, looked a bit strange with his fancy suit, but he didn't care if he offended anyone's fashion sensibility. Tonight was about protecting Olivia at all costs.

Seeing the Colt, Ben's eyes widened. He shook his head. "You should never get mixed up with the blue bloods. Their kind only means strife for us."

"Olivia ain't one of that 'kind,'" Will said, squaring his sore jaw. He buckled the belt.

But Ben continued to look unhappy. "She's not like us, she's one of them. The upstairs. Every time one of us belowstairs tangles with them, we're the ones who wind up paying for it. We're the ones who get hurt."

Will took out his gun and carefully checked the bullets before reholstering it. He put extra ammunition in his coat pockets, then slipped his knife into his boot. He needed to get his mind ready for everything that was going to happen tonight, and his granddad's small-mindedness wasn't helping. So he kept his own council.

"Listen, Will," Ben said, more urgently, "the upper crust, they're not like normal folk. They've got their own rules, they live in their own world, sheltered, caring for no one but themselves. I've seen it time and time again. And that widow of yours is no different."

"Olivia's different," Will exploded. Ben stepped back from the violence of Will's temper, which filled the narrow room. "She's the best woman I've ever known and I ain't gonna stand here and listen to you tear her down. God*damn* this country. Everyone hidin' away from each other, drawin' lines and screamin' 'bout it if a body crosses 'em. Well, ya'll can kiss my damned spurs." He started for the door, but Ben's voice stopped him.

"If she's so different, why are you staying here with me and not with her?"

Will's laugh was hollow. " 'Cause I can lead a thousand head a' cattle through rough Indian territory and not bat an eye, but I'm still a goddamned coward when it comes to breakin' that woman's heart."

And he left, without closing the door behind him.

* * *

Surveying his appearance in the mirror, George Pryce smiled at himself. Oh, he looked absolutely cunning. He had to credit Roddam & Sons—their work was impeccable. And the beautifully severe black wool of his evening clothes was so appropriate for an execution.

"Wonderful work, Crawcook," he said to his valet.

"Thank you, sir." The poor man was so unused to compliments, he nearly blushed. Pryce liked it that way. Kept the man in his place and on his toes.

"That will be all."

With a grateful bow, Crawcook scurried out of the room. No doubt to go running to the other servants to regale them with tales of his master's resplendent appearance. Well, Pryce thought magnanimously, let the little people have their fun.

Checking his jewel-encrusted pocket watch, Pryce saw that it was nearing eight o'clock. Lady Xavier's little gala would be starting in an hour, which would leave him ample opportunity to grab supper at his club and leisurely make his way to Bayswater.

"Are you sure you won't join us at the opera tonight?" his mother asked, coming into his room. She wore ropes of pearls over her Worth gown, and had even tucked feathers in her graying hair. She was, Pryce thought approvingly, the image of a countess.

"Mother, you look lovely," he said, pressing a kiss to her dry cheek.

She only sniffed. "Your father will be quite disappointed if you don't accompany us."

"Both of you go on without me," he said blithely. "I have my own entertainment scheduled for tonight."

"I declare, George," his mother sighed, "you are becoming more peculiar every day." With an artful, practiced shrug, she sailed out of his room.

He turned back to his mirror and gloated over his flawless, refined appearance. There was something delicious in keeping secrets, he realized, particularly from people so close by. Once this whole business with Lady Olivia Xavier was settled, he decided he would investigate some other interesting opportunities Maddox had told him about. Wonderfully nefarious schemes involving smuggling and double-dealing, made all the more gratifying because they would happen right under his parents' noses. And he would still be written about in the newspapers in the most glowing of terms. Why, he thought with a grin, the possibilities were endless.

The notion had him whistling all the way to his club.

"You're looking quite lovely this evening, madam," Olivia's maid said as she finished dressing her hair. "But perhaps you ought to wear just a touch of rouge. Your cheeks are so pale."

Though she wasn't much interested in cosmetics, Olivia understood that if she wanted to present George Pryce with the illusion that all was well in her world, she needed to amend her appearance. So she dabbed on the smallest amount of red to her ashen cheeks. Satisfied, at least, with this small feature, Olivia put on her sapphire and diamond earrings, which accented the dark indigo of her bare-shouldered gown. She thought that she might have worn one of her more celebratory dresses, something in a lively color, but it seemed the height of duplicity to dress festively when she felt funereal.

As Olivia stood, Sarah straightened her train and nodded approvingly.

"Good luck tonight, madam," she offered.

"Thank you, Sarah."

"Is . . . Mr. Coffin going to be here, tonight?"

Ice flooded Olivia's veins. "I believe so."

Sarah looked relieved. "That's good. We all feel so much safer when he's around."

"I know how you feel," Olivia said to herself as she made her way to the ballroom. She watched as the footmen put the last touches on the room. It wasn't by any means a large one—there were far grander houses with ballrooms to rival Versailles—but she only wanted enough space to accommodate her guests, who would number around fifty.

Everything was in order. A special bar had been assembled where glasses of Greywell's would be offered to the guests, and the orchestra was setting up in the far corner. Her cook had prepared a variety of small bites that would taste pleasing with beer. It looked like a very elegant but entertaining little party.

Graham had played his part quite well, ensuring that George Pryce would be in attendance. She was betting that Pryce would not be able to resist watching what he hoped would be a spectacular disaster. And if anything should go wrong—if Pryce should bring his mercenary—Will had agreed to stand by.

Olivia examineed the kegs of beer to distract herself. Seeing him tonight would be the most difficult part. In a ballroom, surrounded by the people who judged her and had the ability to make her life either endurable or miserable, she could not show how much being apart from him devastated her. He had come to mean so much to her, and then, to tell her that he loved her . . .

She blinked furiously to clear her eyes. It had taken all the strength she possessed to pick herself up from the floor of Will's bedroom and drag herself to Greywell's yesterday. Somehow she had managed it, and managed to sleepwalk through the important preparations for this evening. Soon she would reap the benefits.

Yet, as she watched her servants finish readying the room and adjusting their own spotless uniforms, Olivia wondered what she was fighting for.

Will stepped into the ballroom, so handsome in his evening clothes it made her eyes burn. She saw his gun immediately and realized just how dangerous tonight would really be. If her guests commented on the fact that Will was dressed for a ball but armed for a showdown, she could explain it as Western custom, and they would shrug it off as American eccentricity. But Olivia's attention quickly made its way back to Will's face. His right eye was slightly swollen and bruised. It looked as if he'd been in a fight.

Alarmed, she quickly approached him, her heeled slippers rapping on the polished floor. His face was impassive, chiseled and sharp in the glow of the chandeliers. His eyes flicked over her without really seeing her, a quick survey that betrayed no emotion.

"What happened?" she asked, reaching up to gently touch his face with her satin-gloved hand. Her heart sank as he pulled back sharply from her. "Did Pryce's man do that to you?"

He shook his head, still cool. "Little fun I had last night."

"I wonder at your definition of fun," she murmured. He could defend himself; she had seen it several times in the past. He was an excellent fighter, but it still disturbed her to think of him being hurt. "Thank you for coming back."

His gaze was sharp and piercing. "You thought I wouldn't show?"

"Of course not. I just . . ." Her shoulders rose and fell in a gesture of complete loss. "You have more honor than any other man I know, and I'm glad."

"Honor," he snorted. "Yeah, I got that in spades." He looked around the room, taking everything in but her.

Olivia felt chilled by his detachment, but clearly he was wiser than she. Things would hurt less if they began distancing themselves from each other. Standing beside Will in her elegant ballroom, ready to greet the privileged citizens of London for an elaborate and risky charade, Olivia felt a gulf as wide as the Atlantic and as tall as the Rockies open between them. And it was a distance that could never be breached.

Chapter Eighteen

The ballroom was full of the most influential and well-regarded people in London. Several members of Parliament, a handful of titled nobles, the editor of the London *Times* and high-ranking government officials, along with their wives. Charlotte and Frederick were in attendance. Graham stood in the corner, his dark eyes glittering like obsidian as he scanned the room. Olivia felt she ought to be reassured by his presence, but the one man she wanted close to her wasn't in the room.

Even though Will was dressed for the gala, he had insisted that he keep watch outside.

"Pryce ain't a fool," he'd said just before the guests had begun to arrive. "He won't try nothin' inside. But I'll bet my saddle that feller Maddox'll be around, and I aim to clean his plow."

"But Maddox's work is done," Olivia had protested.

Will shook his head. "He's like Pryce, wantin' to

see how everythin' plays out. When he does show, I'll make him as welcome as a Comanche war party."

Somewhere outside, Will patrolled her house. She trusted his judgment, but it would have made her heart hammer less painfully if she could at least see him. She feared for his safety. Maddox was no ordinary thug. He was a professional, and she didn't know whether Will's natural skills as a fighter could outmaneuver a trained mercenary.

Olivia mingled with her guests, falling back on the years of instruction she had received, letting careful education guide her like an invisible hand at her back. She murmured greetings and pleasantries to the men and women who filled the ballroom.

"Everything will be all right," Charlotte said to her, placing a light hand on Olivia's arm. Frederick nodded in agreement.

"Of course it will," Olivia answered with an artificial smile before drifting away. It was strenuous being in the company of friends, whose eyes saw too much.

"I say, Lady Xavier," a member of the House of Lords asked her, "where is this American I have been hearing so much about?"

"Tending to important business," she answered.

"He is rumored to be so very *entertaining*," the man's wife chimed in. She gave a little shiver of horrified delight. "So very uncouth and wild."

"If you wish to amuse yourself with something uncouth and wild," Olivia found herself saying, "you might try visiting the monkeys at the zoo instead of gawking at a fellow human being."

The other woman blushed deeply. "I . . . apologize, Lady Xavier. I didn't mean—"

Olivia held up a hand. "Please help yourself to some of the refreshments. I must see to my other guests." She walked away before she could say anything else, something she might regret. Although she did not regret putting the Parliament member's wife in her place. The nerve of that woman, speaking of Will as though he were some kind of Barnum attraction. Olivia took a glass of beer from a passing servant to steady herself, then set it back down again, finding no interest in drink.

"This ale is delicious, Lady Xavier," the *Times* editor said. "And I must admit, there is something especially novel in drinking something as wholesome and convivial as beer in such an elegant setting."

Many guests standing nearby murmured their agreement as Olivia gave a grateful curtsey. They smiled at each other self-consciously, dressed as they were in their most formal attire but holding pint glasses instead of snifters or long-stemmed wineglasses.

"May I propose a toast?" a familiar voice asked from behind her.

Olivia briefly closed her eyes. She steeled herself for what would be a difficult and dangerous performance.

Slowly, she turned to face George Pryce. Like the other men at the party, he was wearing evening clothes and had chosen on this occasion to wear a monocle that gleamed whitely in his eye. He smirked at her. She clutched the fan in her hand to keep from launching herself at him.

"Mr. Pryce," she said tightly, "what a pleasant surprise."

"The pleasure is all mine," he gloated.

Hers was a challenging performance; she had to

pretend that his appearance was unexpected, which it was not. Further, she had to convey her displeasure at seeing him but in a manner fitting for a social event. She knew he was banking on her ingrained skills as a hostess to keep from throwing him out, and she fully intended to play on this. Out of the corner of her eye, she saw Graham tense, ready for a fight.

"You wanted to propose a toast?" she continued.

"Yes, to your continued success as a brewer." He glanced around the room at people who knew him very well. It repelled Olivia that he was willing to sicken friends and acquaintances merely for the opportunity to humiliate her. Pryce said, loud enough for the whole room to hear, "Let us all raise our glasses in honor of Lady Olivia Xavier."

Everyone in the room did just that, held their glasses high. Olivia, knowing what she had to do but trembling all the same, raised her own beer.

Pryce watched her eagerly as she stared at him with apparent suspicion over the rim of her glass. Before she drank, however, she paused.

"We can't continue this toast," she said suddenly. The guests around her lowered their own glasses, blinking in confusion.

Pryce scowled. "Why not?"

"You have no glass of your own."

More than anything, Will wanted to be inside with Olivia. He saw Pryce step down from his carriage and stand on the sidewalk, looking up at Olivia's house with a smug laugh. Will had wanted to jump out from the side of the townhouse and plow his fist right into Pryce's overbred puss, but that wouldn't fly with

Olivia's plan. So he kept his hand lightly balanced on the handle of his Colt as Pryce ascended the stairs and went inside.

As he moved to the back of the house, Will knew that Olivia's scheme was being played out right now. And as much as he hankered after being in that ballroom with her, he had his own job to do. Olivia was a strong woman. She might not realize it, but she could take care of herself better than most people Will knew. He didn't doubt her strength tonight.

He slipped into the shadows by the servants' entrance, waiting, searching the dark. He knew, as well as he could sense a stampede before it happened, that Maddox would make his move soon, but Will needed to be patient. For a long while, he could see only the empty courtyard and hear the sounds of traffic, the servants bustling inside and the music from the ballroom above. Then, something moved.

"Couldn't keep away, huh?" he asked as Maddox slunk toward the door.

Maddox turned, straightened. He didn't seem much surprised to see Will. "When I take on a job, I see it through."

Will stepped out of the shadows. "Same goes for me."

"That makes us two of a kind," Maddox said.

"I don't kidnap women," Will countered. "An' I don't poison wells."

Now Maddox did look surprised. "You know about that?" He glanced up, two stories above, where the party was being held. Will saw the quick calculation in Maddox's eyes. He meant to warn Pryce.

"You ain't going anywhere," he drawled.

"That so?"

They faced each other across the narrow yard at the

servants' entrance, a small square of light thrown onto the pavement from the kitchen window.

"Never shot an American before," Maddox mused. Will heard the click of a gun's hammer being cocked.

Will didn't waste time with palaver. He drew fast and fired. Maddox yelped as the bullet from Will's Colt slammed into the barrel of his own gun, knocking it from his hand and sending it skittering into the darkness. But as Will's hand went back to cock the Colt's hammer again, Maddox lunged.

They both struggled to gain control of the Colt. Maddox tried to pry Will's fingers off the handle, but the American held fast. As they scuffled, Maddox backed Will to the wall and, with brutal strength, slammed his hand against the bricks. Will managed to wedge a boot into Maddox's gut and push him off, but not before his own gun slipped from his fingers and landed deep in the tangle of hedges growing along the wall.

"I thought I heard a shot . . ."

"What in the world—?" The cook opened the door to peer out in confusion, one of her assistants behind her.

Maddox managed to gain his feet and dove for the open door, knocking the servants to the ground. Will sprinted after him, oblivious to the women's shrieks. He wasn't thinking anymore, letting a lifetime of brawls and fights guide him through instinct. And it felt good, at last, to hurt someone who deserved it.

"A glass?" Pryce repeated blankly.

"Of course," Olivia answered with a tight smile. "How can you toast my success without a glass of fine Greywell's beer in your hand?"

Pryce blanched, but then managed to collect himself enough to force a laugh. "In truth, Lady Xavier, I am not overfond of beer. Perhaps if there is a glass of wine . . . ?"

Olivia shook her finger at Pryce as if annoyed. "Come, come, Mr. Pryce. You cannot attend a gala celebrating my brewery if you do not sample even a little beer. In fact, I had my brewers create a special pale ale for the occasion, which is what everyone is drinking tonight." She gestured at the light, sparkling beer that filled numerous glasses.

Pryce saw the opening Olivia offered and took it. "Ah, there you go. I admit that pale ales are too colonial for my liking. Now," he elaborated, "if you had something more English, like a porter or a stout, I might be persuaded to have a drink."

Sighing, Olivia looked disappointed. "Oh, dear. I'm afraid I didn't provide any Greywell's porter or stout this evening. What a dreadful hostess I am." She almost jumped when she could have sworn she heard a shot fired outside, but a guest also accidentally knocked into one of the servants passing canapés at the same moment. She continued her drama with Pryce.

"The toast?" Pryce urged. "I don't mind being empty-handed."

"Wait a moment," Olivia said suddenly. "It nearly slipped my mind. One of my competitors sent over a keg of bitter today to congratulate me on my unexpected success. Will that be to your liking?"

Pryce looked annoyed at the delay, but then he began to smirk. "Yes, Lady Xavier, I do believe it shall."

She made a great show of having two footmen produce the keg with the competitor's icon boldly printed on its side, then tap it. A glass was filled with the dark beer and handed to George Pryce, which he promptly held high.

"To Lady Xavier," he said, turning to the assembled guests. "May she get what she deserves."

There was a chorus of agreements and then silence as everyone took a drink from their glasses, including Olivia and Pryce. He watched her from behind his glass, barely containing his mirth, and she continued to feign ignorance.

Outwardly, she made herself appear calm, but inside she seethed like a mashing tun. Pryce had done everything as intended, and now it was time for her to put the second and most risky part of her plan into action. She hoped that Will was finding success, even if she did not.

The servants cried out when Will and Maddox tumbled into the kitchen. Will managed to haul Maddox against the table in the middle of the room, laden with dishes and food, and throw a punch square to his jaw. Maddox reeled, but he'd taken hard blows before and shook the strike off. Reaching behind him, he grabbed a pan and swung it at Will, scattering cooked vegetables across the room.

Will ducked in time, but not quite fast enough to escape a hard knock to the shoulder. As he straightened, Maddox leapt onto the table, crouching low to keep from hitting his head against the ceiling. Seizing a broom from a stunned footman, Will swung the heavy handle at Maddox's legs. Maddox jumped several times, and Will swung without connecting, until a maid entered the kitchen and screamed at the sight of a stranger on the kitchen table, distracting Maddox just enough for the broom to land. Maddox staggered and fell, toppling to the ground.

Dazed as he was, Maddox was a fighter and got to his feet swiftly. He stood in front of the stove, where several pots simmered. He seized a pot and threw the boiling contents at Will, who had edged around the table. Blistering water splashed, sending the servants running from the kitchen, as Will crouched with his arm up to shield himself. He struck hard into Maddox's stomach. The man still held the pot, but it went rolling to the floor as he doubled over. Will followed this with another hit to Maddox's chin.

"Yank bastard," Maddox snarled as he spat blood and a tooth onto the floor.

"Limey sack of shit," Will answered.

Maddox dove to a block of knives sitting on the counter. Before Will could stop him, he drew a long and nasty carving blade and brandished it with a smirk.

"Not so brave without your little gun, are you, Yank?" he sneered.

"I'm from a resourceful country," Will said dryly, unsheathing the bowie knife from his boot. He'd never been more glad of his meager inheritance than he was at that moment.

Cursing, Maddox lashed and Will danced back, light on his feet. Will feinted, managing to catch Maddox across the chest. Fabric tore and a thin ribbon of blood showed through the ribbed clothing. Maddox touched his free hand to the shallow wound. The sight of his own blood seemed to enrage him further. He swung wildly with his blade, causing Will to take cautious steps back.

"Stop this at once!" Mordon shouted at Maddox, coming into the kitchen, "or I shall summon the police!"

Will's warning to the butler never had a chance. Maddox grabbed Mordon and held the frightened servant's body in front of his own, with the carving knife held to his throat.

"Keep back," Maddox warned, edging toward the door. Mordon's eyes shone white and terrified as he stiffly moved with Maddox.

"Let 'im go," Will said, taking slow steps forward.

A bark of laughter leapt from Maddox's throat. His eyes hastily scanned the distance between himself and the door that led to the hallway and stairs. Then, when Will took another step closer, Maddox pitched Mordon forward and darted out the door. The butler fell heavily into Will, who managed to keep his knife well away.

"You awright?" Will asked, shoving Mordon upright.

"Fine," the butler gasped. He added, looking steadily at Will, "Go thrash that bastard."

"With pleasure," Will muttered, and charged after Maddox.

Olivia watched Pryce's eyes move eagerly around the room. He was waiting to see his friends and colleagues double over in agony, hoping for it. She felt the bile in her own throat rise.

After taking a sip of her beer, she said to Pryce, "You may wonder what has helped make Greywell's such a success." She hoped she sounded like a woman attempting to flaunt her accomplishments before her worst rival.

But Pryce wasn't interested in playing games anymore. He'd gotten what he wanted—everyone drinking—and now he simply waited for the desired results to take effect. He made a noncommittal noise, still scanning the room.

"Shall I tell you?" Olivia persisted. "It is the water."

That got his attention. "Indeed?" he asked. He could barely keep the malicious glee out of his voice. "I had no idea water could be so important to brewing."

"Having a clean and wholesome water supply with a good mineral content is one of the most important components to a successful brewery." Olivia made an elegant, practiced gesture. "Greywell's is justifiably famous for having its own well—it's even in the brewery's name."

"Fascinating," Pryce said. He took a long drink of his bitter.

Olivia tilted her head artlessly. "I have had several offers from other breweries to purchase Greywell's water, and ordinarily I refuse such offers. But," she continued, "when one of my competitors came to me the other day and asked to use Greywell's water for a special batch of bitters, in honor of me, I simply could not refuse."

Pryce's glass stopped halfway to his lips. "What's that?"

She nodded. "I was hoping you could tell the difference in that bitter you're drinking, Mr. Pryce. It was freshly made yesterday." She gave him a wide smile. "With Greywell's water."

All the guests turned when George Pryce's glass fell and shattered onto the floor. He began to cough and spit loudly, doubling over. The musicians stopped playing.

"You bitch," he hacked. "You're trying to poison me."

"What do you mean?" Olivia asked.

"You know exactly what I mean." He hiccupped. "Greywell's water is contaminated."

"Of course it isn't!" Olivia said. The men and women in the ballroom began to whisper to each other, glancing uneasily at their glasses. Only Charlotte, Frederick and Graham didn't look surprised.

"Oh, God," Pryce groaned. He staggered to a potted fern and stuck his finger down his throat. The guests backed up in horror as Pryce gagged.

"Please, Mr. Pryce," Olivia cried. "The water is fine!"

"No it isn't," he snarled. He wiped his sleeve across his mouth, leaving a shining trail of spittle on the immaculate black wool.

"You have no proof," Olivia insisted, sounding outraged. "Unless you know something I do not."

Pryce laughed bitterly. "I know many things you do not, Lady Xavier." He spat again onto the floor. "Including the fact that the well water on which you dubiously pride yourself is contaminated."

A dull roar of shock went through the guests.

"I pay an exceptional amount of money to keep the supply pure," Olivia declared.

"Just like a Bayswater parvenu to believe money is the answer to everything," Pryce sneered. "Your purchased title is as polluted as your well."

"And I suppose your inherited title makes you somehow superior," Olivia said, making herself frosty and clipped.

"Of course it does," Pryce snapped. "My family's title can claim hundreds of years of history. The very foundation of England has been built on my title. But you," he scoffed, "you and your kind, throwing filthy money at everything you see, believing that a few pounds sterling can make you somehow equal, or superior, to hundreds of years of history. Our country deserves better."

301

"One business can hardly change the course of nations."

"You and your arriviste kind must learn that the nobility of England will not be humiliated; we will not be denied! Not by the likes of commoners," Pryce barked, spitting his words as if they were base insults.

Some of the guests, particularly those with purchased titles or no titles at all, grew restive, while those who did lay claim to inherited titles shifted uncomfortably and refused to look at George Pryce. Olivia wondered if others shared Pryce's sentiment, but she hadn't the time or interest to discover whether this was true.

"And this has to do with Greywell's water?" Olivia asked.

"As I said, it is just as contaminated as you are," Pryce shot back.

"My water is kept under very tight security. It would take someone quite extraordinary to be able to breach it."

It did not seem to matter to Pryce that moments earlier he had forced himself to be sick; he was still gratified and eager to have his vanity stroked. "Yet I was able to do just that," he gloated.

"*You*, Mr. Pryce? I cannot believe it," Olivia cried. "*You* could never harm the well undetected."

"But I did," Pryce taunted.

As one, the guests gasped in shock. No one could speak except a wordless articulation of horror. Seeing the expressions of dismay and revulsion on the faces in the crowd, Pryce's triumphant jeering quickly faded, to be replaced by a growing agitation.

Olivia found it strange but somehow unsurprising that Pryce would take credit for his thug's deviousness. "So the water I sold to make the bitter was tainted, too," Olivia pressed.

"Bitter that I drank," Pryce said acrimoniously. Louder, to the crowd, he said, "You should all rush home to your physicians before you become too ill to do so. As I intend to do."

The guests began to move to the double doors, horrified.

"It is quite fortunate, then," Olivia said, raising her voice so she could be heard by the panicked crowd, "that this beer was made with water I purchased from another brewery."

The crowd reacted again, stopping by the doors to hear this newest development.

The reporter from the *Times* stepped forward. "Didn't you say earlier that the bitters was brewed with Greywell's water?" he asked, and it almost made Olivia smile to see that his notepad was at the ready, eager for a story.

"That was a fabrication," she conceded. "The bitters came from a completely different water source."

"So you were aware of the problem with the well, Lady Xavier?" the reporter pressed, scribbling furiously.

"My associate, Will Coffin, discovered that my well had been tampered with by Mr. Pryce's mercenary. So I purchased several hundred gallons of water from another brewery. I had hoped Mr. Pryce would reveal his treachery." She looked at him, his face ashen, the front of his evening clothes stained with sick. "And so he has."

Maddox bounded up the stairs, knocking footmen aside. Will was fast after him. The mercenary cleared the basement stairs and charged down the first-floor hallway, heading toward the next flight and up to the ballroom on the second story.

He'd just gotten midway up the flight of stairs leading to the second floor when Will dove and grabbed his feet. Maddox fell hard, knocking against the steps with a grunt. Will scrambled up and turned Maddox over, then let fly with punches to Maddox's face. Maddox's knife came up, catching Will lightly across the shoulder. The blade nicked him, a hot thread, and he bent back just enough for Maddox to wriggle out and continue up the stairs.

Will caught up with him just outside the ballroom. Olivia and Pryce were shouting at each other, the other guests standing around them, their eyes wide as moons.

"She's talking nonsense!" Pryce yelled. "I'm not responsible!"

"You just admitted it not a minute ago," Olivia countered, more calm.

"And everyone here witnessed your confession," Lawford added.

"Outrageous!" one man said hotly.

"Poisoning Lady Xavier's well, Lord Hessay's son— a scandal!" someone else added.

"Looks like you're too late," Will said as he and Maddox faced each other, knives ready.

"I finish my work, no matter what," Maddox snarled. "Poison the well: done. Kill you." He grinned wolfishly. "Nearly done." Then he charged.

Will sidestepped, and both men whirled around to face each other again. Maddox swung his blade, trying to cut Will where he could. Will forced himself to be calm, focused. When Maddox made a wild lunge, exposing his left side, Will moved in fast. He sunk his bowie into Maddox's shoulder. The hired gun howled and dropped to the carpeted floor, clutching his injury. Will grabbed the custom-made hilt and pulled the knife free.

The guests near the ballroom door looked back and forth between Will and Maddox in the hallway and Olivia and Pryce inside with them. They looked stunned. "Someone's been stabbed," a few murmured. A woman fainted.

Olivia came running to the door. "Will," she cried. "Are you all right?"

Before Will could answer, Pryce came charging past. "Get out of my way!" he shrieked. He managed to bolt around Olivia and head for the stairs, but he suddenly jerked to a stop and flopped to the ground, sitting upright like a marionette. Pryce stared dumbfounded at the tail of his cutaway coat, which was pinned to the wall behind him with a coffin-handled knife.

Will straightened himself from his knife-throwing stance as guests crowded around Olivia in the doorway. Exclamations of shock and amazement tumbled into the hall. But Will turned just in time to see Maddox disappear through a second-story window.

Will ran to the window, but Maddox was already on the ground. He ran, limping, down the street. Will was about to charge after him when he felt Olivia's hand on his sleeve.

"Let him go," she said. "We accomplished what we wanted."

The police, summoned by Mordon, were already coming up the stairs for Pryce, who was struggling feebly to get out of his pinned coat. He stopped when Graham stood over him, glowering.

Will looked at Olivia, pride bursting in his chest. She'd done it—she'd managed to snare Pryce through her cleverness, bravely facing him down. Will wanted so badly to scoop her up in his arms and kiss her senseless, but he caught sight of the curious faces of the high society guests staring at them. Tomorrow, the papers and gossip would be filled with nothing but what had happened here tonight.

"Just about," Will said. "We got just about everything we wanted."

Olivia had spent an exhausting hour talking with the police, giving her statement, preparing to testify against George Pryce. Most of the guests had been detained as well, excitedly telling everything they'd heard to the detectives.

"It's like something out of a novel," she heard a member of Parliament say to his wife.

"A very shocking novel, my dear," his wife replied. "Imagine, the Earl of Hessay's son involved in such a despicable scheme! It chills the blood."

Olivia was sitting on a chair in the ballroom, dazed, as people milled around her. But Will was nowhere to be found.

"It went marvelously," Charlotte said. "I'll call on you tomorrow." Frederick draped her cloak over her shoulders and began to lead her from the room.

"Tomorrow," Olivia murmured, dazed. But Charlotte and her husband had already gone.

A cluster of attendees stood nearby, talking.

"Did you see the American?" an industrialist asked.

"Quite astonishing," the *Times* editor said.

"What a brute, as I hear all Americans are," a

woman added. "And clearly a laborer, despite his evening clothes. Did you see his hands?"

"And the bruises on his face," the industrialist put in.

"Leave my house," Olivia said, standing up to face them. When everyone blinked in astonishment, she repeated, forcefully, "Get out."

"But, Lady Xavier—"

"I refuse to sit here and listen to you denigrate the finest man I know," she said hotly. "It doesn't matter what country he's from, and it matters even less whether he has a fortune or works hard for a living. I'm glad he knows what it means to work—because he never takes anything for granted. Because he knows what is valuable and what is not. Because," she added, "he isn't afraid to stand up for what he believes in, unlike everyone else I know. Including myself."

Abashed, the guests shuffled out the door. The police had already gone, promising to contact her tomorrow, and the servants had finished cleaning up. Having won her greatest victory, Olivia stood in the ballroom completely alone.

Chapter Nineteen

"What shall I tell the man from the *Times*, Lady Xavier?"

Olivia looked up from the piles of papers in front of her, her eyes watering from strain and lack of sleep, into the agitated face of Mr. Huntworth.

"Tell him that I have nothing to say, and I *won't* have anything to say, so he might as well go back to his paper before he wastes any more of my time," she answered wearily.

"He is most persistent," Mr. Huntworth added.

Olivia rolled her shoulders to stretch them. After the furor of last night, she had been unable to sleep. She had sat up all night, her mind whirling, staring out her window into the garden as though the orderly flower beds and neatly trimmed hedges could help calm her. She knew she ought to be feeling triumphant—George Pryce was well and truly ruined, no longer a threat, her brewery would recover from the setbacks it had faced—but without Will to share the victory, all Olivia could muster was a vague sense of relief combined with disappointment. Her old fatigue had returned, and the sense that she had a tremendous burden to shoulder on her own, and she felt it as surely as if it were a physical weight pressing on her back.

Will had gone as soon as he could, having fulfilled his obligation. Just before he'd disappeared last night, he had said to her, "I'm leavin' for Colorado tomorrow, Liv."

"But what about your grandfather?" she had asked, startled.

Will had shrugged. "He's a decent feller, but he's just like the rest of this country. Tellin' me who I should and shouldn't care for. An' stayin' here, with you so close by, it'd be like havin' a brandin' iron against my heart."

Her own heart had felt shriveled and dried. "Don't let me keep you from your family."

"It ain't that," he said. "I thought findin' Ben would make me settle, give me somethin' to hold to, but it turns out the person who can give that to me is the one I can't have." He tipped his hat to her. " 'Night, Liv." And then he was gone.

So it was over between them—for good. He would not seek her out, and she would not contact him. He was leaving England for his home. The island would be a small and cold place without him. And so would her soul.

These thoughts had tormented her through the night. At first light, she had dressed and gone to Greywell's. There was still much to be done, and she buried herself beneath stacks of correspondence and paperwork to take her thoughts elsewhere. But reporters seeking a juicy story had been hounding her all morning, distracting her from the comfortable numbness of work.

Mr. Huntworth was still waiting for an answer.

"I am most persistent, too, Mr. Huntworth," she replied. "And I will not speak to the gentlemen of the press. We have already prepared an official statement. They will have to be satisfied with that."

Nodding, the manager hurried off to convey her refusal to the men clustered at the brewery gates. Olivia glanced at the clock. It was after ten. Was Will already booking passage back home? Could he have already sailed? She leaned her hot eyes into her fists to keep the tears at bay.

Gone, gone. He was almost gone, or gone already. She had to keep moving, keep herself busy or she could easily collapse, just as she had done when Will had moved out of Princes Square. She abruptly stood, pushing her chair back and startling some of the clerks in the office, and walked into the brewery itself.

This was all hers. She had fought for it. Every tank, tun, keg and bin. She had shocked society three years earlier by taking active control of the business, but she had made damned sure that Greywell's would thrive. She had been so proud of herself. She had made real progress with Greywell's, and loved seeing her work come to fruition. But beneath it all, she had known something wasn't quite right. She was a businesswoman and a member of society, existing in two worlds that were not particularly compatible. She'd felt that disparity, but been willing to accept it as a natural consequence of being a woman living on the cusp.

Olivia went into the room that held the mashing tuns. Out of habit, she checked the temperature of the steam-heated jackets. They were at a consistent

145 degrees; excellent. Uniformity was vital in brewing, the ability to produce a dependable and unvarying product. Beer drinkers didn't like change.

Nor did England, she realized. It was a land that craved fixity, stability, and woe betide anyone who tried to change that. Ever since she was a child, she had been made aware that there were certain people who did not belong together. Rich and poor. Men and women. The leisured and the workers. In school, and as a young bride, she had not examined this. Yet once David died, she had begun to question these divisions. And since she had known Will . . . everything had become very different.

Peering out a window, she saw Mr. Huntworth speaking to the journalists, and the men's disappointed faces as they were turned away. The reporters would return, though. Their readership would relish the story of Lady Xavier, George Pryce and rumors of a wild American. Everything in the public eye.

But, curse it, what was the public to her? She thought about the values everyone struggled to uphold—class consciousness, excruciating decorum, smothering etiquette—and understood that those things had no value. The one man she loved was leaving England, and all because their love might upset someone's delicate sensibilities.

"Oh, God," she said aloud. She leaned against the window and stared out into the gray sky. "I love him."

When Olivia was with Will, she no longer felt that horrible split within herself. She was whole, united through the generous warmth of his heart. And he accepted every part of her. She didn't care what he did for a living, or who his parents were. All she knew was that he had become her friend, her lover, the one person she couldn't possibly live without. And she had let him slip away, because of her own fear, because she was still too dependent on the good opinion of people who didn't matter.

But he did. And she might lose him forever if she didn't act quickly.

Olivia grabbed her skirts and ran back to the office.

"Mr. Huntworth," she said breathlessly, finding him returning from his errand.

"Yes, Lady Xavier?"

"I want your best clerks to check all the ships departing for America today. I want to know who is on those ships and when they are leaving. And if Mr. Coffin has already sailed," she added, "then book me passage to America immediately."

Mr. Huntworth stared for a moment, then nodded. "Yes, Lady Xavier."

Olivia watched his clerks hurry to do her bidding. She hoped, if she did catch up to Will, that he could forgive her. If she didn't, she would never forgive herself.

Will gave the fancy suit to one of the Donleveighs' footmen. He reckoned he didn't have a use for it anymore, and there was a cut across the front that he hadn't the skill to mend. The cut on Will's front was bandaged up by the housekeeper, who gave Ben a heap of baleful looks. In the two nights Will had stayed with his granddad, he'd returned to the house bruised and bloodied.

"I don't know why you have to leave so soon," Ben said, sitting on the bed and watching Will pack.

"You could come with me to Colorado." He folded a shirt and put it into the open bag on his cot.

Ben shook his head. "Me home's here, in England. I'm too old to start over."

"An' I'm too old to start livin' like an Englishman," Will answered. He buckled on his gun and laid the Colt next to his luggage. "America's got its share a' troubles, but there's freedom to be had."

"That's why they went, too," Ben said softly.

Will turned and looked at his grandpa, a questioning frown on his face.

" 'I can't breathe,' Luke said to me," Ben continued. " 'We've got to go.' It could be stifling for a young man trying to make his way in the world. He didn't want to be in service anymore, didn't want his children to be anyone's servants. He said, 'There's fair land for the taking, and nobody to tell me or Hetty what we can and can't do, how high we can rise.' And he wanted to go as high as he could." Ben smiled sadly. "I suppose that's why he picked Colorado."

"It touches the sky," Will said with his own smile. He was about to close his bag when Ben got up and put the daguerreotype of his parents into the duffel.

"You take them with you," he said. "I've spent nearly thirty years staring at them, wishing they could come back, and in a way I guess they have. In you."

"Thanks," Will said, humbled.

Ben put his old, broad hand on Will's shoulder. His bright blue eyes glimmered. "They would have been proud of you, Will. I know I am. You turned out straight and strong, and you fight for what you believe in."

Will stared at the browned picture of his father and mother. Luke Bradshaw's hand rested on his wife's shoulder, protective. "Not everything."

Ben peered at his grandson with a frown Will had

seen in mirrors on his own face. "You love that woman, don't you?"

"Yeah, I do," Will said, without pause.

"And how does she feel about you?"

"I . . . I don't rightly know. Guess I never asked her." Will realized that he hadn't given her much of a chance to say one way or the other. He was always so dead certain that they didn't have a chance, he just plowed on ahead.

"Maybe now is the time to ask," Ben suggested gently.

Will ran a hand along his jaw, still a mite tender from the working-over it had gotten the other night. "She didn't try to stop me when I left," he began.

But Ben gave Will's shoulder a little shake. "What's that word you use? That's bosh. Do you love that woman?"

"Hell, yeah."

"She loves you. Don't argue with me; I saw it the night she came over with you. I just couldn't believe that someone of her class could really feel that way, and tried to convince myself her feelings weren't true. But I was wrong. Servants' gossip tells me she's been wretched since you left."

That stabbed Will right through. "I can't help her, Grandpa. That's what kills me."

"Like hell," Ben snorted, shocking Will. He'd never heard the soft-spoken old man speak so plainly. "Think about what your father died for—the freedom to do as he pleased for no one but himself. And think about that miner who raised you. They wouldn't want their boy to lose out on his chance at love because society told him no."

"Goddamn it," Will said, pacing around the room.

He cursed again. He'd spent his whole life fighting to survive, struggling to take the herd from Texas to Colorado, doing whatever it took to get by. He thought about all the dangers he'd faced down: snowstorms, floods, Indians, fools with guns looking to kill. None of it had stopped him. But the most important thing in his life, the woman he loved, he'd let go without so much as a peep. "I've been a jackass."

"Well, yes," Ben answered with a smile. "What do you intend to do about it?"

Will stopped his pacing and stared at his granddad. "I need a horse."

Not content to sit idly by while her clerks labored, Olivia had joined in on the search. Some of the ships wouldn't release their passenger manifests right away, but Olivia soon discovered that notoriety had its benefits. As soon as the name *Lady Xavier* was mentioned, the shipping firms were eager to help. They wanted to be a part of the public drama of her life, titillated by her infamy.

Still, it took an agonizingly long time to get any real information. By the time one of the junior clerks stood up and announced, "I found him!" it was already after noon.

"Where is he?" Olivia demanded.

"Leaving on the Cunard ship *Gloriana* at two this afternoon."

"Mr. Huntworth—" she began.

"Your carriage is waiting in the loading dock, Lady Xavier," her manager said with an enigmatic smile.

She was already running and didn't have time to thank him properly. *Please,* she thought, *don't let me be too late.*

315

* * *

"She's at the brewery, Mr. Coffin," Mordon said. "And if I may say," he added, as Will bounded down the front steps to his waiting horse, "it's good to see you at Princes Square."

Will took the horse at full gallop through Hyde Park, startling the genteel ladies and gentlemen taking polite equestrian exercise. They reined in their horses and stared as a cowboy in full Western dress hurtled at breakneck speed down Rotten Row. Even to jaded Londoners, this was a novelty.

But Will didn't bother with their gaping. He had to get across the river to Greywell's as soon as he could. It had taken him from Mayfair to Bayswater to get the horse used to a strange saddle. He'd had his chase with Maddox back in Kent to get himself familiar with the English reins. So it was a lifetime of practice that had him pounding down the streets of London, heading south. Thank the Lord that Ben knew horseflesh; he'd picked a fine distance runner that ate up the ground like sugar lumps.

Will crossed the Battersea Bridge, the gray Thames beneath him. He'd come to know London powerful well, could recognize the landmarks. Maybe he'd wind up making it his home. He wasn't much for city life, but it didn't matter where he hung his spurs, so long as Olivia was with him.

If she'd have him.

He almost slowed his horse as doubt darted through his mind, but he shook it off. He'd had his share of uncertainty; now it was time to act.

He didn't allow himself to breathe easy when he saw the gates of Greywell's. Will urged his horse to the loading docks in the back. He had the crazy idea of riding the horse right into the brewery through the large loading doors. As a cowboy, Will trusted the speed of a horse's hooves far more than his own feet, and he didn't want to waste a minute getting to Olivia.

But as the horse clattered over the cobbled loading yard, stacked high with kegs, he almost rode straight past Olivia's carriage pulling away.

"Liv!"

The carriage slowed, and Olivia jumped out before it could stop completely. Her feet tangled slightly in her skirts, causing her to stumble a bit as she started toward him. But she pushed against the ground with the heels of her palms, righting herself, uncaring of the mud that stained her lambskin gloves.

"I was coming to find you," she called to him.

Will swung down from the horse, his heart knocking inside his chest. He wasn't too late. He'd been blessed. "An' I was comin' for you." He started striding toward her.

"I couldn't let you go, Will. I won't." She smiled, so full and beautiful. She started to reach for him across the few yards that separated them.

"Have you no shame, Lady Xavier?"

Olivia's arms dropped as the shrill voice of Prudence Culpepper rang out. The *kibitzer* was staring at them across the courtyard, in a snit.

"I will not tolerate any further outrageousness from you," Mrs. Culpepper sniped, "including such public displays of immorality."

"There is nothing immoral in loving someone," Olivia answered. "Especially a man as wonderful as Will. And I would pity you for having such a cold, bovine heart if I cared even a little about you. But I don't. So go bugger yourself, Prudence."

With a squeal of impotent outrage, Prudence Culpepper stalked off. Will knew that was the last he'd see or hear of the old hen. But he barely spared the battle-ax another thought. His heart nearly shot to the moon with happiness, hearing Olivia's words. She loved him. And that smile of hers glowed with it.

He couldn't stand not having her in his arms. They were only three feet apart, but it was three too many.

But he had to freeze when he heard the unmistakable sound of a gun's hammer being cocked. Seeing him halt, Olivia did likewise, a puzzled frown on her face. Will turned and saw Maddox, bruised and filthy, step out from behind a stack of kegs. Every part of Will went numb as he saw Maddox's gun trained on Olivia.

"What the hell are you doin', Maddox?" Will demanded. His hand hovered near his gun, but he wasn't willing to take the chance that Maddox could beat him to the draw. "It's over."

Maddox took a few steps forward, closer to Olivia. "I've got a reputation, Yank," he snarled. "I always get my job done."

"But Pryce is finished," Olivia said, and Will was amazed by the steadiness of her voice, considering there was a big Webley revolver aimed at her head.

"Doesn't matter," Maddox said. "If I say I'm going to do something, I do it. And that includes killing you, Yank."

"Then quit pointin' that thing at the lady," Will commanded.

Maddox shook his head. He reached into his pocket and pulled out a battered book, then threw it on the ground near Will's feet. He saw that it was a Wild West dime novel, and on the cover were two men facing each other in the middle of the street, guns drawn. At that moment, Will wanted to burn down all publishing houses that produced such claptrap.

"I've been doing a bit of reading, Yank. I like to know who I'm up against. It says in these books that when two men want to finish something, they have a showdown. And that's what I'm here to do."

Will almost groaned. "Nobody does that, Maddox. It's all made up."

"What about Wyatt Earp and the Clantons at the OK Corral?" Maddox insisted. "That was genuine. And if you make a play for that gun right now," he added, seeing Will's hand hover near the handle of his Colt, "I'll shoot this lady. She won't be the first."

Will pushed back the white rage that clouded his eyes. He needed to keep himself steady, since it was clear Maddox was playing a few cards short of a full deck. Men who had been pushed to the edge were always the most dangerous.

"So how about it, Yank?" Maddox taunted. "Are we going to do this properly, or will you make me ruin this pretty woman's face?"

Will's eyes flicked over to Olivia, who managed to keep herself steady. She looked almost as mad as Will felt, her jaw tense and her lips pressed tight. A born fighter. One he wouldn't lose to some crazy Englishman's idea of honor.

"Fine," Will said.

"No!" Olivia insisted. She took a step toward Will, but Maddox raised his gun higher.

"That's far enough, Lady Xavier. This Yank and I have a score to settle."

She turned agonized eyes to Will, and he gave her just the smallest nod and a wink. "*Es vet zich alles oyspressen*," he said. Everything will be all right.

"None of that filthy foreign talk," Maddox shouted.

"*Abi tzu zein mit dir*," she answered. As long as I'm with you.

"That enough!" Maddox screamed, nettled. His focus was gone, unnerved by Will and Olivia speaking Yiddish, and he swung his gun back and forth between them. Will had his opening.

The world slowed as Will's hand darted to his hip. He saw the barrel of Maddox's gun suspended midway between him and Olivia. Then his hand grasped the handle of his Colt and drew it from the holster. In one motion, Will drew back the hammer and fired.

Maddox gaped at the growing stain of bright red in the center of his chest, choking and sputtering, before falling to his knees. His Webley dropped from his fingers.

"That's not . . . how they did it in the books," he managed to gasp.

"I told you," Will said, walking over and picking up Maddox's gun, "them books is full a' lies." Will looked over at Olivia, whose hands were pressed against her mouth in shock. She was pale, but sweet almighty, she was safe. " 'Sides, if you'da read 'em better you would've learned somethin'—out West, a man protects what's valuable to him, any way he can."

Maddox's eyes rolled back as he pitched forward, landing face-first on the muddy cobblestones. Olivia came forward gingerly as Will reholstered his gun.

"Is he . . . ?"

Will eased the hammer of the Webley back, uncocking it. "Yep."

By then, everyone had run out of the brewery to stand on the loading dock, drawn by the sound of gunfire. Excited and stunned murmurs filled the air as they stared at Maddox's lifeless body lying amid the stacked kegs, and Will holding a revolver. And then the murmurs rose to a babble as Olivia launched herself at Will, throwing her arms around him.

"You came back," she said, clasping him tightly as his arms came up to hold her close. "I was going to get you. I thought you would leave."

He cradled the back of her head with his free hand. "I can't leave you, Liv, darlin'. I love you."

"Will." In full view of all the stunned employees, she pressed her mouth against his. "I love you. That's all that matters to me."

"Marry me, Liv," he said. "I don't care if I gotta hog-tie the devil himself. I don't care if I gotta herd inchworms or live in a shed on the side of a smokestack. I just want you to be my wife."

She placed her hands on either side of his face, her violet eyes shining, tears glinting on her short black lashes. "And I don't care if I have to wear evening gowns made of newspaper or drink tea out of a tin can," she said, laughing. "I will marry you, my sweet cowboy."

Epilogue

Golden, Colorado
1887

Olivia checked the figures in the ledger one final time and smiled to herself. At last, the Coffin Brewery was showing a profit.

Sitting at the desk in the small office, she stretched and looked out the window that opened into the brewery. Compared to Greywell's, it was a small operation, but there was a growing market in this town at the foot of the Rockies, and nearby Denver, for quality beer. The Coffin Brewery was one of the few in the region, perhaps in the whole West, that could claim its yeast from a centuries-old strain originating in England. Perhaps that was part of its appeal. In any event, the four years of hard work she and Will had dedicated to their business were finally starting to pay off.

Starting their own brewery had been Will's idea. She had been willing to be a rancher's wife, or just about anything, so long as she and Will could be married. As they were lying in bed debating exactly what they would do, the idea hit him. And it sounded splendid to her.

To everyone's surprise, she sold Greywell's soon after George Pryce's treachery had been uncovered. Mr. Huntworth remained the manager and became a major shareholder, but the deal stipulated that Olivia could take a sample of the yeast with her to America.

As for Pryce, his father's influence had succeeded in keeping him out of prison. Instead, the Earl of Hessay had sent his youngest son to malarial South America, where, the last Olivia had heard, George Pryce had disappeared while trekking in Brazil.

She loved her life here. The winters seemed to last an extra six or seven months, but how could she find fault with something so minor when everything else was so miraculous? Will continued to astonish her. It seemed amazing that a man who had made his life on rough and dangerous cattle trails could be so unfailingly generous with his heart.

And he took well to running a brewery. She focused more on the accounting and record-keeping, but every day Will was out there with their five employees, hefting sacks of barley, stirring the mash, doing whatever was needed. He said to her one night, "I didn't think I'd like stayin' in one place, Liv, but it's jim-dandy. An' I get to see your pretty face every mornin'. A man couldn't ask for more."

Their house in Golden was much smaller than her townhouse in London, which had been long since sold, but she liked its coziness. They had a small parlor with a baby grand piano and a library stuffed with books and paperback novels. She liked the two women who helped cook and clean, their gruff good humor and teasing of her accent. The people of Golden were likewise outspoken and affable. She couldn't recall laughing more than she had at her first barbeque.

When she and Will had time and the weather was good, they would take a picnic hamper and go horseback riding along the high green trails. Will would spread out a blanket on some bluff overlooking the ripening valley, and they would make love until it began to grow dark.

So when Charlotte asked in one of her letters if Olivia missed England at all, the answer was an uncomplicated no. She did miss her parents, but they had come for a visit a year ago, and promised to return the following summer. Her brother had written to say that Graham would happily fetch her back if she was unhappy, but Olivia couldn't remember a time when she had been more satisfied.

The door behind her opened, and Olivia turned to see Will come in from the yard, grinning.

"Mommy!" Little Jake, just turned three, came racing past his father and right into her arms. As he burrowed close, she pressed kisses onto the top of his black, curly head.

"Where have my two men been?" Olivia asked.

"Post office," Jake said. "Pop got a package."

"Is that so?" Olivia turned up her face and Will bent to kiss her. He ran the pad of his thumb under her chin and she still felt how just a touch from him could stir embers.

"Special delivery from England," Will said. He reached into the pocket of his duster and handed her a small paper-wrapped parcel.

"England," Jake repeated. "Where Mommy's from."

"But she lives here now," Olivia said.

"Can I open it?" Jake asked, looking eagerly at the parcel.

"Of course, sweetheart."

Olivia and Will exchanged smiles as their son tore at the brown paper around the package. A year after returning to Colorado, they had adopted their son, naming him Jacob Luke Coffin. And, recently, they had begun the paperwork to adopt a little girl.

"It's a book," Jake said with obvious disappointment. He slid off his mother's lap as she plucked the book from his hands. Will hefted him up and grinned down at his wife as she looked at the cover of the novel.

"*Lady X's Cowboy: A True Tale of Adventure and Romance*," she read aloud. "*By Benjamin Bradshaw, Retired Coachman.*" With a laugh and a shake of her head, she set the book down on the desk and rose to embrace her son and husband.

"Ain't you gonna read it?" Will asked.

"I already know how it ends," Olivia answered. "Happily."

Kissing in the Dark
WENDY LINDSTROM

Her first lie is that she is a widow, but Faith Wilkins sees little choice in telling it. She moved to Fredonia to escape a deadly past, and safety depends upon maintaining the charade: She is a simple healer who moved to town to erect a greenhouse. She has to fool everyone, including Sheriff Duke Grayson, and she'll do whatever it takes to do so.

But Duke is persistent and clever, and Faith knows it won't be long before the handsome lawman uncovers all he wishes. And he wishes for Faith as his bride. But the sheriff is a protector of truth and justice. What will he do when he discovers her lies? It is one thing to kiss in the dark, but in the end, love has to withstand the light of day.

For the first time, Faith believes it is possible.

DEAR PENELOPE

SHARON IHLE

Dear Penelope,
My intended left me for another woman after I traveled to a strange town to marry him. Is leaving him without certain parts of his anatomy letting him off too easy?
                    Signed, Angry in Emancipation, Wyoming

Dear Angry in Emancipation,
You need to cut all ties with your former beau—not cut off parts of him! When my fiancé jilted me, I was left alone and penniless. Luckily, I was offered a position as a hostess at a reputable saloon. Perhaps proposing marriage to its owner was a tad rash, but my soon-to-be husband handled the idea and the arrival of my overprotective family with true grace. Be warned: A marriage of convenience can be anything but. Proceed with caution.
                    Happier than I ever imagined, Penelope